LOOK
BEHIND
YOU

ALSO BY SIBEL HODGE

SIBEL HODGE

LOOK BEHIND YOU

THOMAS & MERCER

Text copyright © 2014 Sibel Hodge
All rights reserved.

Published by Thomas & Mercer, Seattle

www.apub.com

Amazon, the Amazon logo, and Thomas & Mercer are trademarks of Amazon.com, Inc., or its affiliates.

ISBN-13: 978-1477826577
ISBN-10: 1477826572

Cover design by George Adams

Library of Congress Control Number: 2014942968

Printed in the United States of America

LOOK
BEHIND
YOU

PART ONE
TAKEN

Chapter One

Pain everywhere. My back, my wrists, my legs. Even my hair hurts.

The worst of it is in my head. Hot, white shards of pain stabbing my skull. The effort of opening my eyes sends waves of nausea crashing through me.

Engulfing darkness. I can't tell where the blackness ends and I begin. Why is it so, so dark?

I try again. Close my eyelids. Open. Close. Open. Nothingness still smothers me. I can't see a thing.

Where am I? Am I dead?

Slowly, my senses return. Cold, rough hardness below me, against my back. The musty smell of damp earth. The sound of . . . I strain to listen, but all I hear is the pulse roaring in my ears, my heartbeat banging against my ribs, air whistling through my nostrils. And something else now. Drip. Drip. Drip.

I can feel and hear, so I can't be dead. But what's happened to me? Have I been in an accident?

That's it. An accident. I'm in hospital. I'm lying on an operating table, and the anaesthetic is wearing off, leaving me in between sleep and wakefulness. That's why I can't move. That's why I hurt so much. The same thing happened once to someone I knew. She was in the middle of an appendectomy and woke up. Just like that! She couldn't feel a thing and couldn't move, but she could see everything the doctors were doing. She could speak, too. They were shocked when she told them all she could see them.

Can I speak?

'Hello?' I try, but my mouth feels stuffed with cotton wool, my voice distorted and muffled.

So why can't I see? Why is it so dark? Was it a car accident? A bomb blast? A terrorist attack?

I inhale a shallow breath. It doesn't smell like a hospital. There's none of the usual disinfectant and antiseptic odour. And what am I lying on? A trolley? A bed?

I move my right hand away from my stomach to touch what's underneath me, and my left hand moves, too.

How can that be? Why are they stuck together?

I lift my head up instinctively, even though I can't see a thing, and the pain surges forward, piercing through my eyeballs. The fingers on each hand seek out the opposite ones, touching, feeling. Something rough binds my wrists together. A rope, I think. I touch the scratchy material. Yes, definitely a rope. I pull my hands apart. No, they won't budge.

Why am I restrained? What have I done?

A fragment of memory hovers on the edge of my consciousness. Something about . . . being held down in a bed. Tied to a bed. Screaming. No . . . it's gone.

So, again, think. Why am I restrained? Have I tried to hurt myself? Hurt someone else?

I feel around my right side with both hands. Is that concrete I'm lying on? Brick? I'm not sure. It's not smooth like a trolley. Not comfortable like a bed. I can't feel sheets underneath me. I bring my hands up to touch my face and head. Running them over me, I can feel something gritty. Dirt, maybe. I wince as my hand touches a huge, swollen lump on the side of my head just above my right ear. Scalding pain sends black and white stars flashing before my eyes. My stomach lurches, and I roll onto my side and vomit. Hot, acidic bile burns my throat. Tears sting my eyes. I groan, clutching my head in my hands, and roll onto my back again with rasping breaths.

Then the blackness isn't just in front of my eyes anymore. It's in my head, too, as I sink into unconsciousness.

How long have I been asleep? An hour? A day? Two days?

I've got hunger pangs, but I'm not hungry. Far from it. My stomach contracts in spasms at the thought of food. I'm thirsty, though. My throat is as dry as an African plain. I swallow. Lick my cracked, dry lips.

I try to move, but I'm stiff. So stiff. The parts that don't hurt are either numb or tingling with pins and needles. I move my legs only to find they're restrained, too, and won't budge. More rope? I wiggle my toes; that's about all I can manage.

If I'm not in hospital, I must be in prison, then. Solitary confinement. But something is wrong with that theory. Prisoners aren't restrained with rope. They'd use handcuffs.

Right. Think.

My ankles and wrists are tied. I'm somewhere damp, mouldy. Lying on the bare ground. Slowly, I bring my knees to my chest. My left ankle screams in pain.

'Argh!' I cry out, my voice echoing off walls I can't even see. I'm fully clothed. Wearing . . . a dress . . . flat ankle boots. OK, good. What else?

I don't know.

'Hello?' My voice is hoarse, croaky.

No reply. Just the sound of dripping somewhere.

I must be underground. That's what the earthy mouldiness smells like. Underground with darkness suffocating me. And I'm tied up. My body hurts. My head is killing me. But I can't be in hospital, and I can't be in prison, so what does that leave me with?

I've been kidnapped!

As the thought pops into my head, my stomach clenches. My heartbeat thumps wildly. I fight the urge to vomit again. I gulp in deep breaths of stale air. In. Out. Come on; breathe. In. Out. *Don't panic. Think!*

Who would kidnap me? Why?

Think!

We're not rich. Comfortable, I suppose you'd say. Not well off enough for someone to want a ransom. That means there's some other, sinister reason. Am I being buried alive in this darkness? Or kept for . . . Oh, my God! Kept here to be raped and murdered. Or tortured and murdered. Is it a good sign I'm not already dead, or does it mean things will get much, much worse?

I shiver uncontrollably. I don't know if it's from the cold or fear. Maybe both. I'm damp between my legs. I've wet myself, so I must've been here awhile.

Clenching my hands together, I concentrate on trying not to hyperventilate while I think about what I really know.

I know I'm Chloe Benson. I'm twenty-seven years old. Married to Liam. I live at 16 Poplar Close in the Hertfordshire town of Welwyn Garden City. I teach English at Downham College. Liam works for Devon Pharmaceutical. So, as I said, we're comfortable, but not *rich* rich.

Liam will be wondering where I am. He'll call the police. They'll send out a search party for me. They'll find me. Won't they? But where the hell am I? How will they know where to look?

I bite down on my lip to stop a scream escaping.

Quiet. I must be quiet. If someone's keeping me here, I don't want him to know I'm awake. He might be close by, listening to my every move. I'm alive, at least for the moment. I want to keep it that way.

What's the last thing I remember?

The pain in my head makes it hard to think. My memories are hazy, fuzzy round the edges, like an out-of-focus photograph.

I remember . . . a party. Drinks flowing. An unseasonably warm March evening. Someone's house. My house. Yes, that's it. Liam's fortieth birthday party. A surprise for him. Something I hoped would cheer him up. Make things better between us. It's been . . . difficult lately. Whatever I do isn't right for him. Shouting, swearing at me. Those looks he gives me. He's stressed with work. Stressed with life, I suppose—the usual. So, the party . . . yes, the party was to show him how much I still care about him. And afterwards . . . I was going to tell him something. Something important. I try to grasp for more, but I can't find it. It's hidden somewhere in my head. My best friend, Sara, wasn't there. She was leaving for India the day before. Not that I could've invited her anyway; Liam hates her. Just Liam's friends and work colleagues were there. I can't picture anyone specific, though.

Is it still March now? The party is the last thing I can really remember. The rest is just dense muchness.

Muchness? Is that a word? No, *mushiness*.

I curl up my toes. Clench and unclench my fingers. Must bring some warmth back. Stop the cramps. Must move. Must keep calm. Must get out of here. I want to stay alive.

I roll onto my side, brace my palms on the cold ground and push myself up into a sitting position. My head throbs. Dizziness engulfs me.

Breathe slowly. Come on, Chloe. In. Out. You can do this.

I swallow away the bile scorching my throat and wait. Five minutes. Ten. *Just breathe. Adjust. Take your time.*

But I don't know how much time I have before whoever has taken me comes back.

Move. I have to move. Do something. I will the pain in my head to stop, but it doesn't.

I shuffle forwards along the floor, on my backside, with slow, shaky movements. I don't get far before my feet hit something. I reach out and touch the obstruction with bound hands, my fingers connecting with cold roughness. Brick. A brick wall.

I roll onto my knees. Pressing my hands into the floor, I lift up until I'm standing. Everything sways. I rest my palms on the wall for support and take more gulps of air. I'm weak, and the adrenaline coursing through me is the only thing stopping me from collapsing.

The rope around my ankles is tight, and my feet only move about a centimetre independently of each other as I shuffle left along the edge of the wall, touching it with my hands. It doesn't take long to meet the corner of another wall. I stop and breathe deeply before going back the way I've come. When I get to another corner, I calculate the wall is about seven metres long. I carry on about five metres, going to my right, along this new wall, then another corner. It's painstakingly slow. Round I go, until I'm pretty sure I've ended up where I started.

That's when it really hits me, and a guttural cry escapes from my throat. I collapse to the floor, banging my knees on the solid ground.

I'm in some kind of underground tomb.

Chapter Two

No, no, no, no! This is a dream. A nightmare. It has to be.

Or maybe I'm going mad. This is a hallucination of some kind. Have I taken drugs that have messed with the chemical reactions in my brain?

Reaction, reaction, reaction. That seems familiar somehow.

No. I can't be asleep, and I can't be drugged. I can feel pain. I can hear dripping. I can smell dankness and decay. Therefore, I must be awake, and I must be *compos mentis*.

Fingers of dread squeeze my insides. Fear slices through me. Someone has put me in this place. Someone has kidnapped and abandoned me in an underground tomb. Have they left me here to die, or are they coming back? Which would be preferable? To die down here alone, or be tortured, raped, and killed?

I cram a fist in my mouth to stop from yelling out. Hot tears slide down my cheeks. I have to get out of here. Somehow. But my head . . . oh, my head.

I roll onto my side, clutching my head in my tethered hands. It just hurts so much. And . . .

I open my eyes and stare into the black void that's dark as a grave. I've been asleep again, dreaming of my honeymoon in Minorca. How many years ago? How long have we been married? Two years, I think. Depending on what date it is now.

Shit! Why can't I remember?

Anyway, the dream. Yes, we rented a villa in the middle of nowhere and stocked up on supplies for BBQs. Salad, locally caught fish, wine, regional cheeses, fresh bread. Just us and our little hide-out in the sun. Things were perfect between us then. Every day Liam told me how much he loved me. How the minute he saw me, he knew I was the one for him. How proud he was that I was now his wife. We made love every chance we could get. We drove to the beach a couple of days and swam in the clear sea, so warm it was like a bath.

Sea.

Water.

How long can you survive without water? If you're stranded in a boat in the middle of the ocean, you can't drink the water. Too salty. I've heard of people drinking their own piss to stay alive. The thought makes me gag.

My throat is so dry my tongue feels swollen, as if it's too big for my mouth. I wiggle my tongue around frantically, working up some saliva, then swallow. Wiggle. Swallow. Can you last on saliva alone?

I stretch my trembling arms above my head. Flex my legs and toes. Sit up. The dizziness is back again, so I rest my head in my hands until it subsides. I shiver, teeth chattering, biting my tongue. I taste blood.

Right, Chloe, move!

'Yes,' I say aloud. The sound bounces back, mocking me in the darkness. I breathe on my hands, hoping to bring some warmth back. If I can stop the shaking, I can think calmly, rationally. I can't die down here. No. No, no, no. 'So . . .' I say to myself, 'move.'

I manoeuvre into a standing position again and stumble straight ahead to the nearest wall, hands outstretched.

There. Rough brick.

I reach up and can touch the ceiling if I stand on tiptoes. Could it be a basement? A tunnel? A cellar?

I strain to listen again. No sounds apart from the dripping somewhere. Is it in here or behind the walls? Water, dripping.

No, don't think about water. I wiggle my tongue again. Swallow.

A thought strikes me through the terror. If there's a way in, there must be a way out. Unless I'm bricked up in here. But the walls feel old, covered in grime and slime. The render between the bricks crumbles slightly as I dig in my fingernails.

I start at the top of the wall, fingers splayed over it, trying to find something. *What am I looking for?* My brain is fuzzy for a moment. *Oh, yes, an opening.* The only way I can get out of here is to stay alert. Think. Be methodical. I'm used to being methodical. At home, anyway. That's how Liam likes things. A place for every-thing and everything in its place.

A picture of my kitchen cupboards flashes into my head. Tins, jars, bottles, everything in a perfect line, as if placed there by a magic, ruler-toting fairy. Labels facing outwards. A regulation cen-timetre gap between them. No clutter in sight. Just the way he likes everything.

Fingers moving over the wall for I don't know how long.

Nothing.

I come to the corner and rest the lump on my head against the cold wall. Relief from the pain for a minute. Numbness. Ah, that's nice.

Come on. Come on. Move.

I work my away along the wall. About halfway across, right at the bottom, my fingers hit a rough edge. Part of the brick is broken and protruding out.

My heartbeat flutters, stops, and kick-starts again.

I sit awkwardly on the floor and press the rope around my wrists against the jagged brick, working my arms back and forth. Saw, saw, saw. It's tiring. I'm tired right down to the marrow of my bones. Want to sleep.

My head grows heavy. My eyes roll back.

I jerk awake. Where am I?

Blackness.

Omigod. It all comes back to me. I'm going to die. I'm going to die. I'm going to die.

Something furry touches my hand. I shriek, scrambling away on my backside across the floor. What was that? A rat? A mouse?

'It won't kill you,' I say aloud. No, the rat won't kill me.

Don't want to die.

Think!

I wiggle my tongue. Swallow.

The brick! I shuffle back and attack the rope against it again, moving my hands back and forth. Rub. Rest. Rub. Rest. Wiggle. Swallow. Rub. Rest.

I don't know how long I've been at this. It doesn't matter. I can't give up.

It's too slow. I'll be here forever. They might come back before I manage to free myself. I rub in a frenzy then, counting each movement back and forth against the brick. I need to focus my mind on something that won't make me completely fall apart.

One. Two. Three. Twenty. Counting, counting. Sixty. Two hundred.

My arms seize up with cramp. I'm going too fast. Lying on my side to rest, I listen to the terror screaming within me. I start counting again. When I get to a hundred and fifty, I'll start rubbing once more. One. Five. Eighty-one. Three. No, I'm going backwards.

Wake up!

I blink rapidly to stop my eyes closing.

Come on. Try again.

Rub. Rest. Rub. Rest. Wiggle. Swallow.

After what feels like an eternity, part of the rope gives way a little. Yes, I'm getting somewhere!

Drip. Drip. Drip. *Fucking dripping noise pressing into my ears! Shut up!*

Rub. Rub. Rub.

Finally, my hands come apart from each other as I break through the rope. I take a deep breath and remove the rest of the binding still around my wrists. My hands shake, and I wonder what will get me first. Hypothermia. Dehydration. Starvation. Fear.

No. Nothing will get me. I'll find a way out.

I circle my wrists, attempting to get some circulation back. Pump my fists, and the blood rushes to my fingers. That's a little better.

My ankles. Untie them. Yes, that's it. I find a knot on the rope, my fingernails digging in, trying to lift up an edge.

Come on!

There. A knot.

Wiggle. Swallow.

Drip. Drip. Drip.

After I manage to claw the knot loose, I unwind the rope from my ankles and try to stand up, which sends stars exploding behind my eyes again. My legs tremble, and I immediately fall onto all fours.

Breathe. In. Out. In. Out. That's it.

I get up slowly and hold the wall for support. *You can do this. Don't give up now. If you give up, you die.*

13

I wait. One minute passes. Two.

I resume my searching of the wall. It's easier now that I can walk properly, even though I have to concentrate on telling my legs to stop shaking. I run my hands along it and get to the next corner. Nothing.

'There must be an opening somewhere!' My voice sounds like the screech from a murder of crows taking flight.

Murder. Why would someone want to murder me? Leave me down here to die? Or are they coming back? Is anyone looking for me yet?

What will Liam say if I don't come home?

I picture my funeral in my head. Not many people there. Liam, of course, with a look of . . . what's that on his face? Pity? Regret? Anger? A few colleagues who work at the college. My boss, Theresa. Jordan. I smile when I think about Jordan. His kind smile, the warm hazel eyes that seem to see things I don't tell him. Sara will still be in India somewhere. Is that it? The sum of my life boiling down to just a few people? I know why, of course. Liam never liked my friends, so gradually it was easier just to let them drop off one by one. Easier, yes. Anything for a quiet life.

Would anyone really care if I didn't make it out of here? Would they miss me?

Yes. I would care. Chloe Benson would care. That's all I have to cling to.

In the middle of the next wall, I find what I've been looking for. I don't know how I missed it the first time around. Too much fear pumping through me, perhaps. And I didn't examine it all closely. Maybe being methodical works. I must tell Liam how right he is about that. It will make him happy.

It's a patch of texture different from the brick. Wood, rough and solid.

A doorway.

I examine every part of it. No keyhole. No handle. The door is maybe a couple of metres high and less than a metre wide. On the outside edges of the door is more crumbly, gritty render before the brick starts again. Where the bottom right hand corner of the door meets the ground, I can just about fit my hand through a small hole. Maybe animals have burrowed it out over the years, or part of the wall has collapsed. I wiggle my hand on the other side of the gap but can't touch anything except air and the concrete floor. I wonder if another tomb is behind this one, or something else. A corridor. A path to safety.

I push my hands against the door, crying out with the effort.

It doesn't budge. I press my shoulder against it. No, not working. Frustrated, I kick it.

'Let me out! Let me out of here!' Tears stream down my cheeks.

Drip. Drip. Drip. That's the only answer I get, and maybe it's a good thing. At least no one has come back to kill me yet. Panting, I slump to the floor. My hand connects with something cold and hard. I recoil instantly, remembering the rat. But this isn't an animal. This isn't something alive.

I pick it up and feel along its length. It's about half a metre long. One end is rounded, and the other is sharp, jagged. No, this is definitely not something alive.

It's something very, very dead.

Chapter Three

I'm rigid with fear. A sob rises in my throat, lungs struggling for oxygen. It's a bone. It *must* be animal. Can't be human. Can't, can't, can't. *Don't think about that.*

I try to remember my biology lessons at school. Dissecting a rat. Studying a cow's knee joint. Yes, this must be a cow bone. A femur, probably. I don't know why a cow bone would be here, or how it could wander underground. Maybe not a cow then. A dog. A big dog.

I pick it up, pushing the thoughts away. No time to think where it came from or what it really is. To me it's a weapon. No, not a weapon. A tool. That's all. I scrape at the render between the doorframe and the brick with the sharp end of bone, starting where the hole is. Dig, scrape. Dig, scrape, gouge. Cold, silent tears stream down my face. In the blackness, I hear the sound of falling grit. It's working.

Wiggle. Swallow. Bitter saliva in my mouth. Gouge. Scrape. Drip, drip, drip. The sound could drive you mad. Or was I already mad?

A hint of memory struggles to work its way to the surface. A hospital again. Me and . . . something. I don't know. It's gone.

What's wrong with my brain? Why can't I remember how I got here? Is it the lump on my head? Do I have some kind of brain damage?

Who am I? What do I really know?

I'm Chloe Benson. I'm twenty-seven. That's what I know. That has to be enough for now.

My arms shake. Everything shakes. I'm one big shaking vessel.

Am I really here? Am I dreaming, fast asleep in my bed? *I want to wake up. I want to wake up!*

'Stop it!' I say. 'Mind, stop wandering. Concentrate.' So I do, because I don't want to die down here. Don't want to be poor Chloe Benson who died in a hole underground.

I work down one side of the door. Scraping, gouging, digging at it with my nails and the bone as I go. Something sticky on me now. Blood on my fingertips and knuckles, mixing with the render. Pain. Sweat cooling on my already freezing body.

Ignore it!

I try to visualise something that calms me. A hummingbird hovering in the air as it sucks in nectar from a bright purple flower. Sunset over mountains, the sky streaked with gold, red, and orange. What is it they say—*'Red sky at night, shepherd's delight'*? There, see? I'm relaxed. Not a care in the world. Dolphins gliding through the ocean in perfect time with each other. A beach in the Caribbean, white sand, turquoise water. I'm back to water again!

How long have I been here? No clue.

How long will it take?

There's now a gap along one side of the doorway where the render has crumbled away. *OK, good. You can rest now.* I slump to the floor. Cold. So cold. I wrap my arms round me.

I must fall asleep again, because the next thing I know someone wakes me up, screaming. It's me.

How long have I slept? How can I sleep when I'm trying to survive?

Slapping myself on my cheeks, I stand up again. I must try. Must do this.

I work my way down the other side of the door. Render falls out between the frame and the brick wall. Slowly. Painfully slowly. I think about icy cold bottles of water. I picture opening the top and swallowing. Swallowing and swallowing. I can't stop. Can't get enough. Diving into a swimming pool and drinking the whole thing. I wiggle my tongue again and wonder how much saliva a human can produce. Is it infinite?

I'm halfway down the door now. The muscles in my arms burn. Fingers numb, hope sliding away.

Maybe I'm in hell. I've done something really bad, and I'm in hell. No, surely hell would be warmer than this. What have I done? How did I get here?

Don't know. Don't know. Can't think.

I imagine being in front of a roaring log fire. The wood crackles and spits. I know it's not real, though. I can tell by my teeth chattering.

A waft of my own stale sweat and rancid breath hits me.

Jump into a bath. A scorching hot bath. Those winter days when you're so cold to the bone that only a bath will do. Not a shower. A bath. With jasmine essential oil. Fluffy towels heated on the radiator. Mmm, lovely, and . . .

I stop mid-thought as I reach the bottom of the doorway. Most of the render along the sides and top is gone now, apart from some small bits. I breathe deeply in and out, trying to regain some energy.

OK, this is it. Push!

I brace my feet firmly on the floor, one in front of the other. I bend my front knee for stability and push as hard as I can. The door creaks and groans.

Push. Come on, Chloe Benson who wants to stay alive.

It shifts slightly. Then it's falling through inky black and landing somewhere on the other side with a thud. The momentum propels me forward with it, and I'm flying until my outstretched hands hit another wall.

I spin around, fingers skimming more brick. I'm in a corridor or tunnel, but I still can't see a thing.

OK, this is good. This is very good. Go. Run. Escape!

Left or right? Which way?

Who cares? Just go!

I hurry along the corridor, arms out in front of me, hoping to seek out another doorway somewhere.

Smack! My hands hit the end of the corridor, which shoots me backwards, and I land awkwardly on my right leg. I stand up. I'm sore, but nothing's broken.

There's a doorway here, too. Not wood. It's smooth. Metal. I search for a handle and find one. I lift it up and pull. It groans as it opens, like a wounded animal screeching.

And I'm through it and into another corridor. Steps going up.

Hazy light in the distance, a million miles away.

I'm running towards it, legs like rubber.

When I get to the end there's another doorway. Metal again. I heave it open.

Darkness, but not complete. Stars shimmer between shapes of trees. I smell air. Not stale dampness, but fresh air. Forest. Leaves. Owls screeching, out hunting for the night.

Then most things are a blur. Heart thumping. Legs pumping. Running, running, running. Puffs of breath. Blood surging in my head. Woods. Bushes. Slipping on a fallen, slimy log. Pain in my ankle. Up and running. Stumbling. A bat's wings flapping nearby. Pulse hammering in my ears. Animals snuffling, scratching. Rabbits scattering. Branches scraping my face, my arms, pulling hair. Lungs burning. Twigs cracking under my heavy feet. An owl hooting. Muscles screaming. The moon high up.

Then a tarmac road.

I jerk to a stop and lean forward, resting my hands on my thighs, trying to breathe. My chest rises and falls with the exertion, exhaustion. I can't afford to stop.

And I'm running again, along the side of the road. Headlights in the distance. Running towards them.

I wave my hands in the air wildly and move into the middle of the road. The lights get closer, slowing down.

I sink to the asphalt on my knees and slip into more blackness.

PART TWO

SKELETONS IN THE CLOSET

Chapter Four

Voices filter into my unconsciousness. Echoes of voices.

No—not voices. Beeping. Slow and steady. Beep, beep, beep, beep.

Pain everywhere.

For a moment, everything is blank. Then I remember the tomb. I'm still there.

My eyelids fly open and I gasp for air, sucking in more than I can breathe. I cough and splutter. The beeping accelerates.

A nurse appears in front of my eyes as my vision returns. 'Nice to see you awake,' she says, a pleased smile on her face.

'What happened?' I look down at my hands, bandaged with gauze.

'We're hoping you can tell us. A motorist found you collapsed in the road.' She examines the machines monitoring me. 'Your vitals are stable. You've been unconscious since they brought you in.' After scribbling something in a folder of notes at the end of my bed, she stands at the side of me, looking down. 'How are you feeling, pet?'

'My head hurts. My throat. Hands.' I notice a drip attached to a vein in the front of my elbow via a big needle taped down.

'You're mildly dehydrated, with some kind of bump to your head. You've had a CT scan and an MRI, but the doctors couldn't find any damage to your brain, which is good.'

'What . . .' I lick my lips. Try to swallow past the lump in my throat. 'What . . . date is it?'

'It's Thursday.'

'No.' My voice is a hoarse whisper. 'What date?'

'Ninth of May.'

Ninth of May? What? No, it can't be.

'Did you say the ninth of *May*?'

'Yes, that's right.'

But if the last thing I remember is Liam's birthday party on the twenty-third of March, I've lost about seven weeks of memory.

I lift a hand to the side of my head, touching the lump there. The pain brings nausea bubbling to the surface. 'I'm going to be sick.'

The nurse grabs a cardboard kidney-shaped bowl from on top of a cabinet beside my bed, thrusting it under my face just before I vomit. After the final spasms wrack my body, she wipes my face with a wad of tissues, also from the cabinet.

'You're OK—don't worry. I'm going to page the doctor, and he'll come and see you.' She wheels a bedside table next to me and places a jug of water from the top of the cabinet on it, along with a glass that she fills. 'You can have some water, but don't drink too much at once. Slow sips, OK?'

I nod. 'My husband. Does my husband know I'm here?'

'I'm afraid we haven't been able to tell anyone where you are. You had no ID when you were brought in, you see, so we didn't know who you were.' She takes a pen and pad from her top pocket. 'Give me your name, address, and phone number, and I'll get in touch with him.'

'I'm Chloe Benson. My husband's name is Liam.' Instinctively, I reach my sore hands to my raspy throat as I tell her our address, home phone number, his mobile number.

She pats my shoulder so gently I can't actually feel it. 'I'll contact him. And the doctor will be with you soon.'

'I was kidnapped.' My eyes water as the full realization of everything that's happened sinks in.

Her mouth falls open. 'Kidnapped?'

I can only nod, tears streaming down my face. Even to my ears, I know how it sounds. Crazy. Ridiculous. Who would want to kidnap a suburban wife and teacher?

'Right. Well, I'd better add calling the police to my list then, too. Don't worry; you're safe now, pet.' Her shoes squeak on the lino as she marches out of the room with purposeful strides, carrying the sick bowl.

I pick up the plastic cup of water in my bandaged hand, wincing at the throbbing pain in my fingertips. I intend to take a few sips, but I can't stop myself. I gulp the whole thing down in one swig, then pour some more. A wave of nausea rises inside, but I swallow it down and sip the next cup slowly, looking around my private room off the main ward.

From my bed, I can see out to the nurses' station. The nurse who just came in is on the phone, but I can't hear what she's saying. She frowns, looks up at me, and says something else into the phone, shaking her head. My gaze wanders past her, out into the rest of the ward. Someone wails in pain. Someone snores loudly. Chairs scrape against the floor. Footsteps echo.

I wipe my damp cheeks with the back of my hand and lean my head against the pillow, closing my eyes.

The next time I open them again, a man is standing at the end of my bed, reading my notes. He's wearing a white coat over a suit.

A doctor, then. He's got wavy ginger hair and a smattering of freckles across his face. Another folder about four centimetres thick is tucked under his arm.

'Who are you?' I lift my head slightly from the pillow and feel dizzy. I rest it back again, eyelids fluttering as I try to keep them open.

'Ah, glad to see you're awake.' He smiles, puts the notes he's reading into a slot at the end of my bed, and sits down in the plastic chair next to me. He places the folder from under his arm onto his lap. 'I'm Doctor Traynor. I'm a neurologist. And you are Chloe Benson, is that right?'

'Yes. Did you get hold of my husband? The police?'

'Yes. Apparently, your husband is in Scotland, but he's making his way back now. The police are also on their way.' He takes a slim-line torch from his top pocket and shines it into my eyes. The sudden brightness makes me blink and lean further back into the pillow. 'It's OK; I just want to examine you.' He holds my eyelids open until he's finished. Clicking off the torch, he says, 'Good. Can you follow my finger with your eyes?' He holds up his finger, moving up, down, side to side. 'Yes, very good. Do you know what happened?'

'I was kidnapped,' I say in a shaky voice. 'I woke up underground somewhere and managed to escape. Then I just kept running and running. I don't know how I got there. I don't—' I break off to take a calming breath. 'I don't remember what happened.'

He frowns, nods, and looks at his folder. 'Can you confirm your date of birth for me, please, Chloe?'

I tell him.

'And your address?'

I tell him that, too.

'Before you were . . . er . . . kidnapped, what's the last thing you remember?'

'A party. My husband's birthday party.'

'And when was that?'

'The twenty-third of March.'

He narrows his eyes slightly. 'You can't remember anything since the twenty-third of March?'

That's what I just said, isn't it? 'No,' I say calmly, fighting the frustration.

'Do you know what date it is today?'

'The nurse told me it's the ninth of May. Which means I've lost seven weeks of my life somewhere. Have I got brain damage? Is that why I can't remember?' I touch the lump above my ear.

'When you were brought in unconscious, we carried out some scans. Apart from the bump to your head and a few abrasions on your wrists and hands and face, we couldn't find anything significantly wrong with you, which is good. There's no brain injury or damage. You are a little dehydrated, but the drip will sort that out now, and there should be no lasting effects. But . . .' His smile erodes as he studies me for a moment before tapping the file in his lap. 'These are your medical notes.'

I frown, confused. 'Yes?'

'Do you remember being hospitalised in April?'

'What? No? I just told you. I remember my husband's party, and then . . .' I stop, wondering what the hell he's talking about. 'Did I have an operation or something?'

'No.' He flicks open the folder and reads to me. 'You suffered a miscarriage on March the twenty-fourth. You were apparently very depressed afterwards, and your GP prescribed Zolafaxine. It's an antidepressant.'

His words trigger a memory to hit me with the force of a wrecking ball. Of course! It's what I was trying to remember when I was held captive. The important thing I was going to tell Liam about after his party. I was pregnant. I don't know how I could've possibly forgotten that.

27

I tune him out as my hands instinctively touch my stomach. An empty stomach, devoid of any life that was in there. I gasp. Tears sting my eyes. But I have no time to reflect on what I've lost, because he carries on talking and I have to concentrate on what he's saying. This is important.

'. . . a bad reaction to the antidepressants, apparently. It can happen occasionally.'

'What do you mean "a bad reaction"? What kind of reaction?'

'You were suffering from psychosis-like side effects.'

My blood turns to ice in my veins. 'Wh-what does *that* mean?'

'You were having hallucinations. You were confused, agitated, and paranoid. Your husband and the hospital thought it best for you to be admitted for your own safety until the drugs wore off.'

'My own safety?' I shriek, not believing what I'm hearing.

He looks up sharply. 'Yes. You were sectioned under the Mental Health Act and admitted to the psychiatric ward.'

I shake my head, and the movement sends throbbing pain through my brain.

'You don't remember any of this?'

'No!' I struggle to keep calm.

'When you were released from hospital and sent home, the effects of the drugs had completely worn off. You were functioning normally, although you were still a little sad. We were certain there would be no lasting side effects from the drugs, but were not prepared to prescribe any more for obvious reasons. Even if a different antidepressant were prescribed, you're probably more susceptible to another reaction from it.'

'Why can't I remember that?'

He closes the folder and looks me in the eye. 'I'm not sure. You could have experienced another delayed side effect stemming from the Zolafaxine, or you could be suffering from amnesia brought on by the bump you have.' He points towards my head. 'Either way, it's very worrying.'

Worrying would be an understatement in my book. 'What happened after?'

'After?'

'When I was released from the hospital. When I was better. What happened then?'

He skims through more notes. 'You had a follow-up appointment with your primary care psychiatrist, Dr Drew, the week after. Everything seemed to be going well. He made a note that you were still grieving after the miscarriage, but he didn't believe you were depressed. He signed you off work for a further three weeks. You declined a weekly session with him and said you were able to cope with life. He was happy that the psychotic episode was sparked off purely by the drugs and you had no underlying mental illness.'

'What did I do when I was hallucinating?'

'Your husband found you at home on his return from work. He said you were in the garden, scratching and digging the path with your fingers. You were hallucinating that a man was chasing you, trying to kill you. You were digging to try and get away from whoever you thought was after you.'

All the blood drains from my face. My skin turns clammy with sweat. He's just described someone who isn't me. Hallucination? Paranoia? Maybe I'm really hallucinating now. This is just some bizarre and incredible nightmare.

Isn't it?

I stare at him, open-mouthed, trying to wrap my thoughts around this.

He looks down at my hands. 'Apart from the abrasions on your wrists that you have now, your hands looked like that when you were brought in before. Bloody, scraped skin and broken fingernails.'

'How is that possible? How could I hallucinate like that? How could I go from a sane person to having a psychotic episode?'

'As I said, it was a reaction to the drugs. It's very, very rare, but it can happen. We filed a pharmacovigilance report with the manufacturer as soon as we were sure.' He appears uncomfortable, as if I'm about to threaten the hospital with legal action.

'I don't even know what that means.'

'We are required by law to report any side effects to a drug. Especially when they're as severe as you experienced.'

'So . . .' I take a deep breath and lean my head against the cool pillows. I'm exhausted. Want to close my eyes and sleep. Sleep forever. 'I was released from hospital and I was fine, apart from still grieving because of the mis . . .'—my eyes water—'the miscarriage. And then what happened? What about the kidnapping? I don't remember how I got there. I don't remember any of this. What if whoever took me hit me on the head? What if they know where I am?'

He nods sympathetically in that way doctors do when they don't have a clue what's wrong with you. Thinking hard, he rests his chin between his thumb and forefinger. 'We'll leave that side of things to the police, who will no doubt be here shortly. From a medical point of view, I'll need to do some more tests. I'll come back later, when you've rested.'

And then I get it. The cloud of doubt in his eyes. The concern on his face, as if he's looking at a child who's been caught lying.

He doesn't believe I was kidnapped. He thinks I've had another 'psychotic episode.'

Chapter Five

The sound of shuffling footsteps jerks me awake. My eyelids fly open, heart racing, before my gaze settles on two men standing near the doorway.

'Chloe Benson?' The tall one says. He's broad shouldered, late forties, with dark brown hair flecked with grey around his temples. His black suit is rumpled. The other one is shorter, with the build of a boxer and a nose that looks like it's been broken a few times.

I swallow, my throat dry and scratchy. 'Yes,' I say warily, ready to reach for the alarm button beside my bed.

He takes a step forward and holds out a card with a photo and some writing on it. 'I'm Detective Inspector Summers. This is Detective Sergeant Flynn.' He gestures to his colleague with an upturned palm.

I squint at his police ID. The photo is of a younger Summers, who looks more like a criminal than a police officer. I nod, not sure what to say in these kinds of circumstances. I've never had cause to speak to the police for even a speeding fine. Somehow I feel guilty just being in their presence, as if I've done something wrong and I'm trying to hide it. I always get the same kind of feeling going through customs at the airport. Even though I'm a perfectly innocent traveller without so much as a duty-free packet of cigarettes, I still *feel* guilty going through the "Nothing to Declare" section with all eyes on me, wondering if I really am a drug-smuggling mule in disguise as a casually dressed English teacher.

'It sounds like you've had quite an ordeal.' Summers sits on the only plastic chair in the room, next to my bed.

Flynn leans against the doorframe and pulls out a biro from his top pocket. He's already holding a small notebook in his hand. He flips over a few pages before hovering his pen over the notebook.

'Can you tell us what happened?' Summers asks.

I tell them everything I can remember, from the time I woke up underground until the time I escaped and ran out into the road. I try to stay calm, but my heart palpitates, and beads of sweat break out on my forehead and upper lip. When I finish, Summers looks at me with an expression of impassivity.

'Can you think of any reason why someone would want to abduct you?'

'No! I . . . I'm just a normal, average person. I'm not wealthy. I don't associate with criminals. I've never even had so much as a parking ticket.'

'What do you do for a living?' Flynn stops scribbling and looks up at me.

'I teach A Level English Language at Downham Sixth Form College.'

'Are you married?' Summers asks.

'Yes. I've been married for two years to Liam Benson.'

'What does your husband do?'

'He's a pharmaceutical manufacture product manager for Devon Pharmaceutical.'

'Does he deal with anything sensitive?' Summers frowns. 'Animal testing, perhaps?'

'No, he's responsible for the manufacture of all the drugs they produce. He has nothing to do with the animal testing side of things as far as I know. Why?'

'Some animal rights groups can be, let's say, overzealous when it comes to animal testing. It's not unheard of for pharmaceutical employees or their families to be targeted, which is something to consider. Where is your husband?'

'The nurse spoke to him and he said he was in Scotland, working. Their plant that makes the drugs is in Aberdeen. He's on his way back now.'

'We'll need to speak with him, too.'

'Yes, of course.'

'So you don't remember anything leading up to when you were taken? Anything strange happening?' Summers asks.

I glance down at my hands, my fingers throbbing. 'No. The last thing I can remember is my husband's birthday party, which was March the twenty-third. I can't seem to remember the last seven weeks at all.' I think about what Dr Traynor told me and place a hand on my stomach, as if the act will somehow bring my baby back to life.

Summers leans forward slightly. 'Do you have any financial problems or owe money to anyone?'

'No. I mean, our house is mortgaged, but we don't have any other loans or anything. We're financially secure.'

'Have you received any kind of threats from anyone?'

'No.'

'You haven't been followed recently? Had any strange calls?'

'No.'

'OK, how about any problems with people? Colleagues, family members, friends?'

'No, nothing. Like I said, I'm just a normal person who lives a fairly quiet life.' I pause, wondering how to tell them. 'But . . .' I close my eyes for a moment.

'Yes?' Summers's voice prompts me to open them again.

'Well . . . my doctor just told me something happened to me after the party.'

Summers inclines his head and waits for me to carry on.

I tell him all I know so far, and it's as if I'm talking about someone else, because what Dr Traynor told me couldn't possibly have happened, could it? It's something so bizarre. One minute I would've been happy Chloe, excited about our first baby, and the next, I was crazy Chloe, hallucinating that people were out to get me and injuring myself trying to get away from them.

Summers regards me for a moment with his eyebrows raised. 'Did you have a history of depression before the miscarriage?'

'No, not that I know of.' I wonder what other loose cannons are in my past that I can't remember.

'And no other allergic reaction to prescribed drugs before?'

'Well, I can't take penicillin because it brings me out in hives, but I . . . no, I've never had a . . .' God, I can't even bring myself to say the word 'psychotic.' 'I've never had a reaction like Dr Traynor described.'

Summers glances at Flynn for a brief moment, then back to me. 'What have the doctors said about your memory loss?'

'Dr Traynor said there's no brain injury or damage. It might be something to do with . . .' I wave my hands around, trying to recall exactly what he said, but everything's such a shock. 'Er . . . it might be a delayed reaction to the original antidepressants. They're going to do some more tests.'

'Do we have permission to speak to your doctors about your medical history?'

'Yes. Yes, of course. I've got nothing to hide. I just want to get this sorted out. I won't feel safe until whoever took me is caught. Will you be able to find out what happened? Because this man is still out there, and I don't have a clue who he is or how he managed to abduct me.' I glance at Summers, eyes pleading, my heart rate going through the roof.

'Man? Is there anything that leads you to believe it was a man?'

'Well . . . no, but why would a woman do this? It makes sense that it's a man, doesn't it?'

'It's very possible. Don't worry, Mrs Benson—you're safe here.'

I blink back the rising terror. 'Please, call me Chloe. And I won't be here forever, will I? What if he comes back to get me?'

'We're going to do everything we can to find out what happened,' Summers says, although he doesn't look convinced. 'But with your limited memory of things, it may be a little difficult, I'm afraid.'

'Do you know who found me?' I ask.

'A woman called . . .' Flynn looks down at his notepad. 'Anne Casey. She was driving down the Great North Road, heading home from work at the time. She called an ambulance on her mobile, and they met her at the scene.'

'The Great North Road? That's about five miles from where I live.'

'You were found on a stretch of road that runs along the boundary of Sherrardspark Woods,' Summers says. 'Have you been to that area before? Walked in the woods, maybe?'

I start to shake my head, but the pain stops me. I lean back against the pillow and take a deep breath, willing the nausea to disappear. 'No. Never. Liam's driven down that road before when we've gone to Welwyn village, but I've never been into the woods.'

'Would you be willing to accompany us to where you were found to see if you recognise the area where you might've come from?' Summers asks.

The thought sends a chill up my spine, but I tell myself I'll be safe. I'll be with police officers. Nothing can happen again, can it?

Before I can answer, Liam rushes into the room, pushing past Flynn's bulk in the doorway. 'Oh, Chloe, I was so worried.' He sits on the bed and crushes me to him, enveloping his arms round me. He holds me so tight it's painful.

'Ouch!' I yelp.

He releases me. 'I'm sorry. Are you in pain? Are you OK?' He leans back and studies me, his pale blue eyes darting a concerned look between my face and my bandaged hands. He touches the scratches on my cheeks gingerly. 'I spoke to the nurse on the phone, but she only told me the basics. They said you've lost your memory. Is that true? What happened, darling?'

'I don't really know. I was . . . abducted.' I repeat the story I told Summers and Flynn, and somehow it seems less real the more I tell it.

'What?' Liam's eyes widen. His lips twist into a thin line. 'Oh, Chloe. It didn't happen again, did it?' He shakes his head softly at me. 'I thought everything was going to be OK now. You were doing so much better. The doctors told us there'd be no lasting effects.'

'This isn't from those drugs. It happened. It really happened. I was kidnapped.' I risk a glance past him to Summers, who's looking at me with a blank face.

'But this is exactly what happened before.' Liam's voice quietens.

'Liam, this isn't anything like before,' I say, even though I don't know what it was like before because I can't bloody remember. 'Someone took me and put me somewhere underground. I escaped. I ran for my life and made it to the road where a woman found me and called for help.'

He glances down at my bandaged hands. 'But your hands?' He strokes my forearm softly. 'It's what you did last time.'

'Apparently.' Even though I'm bone-numbingly tired, anger rises within me. I try to bite it back. Anger doesn't work well with Liam, and I need him to believe me. Need everyone to believe me. 'But I know what happened. And he's still out there. The man or . . . or whoever took me.' I start to cry then. Fat tears fall uncontrollably down my cheeks. My shoulders shake. My nose blocks.

'You said you don't remember what happened, though, Chloe.' Liam sighs ever so slightly.

'No, I remember waking up in that place. I remember escaping. But I don't remember how I got there.'

Liam puts one arm protectively round my shoulder and twists on the bed so he's looking at Summers for the first time. 'You're from the police station?'

'Yes. DI Summers.' He holds out his hand for Liam to shake, but Liam ignores it.

'And what do you think?' Liam asks him.

'I'm sorry?'

'Her story.'

'It's not a story.' I wipe my nose on the back of my bandaged hand and look at Summers, trying to send him a silent message that I'm telling the truth. This isn't some kind of deranged flashback. I'm not deluded or confused.

Summers's gaze flicks between Liam and me. 'Your wife has obviously been through some kind of traumatic incident, and it's my job to find out what that is.'

Liam tenses beside me.

I take a big sniff. It echoes in the ensuing silence.

'You were in Scotland for business?' Summers asks Liam, taking charge.

'Yes.'

'For how long?'

'I flew up to Aberdeen three days ago.'

'And Chloe was at home when you last saw her?'

'Yes. Did she tell you what happened when she was hospitalised before?'

Summers nods. 'She did. But it will help to hear things from you, since Chloe clearly doesn't remember the incident. The last thing she remembers is your party.'

'Yes. It was my fortieth. Lots of friends were there. It was a good night. And then . . .' Liam glances at me with sadness. 'The day after the party, Chloe told me she was pregnant.'

I stifle a sob.

'But . . . in the early hours of the following morning, she had a miscarriage.' Liam tightens his arm round my shoulder. 'After the miscarriage, she became depressed. She wasn't eating or sleeping, and she'd lost all interest in life. So I insisted she go to see her GP, who prescribed some antidepressants and sleeping tablets. Unfortunately, she had some kind of reaction to the antidepressants, though, and . . . well . . .' He looks over at me to check that I'm OK.

'Carry on. I want to hear this,' I say. Maybe 'want' is the wrong word. I *need* to hear this. Need to know if I'm going insane. Again.

Liam makes a sound like a sigh. 'Chloe suffered from hallucinations and exhibited paranoid behaviour. She thought a man was chasing her, trying to kill her. I came home from work and found her in the garden, scratching and digging at the path. She was screaming, trying to get away from whoever she thought was chasing her. When I tried to help her, she was confused and disorientated. She just fought back.'

My cheeks burn with embarrassment, self-loathing, disbelief.

'We had to have her sectioned for her own safety.'

An involuntary gasps escapes my lips. If Liam hears it, he ignores the sound and carries on talking about me. I've been reduced to a mere spectator in my life.

'The antidepressants were stopped immediately, and she was given antipsychotic drugs until she appeared to return to her normal self.'

'How long was I in hospital?' I force the question out, even though the words seem to stick on my tongue.

Liam gives me a sideways glance. 'A week. Then you had an outpatient appointment with the psychiatrist. But we all thought you were getting better. They didn't think there would be any lasting effects from the drugs when they were out of your system. But now this has happened, and . . . well, you must know how this sounds, Chloe. It's all so far-fetched. And so much like what happened before. We don't want to waste the police's time, do we?' He strokes my shoulder and looks at Summers with an apologetic expression.

And that's when I really start to question myself. Did I really wake up in that place? Did I really escape? Or have I imagined the whole thing? Is this some kind of relapse?

'I think you can let us be the judge of what's wasting our time.' Summers gives Liam a courteous smile. 'What happened when Chloe was released from hospital?'

'She was signed off work, so she was just at home, recuperating from it all. She seemed to be OK—a little depressed, still, about losing the baby. She still had trouble sleeping, too, but things were getting back to normal, or so I thought.'

'Did you contact her while you were away in Scotland? Maybe we can establish exactly what day you went missing, Chloe.' Summers looks pointedly at me.

'I rang her mobile phone when I arrived, but then I was up to my neck in work and didn't have time to contact her. We're launching a new diabetes drug soon, so it's been a very hectic time.'

'You work for Devon Pharmaceutical?' Summers asks.

'Yes.'

'What does your job entail exactly?'

'I oversee the manufacture of our drugs, amongst other things.'

'Does Devon Pharmaceutical carry out animal testing?' Summers crosses his legs.

'Yes. And I can see where you're going with this, but our company has never been a target for that in the past.'

'So you've never personally received any threats in connection with your work?'

'Absolutely not.'

'Let me just confirm that the last time you spoke to Chloe was on the sixth of May, when you arrived in Scotland?' Flynn asks.

'Yes.'

Flynn writes it down. 'She didn't mention that she was going anywhere or doing anything in particular?'

'No.' He glances at me, wearing a look of concern. 'She hasn't been out of the house much since the miscarriage.'

'And she didn't tell you anything that could be cause for alarm?' Summers asks.

'Definitely not.'

'Did you fly back from Scotland today?' Flynn asks.

'Yes, although I wasn't due back for another four days. I got the taxi to drop me off at home on the way back from Stansted airport. Then I left my suitcase there, got my car keys, and drove here straight away.'

'Was there any sign of disturbance or forced entry at your house?' Summers again.

'No. I didn't notice anything like that, but of course I only had a quick look.'

'I'd appreciate it if you'd do a thorough check when you get home and let me know.'

'Of course.'

'Can you give us the names of any friends or family who might've seen you before you disappeared?' Summers asks me then.

'Liam's all the family I have,' I say. 'And my best friend Sara is in India, travelling.'

'What about your family?' Summers asks Liam. 'Would they have checked up on Chloe while you were away?'

'No. I'm an only child, and my parents were middle-aged by the time I came along, so they passed away years ago. There's only my cousin, Jeremy, and his wife, Alice, but they live in Kent. The last time we saw them was at my party, when they stayed the night and left the following morning.'

'How about any work colleagues?' Summers asks me. 'Anyone you were close to at the college you might've seen?'

I think of Jordan then, but it's not as if he would come to the house. If Liam found out, he would've got angry. 'No,' I say softly. 'They're just colleagues, not friends.'

Summers lets out a deep breath and stands. 'Well, we'll start making some enquiries. I'll liaise with Dr Traynor to see when you'll be fit enough to accompany us out to the woods. And if you think of anything else, let us know, OK?' He pulls a card out of his pocket and hands it to me, but Liam is closer and takes it before I can.

Liam shoves it into the pocket of his suit jacket. 'We will.' He stands up. 'Perhaps I can have a word with you before you leave?' He angles his head towards the doorway, and a look passes between them. Liam leads the way into the corridor, and I see him talking earnestly to Summers and Flynn. Summers looks over at me briefly.

I fidget with the bed sheet as Summers nods several times, and Flynn writes something down in his notepad before leaving. When Liam returns, he sits on the bed next to me and takes my hand in his. I try to look him in the eye but find I can't. Instead, I stare at the sheets.

'Whatever am I going to do with you, my love?' He strokes my hair gently.

Chapter Six

'How are you feeling?' Dr Traynor enters the room, forcing the swirling thoughts of panic in my head to stop abruptly.

'Tired. I've got a headache and still feel a bit sick.'

'That will be the concussion. It's only mild. You'll feel more like your normal self in a few days.'

But what is my normal self? I want to ask. I don't know anymore, not after what he and Liam have told me. I sit up, pushing the bedside table away. The remains of a stodgy lasagne and soggy chips sitting on top of it make me feel sick now. I'd managed to pick at it, but the fear and anxiety has bitten away at any hunger.

'No appetite?' he asks.

'Not really.'

'You need to eat to regain your strength.'

'Have you eaten the food here?'

'Good point.' He smiles and sits down next to me. 'Has your husband left?'

'Yes. He needed a shower and something to eat. He's coming back later with some clothes and toiletries for me.'

'Good. In the meantime, let's carry out a few tests if you're up to it, shall we?'

'OK.'

'I'm going to ask you a series of questions to check different areas of your memory. Just answer them as quickly as you can.' He opens the notes on his lap and clicks the top of his pen. 'What's your full name?'

'Chloe Benson.'

'How old are you?'

'Twenty-seven.'

'Where do you live?'

'Poplar Close.'

'How long have you lived there?'

'Just over two years.'

'Good. Who am I?'

'Dr Traynor.'

'Which year is it?'

'2014.'

'Which month is it?'

'May.'

'Who is the Prime Minister?'

'David Cameron.'

'Can you count backwards in threes starting from five hundred?'

'497, 494, 491, 488, 485, 482, 479, 476, 473, 470—'

'OK, that's good. Can you count backwards in sevens?'

The sevens are harder, but I manage. He recites five lines of poetry and asks me to repeat them back to him, which I do.

He hands me a sheet of paper with various shapes on it. After I've studied it, he takes the paper away and says, 'Where did you grow up?'

'Here in Welwyn Garden City. Then I went to university in London and moved back here afterwards.'

He scribbles something down. 'What did you study at university?'

'English. Then I did a teacher training course.'

'Which shapes were on the piece of paper I just showed you?'

'Stars, triangles, squares, oblongs, something that looked like a palm tree.'

He tells me a sequence of words that I have to repeat back to him. Then a sequence of numbers. He holds up cards with pictures of different animals on them and asks me to call out which one he's holding up. Finally, he closes his notes and places the pen on top. 'Good. Very good.'

'It doesn't feel good from where I'm sitting.'

'You have what is called amnesia. It could be from the bump to your head. After a concussive injury, brain cells not destroyed are sometimes left in a vulnerable state for a time but eventually heal themselves. It could also have been brought on by a delayed side effect from the antidepressants.' He pauses, as if he's making me aware some bad news is coming. What could be worse, though, I have no idea. 'We did a blood test when you were admitted and found Silepine in your system, which is a sleeping tablet. Apparently, your GP prescribed it to you at the same time as the antidepressants to help you sleep. It's possible they gave you some kind of similar reaction to what happened with the Zolafaxine.'

'What? But I . . . they . . . no.' I try to speak, but my mouth just flaps open and closed. It takes a moment for my brain to catch up with my mouth. 'I don't take sleeping tablets. I've only ever taken them once in my life when I was having trouble sleeping at university. They made me feel so terrible and drowsy the next day that I've never taken one since.'

'Silepine aren't like the old sleeping tablets. They don't have the horrible drowsy effect the day after.' He looks at his notes. 'We only found a moderate amount in your system, but nevertheless, if you were allergic to them, it could have caused you to exhibit the same psychosis-like symptoms as before. Hallucinations and amnesia in themselves are also adverse side effects of Silepine, although, again, they're very rare.'

'Yes, but I didn't take them. I . . .' I can't speak then. It's just not possible. Any of this. It's not real. How can it be? But I can't deny I took them when a blood test proves I did.

'When the hospital released you after the incident with the antidepressants, we advised you not to take any other medications. Sometimes, once you have a reaction to one, it makes you more susceptible to have a reaction to other drugs.' Dr Traynor clears his throat. 'But it would appear that you did take them. What other explanation can there be for them being in your system?'

'Why would I take them, then, if you told me not to?' I challenge him.

'I'm afraid we can only advise patients on their care. Sadly, they don't always take our advice. Liam has mentioned you were still having trouble sleeping, so it's possible you decided to take them anyway. Or perhaps the grief became more severe and escalated into depression once more and you wanted to harm yourself.' He shifts uncomfortably in his chair. 'Depression can sometimes be difficult to assess.'

I know all about it being hard to assess. I never knew about Mum until it was too late. But even so, I stare at him with alarm. 'You mean I . . . wait. You think I took them to try and *kill myself*?'

'It's possible. Or it could've been a cry for help. And that's what we're here for. To help you.'

'No, I wouldn't have done that. I just wouldn't.' I must look wild as my gaze flits around the room, hardly resting on one thing while I try to make sense of what he's saying. The bits and pieces of me don't seem to fit together properly anymore. Everything's wrong, out of place, like a scattered jigsaw puzzle.

'Unfortunately, you can't remember exactly what did happen, so it's entirely possible that you did.'

'But I know I'd never try to kill myself.'

He remains silent. Just looks at me in a calm, doctorly way that says he's seen it all before and nothing surprises him anymore.

'What do you mean by a moderate amount, anyway? How much would I have taken?' A tingling sensation starts under my scalp. I rub the back of my head against the pillow.

'Probably only three or four tablets. Enough to make you very sleepy.'

'But will I get my memory back?' I ask shakily. 'I've lost seven weeks. I need to know what happened. I need to know if . . .' What do I say? If I'm mad? If I'm hallucinating? If I tried to commit suicide? 'I need to know if there's someone out there who's going to come back for me.'

'The brain is a very complicated piece of machinery, and unfortunately, there's no cure for amnesia, but many forms do fix themselves. Sometimes patients with amnesia that's not caused by a brain injury experience the return of their memories spontaneously or over time. It's a waiting game, I'm afraid.'

I feel a pain in my chest, as if someone has dealt me a swift blow. 'A waiting game?' Waiting for some unknown person to come back and kill me. Lost in limbo until he's caught and locked up.

'I have no definitive answer for you. Your memory could return in a matter of days, weeks, or even months. It could return in bits and pieces, or it could happen all at once. Both your long-term and short-term memory seem to be functioning correctly. It's just this small period of time that is missing. But I'm very optimistic you'll make a full recovery eventually.'

'And in the meantime, I won't know if this person is still after me.'

'I'm sure the police are doing all they can.' He smiles, as if that's supposed to reassure me somehow. It doesn't. Nothing will until I know what really happened. 'The police have spoken with me about you accompanying them to the area where you were found wandering.'

'They said they would talk to you.'

'I think we need to wait at least a day and see how you're feeling then. Physically, you have no major injuries, although you're still a little weak. We'll take the drip out tonight, but I want to make sure you're strong enough before you leave the hospital, even if it's only for a short while.' He stands up, presses his folder of notes to his chest. 'Try not to worry too much. Getting stressed won't help your recovery.'

How can I not worry? It's already burrowing a dark tunnel beneath my sternum.

'Another doctor will be in to see you later, to do a psychiatric evaluation.'

Too weary to speak, I can only nod.

I'm sipping a cup of tea the orderly has just brought round the ward. I don't usually have sugar in it, but I asked for three in this one. All the better to get my strength up. I don't want to stay in this place any longer than I have to, in case I end up in the loony bin again.

I've been going over and over it in my head, and I'm sure now. Absolutely positive that what I described did really happen. It wasn't a hallucination. It wasn't a relapse.

It must've been the head injury that's made me lose my memory. I just don't know how I got the injury, or how I woke up in that place.

Or was it the sleeping tablets?

Think, Chloe!

But the more I think, the more muddled my head gets.

I flip the sheets back, swing my legs over the bed, and sit up. The room tilts before my eyes. I take a deep breath and gently touch the lump on my head. It's solid, like a hard-boiled egg under the surface.

I wait for my vision to clear, and then stand up, gripping onto the bedside cabinet with my left hand for support. On unsteady legs, I tentatively test the weight on my sore ankle. It's painful, but at least I can support myself. I'm wearing one of those horrible hospital gowns with lots of ties at the back that you can never do up properly yourself. Holding onto the back of it, for modesty, with my right hand, I take small steps around the room. Back again to where I started. When I turn round to repeat the exercise, a man is standing in my doorway, watching me.

I freeze.

He has a shock of grey hair, thick grey eyebrows, and a grey goatee beard. He's wearing dark green cord trousers, a white shirt with a small stain of something that looks like coffee on the front, and a tweed jacket with leather patches at the elbow, giving him a grandfatherly appearance. The look on his face . . . it's creepy, like he recognises me somehow, but I've never seen him before in my life.

'Stay there!' I say, pressing the emergency bell by my bed.

He smiles but doesn't make a move towards me. 'Very good move, Chloe. You want to make sure I'm not a threat, but I can assure you, I'm a doctor.'

49

A nurse rushes to the room. 'Is everything OK?' She glances between the man and me.

I point a wobbly hand at him. 'He says he's a doctor, but he doesn't look like one. Is he?'

She gives me a relieved smile. 'Yes, this is Dr Drew.'

It's then I notice the ID badge pinned to his shirt pocket, although it's too far away for me to read. I sit on the bed, my shoulders relaxing with relief. 'Thanks,' I tell her.

'Do you need anything else?' she asks.

'No. Thank you.'

She walks out, and Dr Drew takes off his ID badge, holding it out for me to inspect. I take it and read: "Dr Albert Drew, Consultant Psychiatrist, Mental Health Unit, Queen Elizabeth II Hospital."

'Sorry,' I mumble, handing it back to him.

'No, that was very wise, under the circumstances.' He nods to the chair beside the bed. 'Do you mind if I sit?'

'I don't mind.' Or maybe I did, depending on what more bad news I was going to get.

'Do you recognise me?' he says after he gets comfortable, resting his hands on his ample belly.

'No. Should I?'

He gives me a warm smile. 'I was in charge of your treatment when you were admitted in April.'

'Oh. Right. I . . . I don't remember that.'

'Yes. So Dr Traynor informed me.' He steeples his fingers. 'Do you think you could tell me what happened before you were brought in this time?'

I flop forward, cradling my head in my hands, my long hair swinging down over my face like a curtain. 'Oh, God,' I groan. I don't want to go over it again.

'I know this is very traumatic for you, but we're all here to help you.'

I lift my head and search his eyes, looking for some kind of trap, but all I can see is kindness and compassion there.

'Tell you what: Let me rustle up some tea and biscuits, and I'll come back in a minute.' He leaves the room.

I swing my legs back into bed, pull the sheets over me, and stare at the ceiling. He returns a few minutes later with two mugs of tea that look like dirty dishwater and a plate of biscuits on a tray. He puts them on the bedside table, then settles back into a comfy position on the chair and waits for me to speak. I ignore the foul-looking tea and tell him what I've told everyone else.

He watches me expectantly, nodding every now and then, without interrupting me.

When I finish, I say, 'Do you think I made this all up?'

'Did someone say you had?'

I think about the look in Dr Traynor's eyes. Maybe I mistook his lack of belief for concern. But Liam . . . no, he definitely didn't believe me. I don't know if the police even think I was telling the truth. 'I don't think my husband believes me.' I bite my lip. 'But I didn't make this up. I know I didn't.'

I know I'm not mad.

Don't I?

I mean, not as mad as I apparently was when I was admitted to hospital.

He regards me for a moment with a kind smile and then leans towards me slightly. 'I don't think you've made this up. What's important is what you *believe*. And you believe this did happen. But . . .' He pauses here. 'What you've described is a reaction very similar to what happened with the antidepressants before when you were sectioned.'

'I know.' I exhale a lungful of breath in defeat.

'On the other hand, you have slight abrasions on your wrists, which could point to you being restrained. You're dehydrated, scratched and bruised, and you have a bump to your head. Something has obviously occurred. In which case, there is a possibility you could still be in danger.'

Chapter Seven

'That's what I'm scared of. I don't know who took me. I don't know *why* they took me.' A rising panic forces my chest muscles to constrict.

'Indeed. It's natural to be scared, but I think we need to leave the investigation to the police and let us doctors handle the other side of things. I was more concerned about finding out if you were a danger to yourself.'

'Myself?' I say cautiously.

He doesn't say anything, but he doesn't need to. I can see everything he's not saying reflected clearly in his eyes. He clears his throat. 'When you were released from hospital before, you had one follow-up appointment with me, but you mainly wanted to talk about the loss of your baby.'

A twinge of grief rips through me so hard it physically hurts deep inside, leaving me raw.

'I encouraged you to write a journal or a letter to your baby as a way to let the grief out.'

'Did I do that?'

'I don't know. As I said, you only had one appointment, but you thought it sounded like a good idea.'

'But I wasn't depressed, was I? I didn't think about killing myself? It was just grief?'

'There can be a fine line between depression and grief. Sometimes the symptoms of depression are similar to the emotions of the grieving process. But in our outpatient appointment, I saw no signs that would indicate clinical depression.'

'But I *was* depressed when I went to my GP after the miscarriage?'

He purses his lips, as if he's weighing up how much to tell me. 'Apparently, your GP believed you were; that's why she prescribed the antidepressants and sleeping tablets. Liam also believed you were depressed.'

'Dr Traynor thinks that after I came out of hospital, the grief turned into depression again. He thinks I tried to kill myself with the sleeping tablets but I had another adverse side effect and that I've hallucinated this whole thing.'

'What do you think?'

'I don't know. I mean, this is all just . . .' I shrug hopelessly. 'It's so confusing. I don't think I would've tried to kill myself. And I know I wasn't hallucinating when I was kept confined in that underground place. I remember it all so vividly. The terror. The feel of the walls when I touched them. The rat. The dripping sound of water. Scraping away at the doorframe. Running down the corridors and through the woods.'

Dr Drew looks sceptical. 'When you had the episode with the antidepressants, you also believed the hallucinations were very real, too.' He pauses for a moment, then says, 'Perhaps we should talk about the time you do remember. The time before the party.'

'Will it help me recover my lost memories?' Hope and desperation emanates through my voice.

'It's possible. It may trigger something in your brain, and it could help us determine your state of mind at the time this new incident began.' He scratches his head. 'I believe you could be suffering from dissociative amnesia, which means amnesia caused by trauma or stress. It's a form of denying a distressing event as a coping mechanism. Since there is no brain injury involved here, it's likely that you may begin to recall the trauma over time, and talking about your past could help with that. It is possible that the trauma of the miscarriage itself has brought this on.'

I frown, confused. 'Wait, Dr Traynor didn't mention anything like that. He said the amnesia could be from concussion or as a side effect of taking the sleeping tablets, the Sil . . . Sil—'

'Silepine.'

'Yes, that.'

'Well, all of our theories are entirely possible.' He sounds a little defensive, and I wonder if there's some kind of departmental rivalry going on about my diagnosis. 'Unfortunately, there is no exact test we can do to prove the correct one, which is why we need to look at everything.'

'I see,' I say, except I don't see at all. I feel like I'm stumbling around in the dark still, blindly bumping into things. I take a sip of water and swallow slowly. My fingertips itch under the gauze, and I fight the urge to scratch them. 'Where do I start, then?'

'How were things going before the miscarriage?'

'Well . . . things weren't perfect, I suppose. I mean, whose life is perfect?'

'I would imagine it depends on your idea of perfection. What was your home life and work like?' He looks at me as if I'm a curious specimen.

'Work was good. I teach A Level English Language to college students. Of course, you get the odd pupil who likes to muck around and have fun, but on the whole, they're a good bunch of teenagers. It's a sixth form college affiliated with Cambridge University. Most of the students are from good backgrounds and want to go on to

Cambridge, so it's not like I'm teaching in an inner-city school, which brings its own set of problems.'

'That must be very rewarding.'

'For the most part it is. Liam doesn't like me teaching.'

'Why not?'

I exhale a deep breath. 'He's old fashioned. He thinks the wife should be at home, taking care of her husband's every whim.'

'And you don't agree with that?'

'Teaching is one of the few things I've managed to hang onto that's mine.'

His brows furrow together. 'Can you elaborate on that?'

I wonder how much to tell him. I don't like airing my dirty laundry in public. This is the life I've chosen, and sometimes you just have to put up with things, don't you? And anyway, every relationship has its up and downs. But I want to find out what happened to me, and talking about this may be the only way to get my memory back. 'Liam can be a bit controlling sometimes. You know, he just likes things done his way, I suppose.' I shrug. 'And then sometimes, he's wonderful. Attentive, loving, thoughtful. It's not all bad, really; it's just normal. No one's perfect, are they?' I let out a mirthless laugh. 'We've all got flaws, haven't we?'

'Of course. We wouldn't be human if we didn't.'

'In the beginning, things were great between us. He was romantic and kind, and funny. After we got married a couple of years ago, things started to change. He was working long hours, and I put it down to the stress of his job that was making him moody sometimes. Then he got a promotion, which made him even more stressed, but now I think . . .'

'Yes?'

'Maybe it's just me that makes him moody. I thought the baby might help get things back on track for us. But, well, obviously that didn't happen. It looks like it's just made things a whole lot worse.'

'Was he happy about the baby?'

'I don't know. I can't remember. I was going to tell him after the party, but that's where my memory ends.'

'Did you talk about having children?'

'He didn't want to spoil things between us if we had a baby. He wanted it to just be us as a couple.' I bite my lip. 'Some men are like that, aren't they? They get jealous when a baby comes along.'

'Was he jealous over you?'

A memory hits me then. About a year ago, Liam had just been promoted. We were having a celebratory meal at his favourite Chinese restaurant. His close work colleagues were there, but none of my friends by then. I was on one side of Liam at the table, and on his other side sat his new boss, Julianne, to whom he was paying rapt attention. He practically ignored me, so I turned to the man on my other side, Paul Etherington, who worked in the department Liam was leaving, and began an interesting conversation with him. Liam was happy, on form, making witty comments and charming everyone. The drinks flowed. At midnight, everyone left the restaurant, and when we got in the taxi Liam wouldn't speak to me.

As soon as we walked through the front door, he accused me of flirting with Paul. The intensity of his anger took me aback as I remembered just how much flattering attention he'd paid to Julianne. I told him I was just being polite, making small talk with people he worked with. Suddenly, Liam grabbed hold of me and pushed me hard against the wall, his mouth on mine, his excitement pressing against my thigh. I tried to push him away, tried to say I wasn't in the mood after his outburst, but in the end, I thought it best to go along with it. I hated the angry Liam, who either sulked and wouldn't speak to me for days, or berated me and made snide comments and told me how everything was my fault. So I did nothing when he lifted up my dress and yanked my knickers down, ripping them in the process. Did nothing when he picked me up and dropped me roughly onto the stairs, the hard wooden corners digging into my spine. And when he shoved himself inside me, I pretended I was as excited as him. It was better that way. Easier for me.

Afterwards, he kissed me roughly, his eyes as dark as the ocean in a storm, and said, 'You're mine, Chloe. Don't ever forget that.' And he walked past me up the stairs, leaving me to wonder what the hell had just happened.

Maybe it *had* been my fault. Maybe I was paying too much attention to Paul and not enough to Liam. I didn't know whether apologizing might just make him angrier, so I crept into our bedroom, undressed in silence as I listened to him singing in the shower, and got into bed, keeping my eyes shut tight.

When I woke up the next morning, it was so unreal I thought I must've imagined it at first, but my back was bruised and I was sore inside, and I knew it really had happened. He brought me breakfast in bed, apologizing profusely. Said he couldn't stand the thought of me leaving him and had just got himself so wound up he couldn't help it.

I justified it by telling myself that hadn't most women done that at some time or another? Had sex when they weren't in the mood for it. Done it because their partner went on and on about it. Done it just to keep the peace. And that's what I was doing. Keeping the peace so the loving, caring Liam returned. He was my husband, after all, and I desperately wanted to please him. Maybe that sounds sad and pathetic, but I'd been without love since my mum died, and now I'd had a taste of it, I craved it like a drug, so I resolved to try harder to keep everything in harmony.

'Sometimes he gets jealous,' I say, answering Dr Drew's question but finding it hard to meet his eyes.

'And how do you feel about that?'

I fiddle with the sheets. 'I used to think it was kind of sweet and protective. As if it proved just how much he loved me.'

'And now?'

'Sometimes it's stifling. I have to be careful who I talk to and who I look at when we're together. It's like I can't be *me* anymore because I'm worried I might upset him.' I risk a glance at Dr Drew, who's tapping his fingertip on the side of his forehead, looking deep in thought. I wonder what else to say. How can you talk about something that's hard to define? 'I suppose things just creep up on you, don't they? Liam's a bit stuck in his ways, I suppose you'd call it. It could be the age gap between us.' I shrug. 'Don't get me wrong, though, it's not all bad. I'm probably making it sounds worse than it is.'

'How old were you when you met Liam?'

'I was twenty-five and he was thirty-eight. I'd just started my job at the college. We met at a nightclub, and he whisked me off my feet. He was intelligent, kind, had a good sense of humour. It was the first real relationship I'd had, and we fell madly in love. We got married after three months.'

'A whirlwind romance?' He smiles.

'Yes.'

'Has he ever hit you?'

'No!'

'Has he ever been verbally abusive?'

'Aren't most men like that sometimes?'

'I wouldn't say that, my dear.' He takes a sip of his tea, grimaces, then sets it back on the bedside table. 'How about psychologically or emotionally abusive?'

I sigh, wanting to put into words things I've never talked about, but not wanting to because it will make it too real. 'I don't really know what you mean by that. Maybe.'

'Are you happy with the way things are?'

'Is anyone *really* happy? I mean, you look at other people's lives and you think they have a great job or a great marriage and they seem so happy, but you're only seeing what they want you to see. When people ask you how you are, the automatic reaction is to say you're fine, isn't it? No one wants to listen to you moaning about the trivial little bits and pieces of your life. So how do you know when someone's happy and when they aren't?'

'I'm only interested in you, not everyone else. What do *you* want people to see?'

'All couples have bad patches. You can't go through life being happy *all* the time. What is the definition of happiness, anyway? I bet if you asked a hundred different people, you'd get a hundred different answers. Ups and downs are part of marriage.'

'True, but do you think your problems are trivial then?'

'I suppose so. I have a good job. A nice house. A husband. What can I have to complain about? You just have to get on with life and make the best of things.'

'Little things have a way of piling up.'

I don't say anything. Don't know if he's expecting me to say something. What can I say? It's a marriage, and all marriages have problems. Then I think I finally get what he's saying. Or not saying. I stare at him for the longest moment until I'm forced to take a breath. 'Do you think Liam has something to do with me being kidnapped? Is that why you're asking about him?'

'No, I'm not suggesting that at all. I'm simply trying to find out about your life to see if it helps jog your memory.'

'As I said, things aren't perfect, but Liam is a manager in a pharmaceutical company, not some kind of lowlife criminal. He doesn't kidnap people and leave them for dead.'

Dr Drew nods profusely. 'Of course not.'

'So what *are* you suggesting? That I've hallucinated the whole thing? That I've made it all up for some reason?' The room becomes stuffy and hot, or maybe it's me.

He smiles at me then. It's a kind, patient smile. 'The problem is at the moment we don't know what happened, so we should carry on exploring all avenues. For example, do you talk to any friends or family? Maybe you spoke to someone about where you were going or what you were doing before you were found near the woods.'

'Not really. Do you know about my mum?'

'Yes. When you were admitted, I discussed what happened to her with you and Liam, as it might've had a bearing on you.'

I voice the fear I've wondered about for a long time. 'Can depression and suicide be hereditary?'

'Depression is a very complex disorder where both genes and environment play a role, but, yes, depression often runs in families. But you don't know if your mother intentionally overdosed on cocaine, do you? She was discovered dead in the bathroom of one of her coworkers' houses when he was having a party, wasn't she?'

'Yes.'

'When we spoke before, I seem to remember you saying neither you nor anyone else saw any warning signs of depression prior to her overdose, so this wasn't something you could foresee. The obvious circumstances point to your mother using the cocaine recreationally. Her death was also ruled as accidental by the coroner.'

'Yes, but I was nine years old when she died. I could've missed a lot of things. No one will ever know what really happened, will they?'

'I agree, but at that age it's not your responsibility to be the parent.'

'No, but that doesn't make things any easier.'

'Tell me about what happened after she died.'

I think back to when the police came to my babysitter's house and told us how Mum had been found dead after a suspected overdose at a friend's party. How I felt numb for a long time afterwards. So long, it felt like it was ingrained in my soul and etched into my bones, as if I'd never feel anything again. One day out of the blue, the disbelief and shock hit me so hard I physically lost my voice. I couldn't speak at all, and that was good. I didn't want to talk to anyone, didn't want to try to explain how I felt. I couldn't.

Slowly the shock gave way to overwhelming grief and sadness. Feeling as if I'd never stop crying. A black cloud hovered over me constantly. It took six months before I started talking again, and even longer for the cloud to blow away.

'It was awful. I never knew my dad. He left Mum as soon as he found out she was pregnant. He's not even named on my birth certificate. I had no other family, so I was taken into care and lived in a children's home.'

'It must've been hard losing your mum at that age and growing up in the care system.'

'"Hard" is an understatement. No one wants to adopt someone that age who's damaged. They all want perfect, sweet babies. So I was basically on my own, and it was tough. I knew education was my key to getting away from it so I could gain my independence and start again. So I worked hard, got good exam results at school, and went to Uni.'

'What about any friends?'

'When I was in the children's home, I wasn't really that close to anyone. Other kids came and went. Whenever I finally did make a friend, they left to be adopted or fostered. And Liam always made a fuss if I wanted to do something with friends, so I suppose in the end it wasn't worth the effort. I do keep in contact with my old school friend, Sara, but that's mainly because Liam doesn't know about it. He doesn't like her, you see. He says she's flighty. She likes to travel a lot. She's a graphic designer, but she only works as long as she has to, so she can save up some spending money. Then she's off again, travelling somewhere else in the world and doesn't come back for months on end.'

'Does that make you feel isolated with no one to talk to?'

I fiddle with one of my hooped earrings, sliding it round and round through the pierced hole as I think about that. 'Yes, I suppose.'

'I think you're a very resilient lady.'

I frown and glance over at him, not sure if he's joking. 'Really?'

'Yes.'

And for the first time in a long time, I feel like someone is actually on my side. The knot in my stomach unclenches a fraction.

'Do you still feel independent?'

'I know what you're going to say.'

'And what's that, my dear?'

'That I've given up independence in my marriage. That Liam was some kind of father figure to me, and I was desperately looking for love when I met him, so I carried on ignoring the obvious until it was too late to change it.'

His eyes soften. 'Is that what *you* think?'

'Look, he *can* be moody and arrogant and controlling sometimes, but he's never hit me, so it's not like I'm an abused wife, is it?' I shake my head for emphasis, and it hurts.

Chapter Eight

I open the overnight bag Liam has just brought in as he hovers by my bed. He's changed from his work suit into a pair of new dark blue jeans and a black shirt. His clothes are crisp, clean, and perfectly ironed. Even in casual gear, he looks groomed and styled, as if he's just stepped out of the pages of *GQ* magazine. He wears his blond hair short at the sides and longer on top, pushed back slightly so it looks like he's been casually running his fingers through it, when in fact he stands in front of the mirror for ages styling it. He takes longer to get ready than me, actually. A fact he likes to point out when he says how messy my long wavy hair looks. Says I should take more care over my appearance. But even when I wear my hair up, it has a mind of its own, tendrils escaping from every direction. My hair is a messy mop. His words, not mine.

I feel Liam's gaze on me and look up into icy blue eyes. He has an expression I can't read. Concern? Exasperation? Disgust?

'This hasn't been easy for me, you know,' he says.

For him? What the hell does he think it's been like for me? But I don't want to start a row. Can't handle that right now. So I bite my tongue as I always do. It's better this way. 'I'm sorry,' I mumble, pulling out some black leggings and a long pink swing top with a scooped neckline so I don't have to look at him.

'It's been hard work holding down my job and trying to look after you, too. I'm up to my eyeballs in the launch of this new drug and under immense pressure.' He blows out a frustrated breath. 'Do you really not remember anything, or is this just some cry for attention?'

I look up sharply. 'How can you think that?'

He raises his eyebrows. 'Because I know you *and* your family history.'

'What does that mean?' My voice jumps louder.

'Look . . .' He glances out to the corridor. One of the nurses at the station is now looking at us through the open doorway of my room. He sits down heavily on the chair next to my bed. 'If you don't remember, then you obviously don't know how upsetting it was for me to find you like that before. It was just awful. You were crazy. Shouting and shrieking and lashing out at me.'

'I *don't* remember. I've lost my memory.' I fight to keep my emotions in check. It won't do any good to lose it. I could end up sectioned again, and then where would I be? Apart from in the mental wing, of course. I twist the edge of the stiff, cold bed sheets into a knot. Untwist. Twist. Untwist. 'When you went back home, did you check for any more signs of a break-in like the police suggested?' I'm hoping for some sort of clue as to how I could've ended up in that place in the woods.

'Yes, and there was nothing, just like I thought.'

I rummage further in the bag and pull out toiletries. Deodorant, shower gel, soap, toothbrush and toothpaste. I would kill for a shower. A sour smell of sweat and vomit and dirt clings to me. I can smell my breath when I talk. The nurse told me I shouldn't get my hands wet for a few days, so she's promised me a sponge bed bath later. Lucky me. 'Thank you for bringing these,' I say.

'You're welcome.' He wrinkles his nose. 'I thought you could do with them.'

I start to cry again, the tears sliding tracks down my cheeks and onto the leggings. 'This man who took me . . .' I trail off. Swallow. Breathe. 'What if he comes back? What if—'

He holds a hand up to stop me talking. 'He won't come back.' He pronounces each word very slowly, as if he's talking to someone who's deaf.

'But how do you know?'

He takes in a deep breath and holds it for a while before he speaks. 'Because it didn't happen, darling. You heard what the doctors said. It was just a hallucination. It wasn't real.'

'Did you see my handbag when you got home?' I wipe the tears on the sheet. 'Or my mobile phone?'

'No. I wasn't really looking for them.'

'My bag would be hanging on the hook on the back of the kitchen door, just where it always is.'

'I didn't notice.'

'It's just that . . . what if he has my bag? My house keys are in there. My bank cards. Things with our address on them. He might know where I live. He might come back!'

The nurse appears in the doorway. 'Everything all right, Chloe?'

I sniff. 'Yes. Thank you.'

Liam sits on my bed, cuddling me and cradling my head on his shoulder. 'She's OK, just a little exhausted, I think.' I hear concern in his voice.

'Let me know if you need anything.' She gives me a sympathetic smile before going back to her desk.

'If it makes you feel better, I'll change the locks and cancel your bank cards. OK?' Liam says in a soothing tone, stroking my back.

'I want to go home,' I croak out.

'Quite honestly, darling, I think this is the best place for you at the moment.'

Chapter Nine

The sun filters through the back window of the police car, warming my bones. I rest my forehead against the glass and close my eyes.

'Are you OK?' Summers asks.

My eyelids flutter open. 'It's nice to be out of hospital in the fresh air.'

'I had a hernia operation once,' Flynn says from the driver's seat. 'Couldn't wait to get out. It's the smell. It gets to you after a while.'

'We're nearly there.' Summers twists in his seat to face me.

I stare out of the window as we drive up a country lane, passing the golf course on our left and Sherrardspark Woods on our right. The trees are thick and lush, an explosion of greenery and moss and branches. At the end of the lane, we turn right onto the Great North Road.

'Just here.' Summers points to a sign at the side of the road that indicates a bend up ahead. 'This is where you were found by the driver.'

Flynn slows the car to a stop, and we get out. The doors closing echo with a metallic bang in the stillness. Birds let out excited chatter and melodic singing.

'Do you recognise anything?' Summers asks.

I look at the road from all angles. Everything looks different in the daylight. 'I think I came from this direction.' I point towards the trees.

'Let's start there, then.'

We walk across the road and enter the woods.

'Did you know the first recorded history of these woods dates back to an entry in the *Domesday Book* in 1086?' Flynn asks no one in particular.

'No, I didn't.' Summers gives him a disinterested look, which doesn't deter Flynn from carrying on with his history lesson.

'I didn't either, until I started checking the maps for any signs of underground structures. Interesting, though, isn't it?'

'Is it?' Summers says in a bored tone.

'Yes. Apparently, fossils and Stone Age artefacts of ancient pottery have been recorded here, although they've never found any evidence of ancient settlements.'

Summers raises an eyebrow. 'How about telling me something useful, like whether you found anything marked on the maps that might actually help?'

'Er . . . no. The whole woods cover 185 acres, but I couldn't see any signs of underground structures or buildings marked anywhere.'

'That's a lot of ground.' Summers looks at me. 'How far do you think you ran?'

'I don't know.'

'How long were you running for, then? A minute? Two? Ten?'

I clench my fists at my side, frantically looking around for something I recognise. I'm not exactly fit. I walk the half hour to work because I can't drive, but apart from that, I don't exercise. I don't know how long could I run under normal circumstances. I've never tried. And these weren't normal circumstances. I was running for my life, adrenaline pumping hard, fear chasing at my heels. 'It's all a bit hazy. Maybe ten minutes?'

Summers glances at me as we walk. 'You said the place underground was made of brick and concrete?'

'Yes, with some doorways in it.'

'And the last door opened up into the ground, like a kind of trap door?'

I stop walking and squeeze my eyes shut, trying to think. It feels like I've got one foot stuck in a past I don't remember and one foot in the present. One false move and I'll be ripped right down the middle. 'I ran along a corridor to a doorway. I opened the doorway, and there were steps upwards. There was a hatch at the top, and I pushed it open. Then I was in the woods, running, and it was dark.'

Flynn and Summers exchange a look. 'How big was the structure?' Flynn takes my hand to guide me over a fallen tree. I slip on the moss covering it, and he grips my arms, holding me upright. 'Careful,' Flynn says.

'I don't know. The room I was in was about seven metres by five metres, but I don't know how big the whole place was.' I scan the area, desperately hoping to see something. Anything I can pinpoint that will help to prove I'm right and that this isn't just a figment of my crazed imagination.

After an hour of walking, Summers pulls some bottles of water out of his rucksack and hands them out. I hold the cool plastic to my forehead, breathing heavily as the world falls apart around me.

'Do you want to sit down?' Summers takes my hand and guides me to sit on another fallen log.

'I must be more worn out than I thought.' Everything swims in and out of focus.

'It's OK. We're not in a rush.' Summers hands me a chocolate bar. 'Here, eat this.'

I wait for my vision to refocus, then tear off the wrapper and stuff it in the pocket of my top. I take a bite of warm, soft chocolate and swallow it down with some water. 'I could hear dripping,' I say.

'That might not help much,' Summers replies.

I swallow another bite. 'The bone I used to scrape out the render in the doorway. I think it was human.' I finally put the thought I've been trying to hide in a corner of my brain into words. 'There might've been someone else down there. He may have done this before.'

'What makes you think it was human?' Flynn asks.

'It was too big to be a cat or a dog or fox. What other kind of animal would be out here?'

'Deer? Badger? Muntjac?' Flynn suggests.

'I'm pretty sure it was a leg bone. A human femur,'

'Just one bone?' Summers gives me a noncommittal look and takes a swig of water.

'I only found one, but it was pitch-black in there. There could've been others.' I stand up, and we resume walking. We trail slowly through the dense woods for another hour, but everything looks the same. Miles and miles of oak trees, silver birch, hornbeam, cherry. A woodpecker drumming at the bark in the distance. Shrubs, bracken, logs. And bluebells everywhere, creating a carpet of soft lilac. I never want to see another bluebell as long as I live. I stand still, trying to pierce behind the colourful veil into the shadows beyond. Somewhere out there is the place I was held captive. 'I'm sorry. I just . . . I'm not helping much, am I?'

'Let's head back.' Summers pulls out his mobile phone and presses a few buttons. 'GPS. So we can find our way out.' He turns to his left and walks in front. 'We made enquiries with the college. I spoke to the principal, Theresa Higgins. She confirmed you'd been off sick since the miscarriage.'

'What else did she say?'

'That you're a good teacher. The students love you. You're professional and competent, but not particularly close friends with any colleagues. She said to give you her regards.'

'We also checked with your neighbours to see if anyone remembers seeing you or anyone else at your house. But no one noticed anything untoward or suspicious.'

My chest deflates like a balloon that's had all the air let out. No one saw anything. No one knows anything. Including me. 'If I did have a reaction to the Silepine and was in a psychotic state, hallucinating, don't you think someone would've seen it? I mean, it's five miles from my house to where I was found. Surely, someone must've noticed me somewhere along the way.'

'You'd be surprised.' Summers raises his eyebrows. 'A few months ago, we were all called out looking for an Alzheimer's patient who wandered off from his residential home. Even the helicopter was out searching. He was eventually found ten miles away, and no one called in to report a confused gentleman wandering around. The only reason we found him was because he ended up in a shopping mall and refused to leave when security was closing up.'

'No one wants to get involved these days,' Flynn complains. 'A crime could be happening right in front of someone's nose, and they'd probably keep their head down and walk past.'

We walk in silence for a while as I digest that. Someone out there must have seen me. Would they ever come forward and help? Or had they already forgotten it?

'Liam said he checked the house thoroughly.' I risk a glance at Summers. 'He said there was no sign of a break-in.'

'Yes, he told me.'

'He did? When?'

'He called this morning from work to see how we were getting on.'

I chew on my lower lip and wonder what else he's told them. 'Did he mention if he'd found my bag and my phone? He was going to have another look for them.'

'No. Are they missing?'

'I don't know. I need to check at home. Liam said he'd cancel my bank cards and get the locks changed.'

'That's a good precaution. We advised him to change the locks yesterday, just in case,' Flynn says. 'We checked your bank accounts. The last time you used your debit card was to withdraw three hundred pounds on the fourth of May.'

'Oh. That doesn't ring any bells. I wish I could tell you more, but I just don't . . . I can't . . .' I stand still, taking big gulps of air.

Summers and Flynn wait for me.

I look Summers dead in the eye. 'I'm not making this up. Despite what Liam may have said to you, and what apparently happened to me before, I'm not lying.'

'I didn't say you were.' Summers gives me a tight-lipped smile.

'Have you spoken to Sara? Maybe I told her something. Maybe I was going to go somewhere, and she knows about it.'

'Sara, your best friend, who's in India?' Flynn says.

'Yes. She was flying out there the day before Liam's party.'

'Liam didn't have a number for her.' Flynn pulls out the notebook from his pocket. 'Do you know it, by any chance?'

'Yes.' I rattle off her mobile number from memory, which he scribbles down and underlines several times. I stare at the trees and blow out a frustrated sigh, long and hard.

'Are you OK? Summers asks.

I shake my head. 'It just seems ironic that I can remember a stupid phone number, but I can't remember anything important.'

When we get back to the car, the hot sun is moving over the horizon. It looks like summer has well and truly arrived early for once. I slide into the back seat as Summers and Flynn get in the front. Summers take his mobile out of his pocket. 'Right, what's Sara's number?' he asks Flynn.

Flynn shows him his notepad, then flicks a few pages backwards and points to something I can't see. Summers nods, punches in some numbers, and listens to the phone. I can hear the dialling tone ringing loudly. It rings and rings, then cuts off.

'Sometimes when she's travelling, you can't get hold of her for days or even weeks. She goes off on all these weird and adventurous trips in the middle of nowhere, and there's no phone signal or Internet access.'

'We'll keep trying her,' he says. 'I spoke to Dr Traynor about your condition when you were brought into hospital. He says you were dehydrated, but not severely so. It's possible you didn't drink for a day or two, which is the only thing we have to go on regarding a possible timeline.'

Two days? Was I underground for two whole days?

'We've done some checks on your home phone number, but there were no calls made to or from your house within that time frame that might give us some leads. We got your mobile number from Liam and checked that, too.' His forehead creases.

'Did I call anyone?'

'There were several calls to and from the number you just gave us. Sara's number. We were waiting for the phone provider to give us information as to whose number this was, but now you've just confirmed it for us.'

At least I'd done something helpful.

'On the twenty-ninth of April, you called Sara's number and spoke for over an hour. There was also a missed call from her to you on the sixth of May, but nothing after that.'

Maybe I had told Sara a vital clue. If I'd phoned her, maybe she could tell me how I came to be in that place. A spark of hope lights up inside.

'You received a call on your mobile phone on the twenty-ninth of April from the college as well.'

'Maybe it was Theresa, asking how I was doing and when I'd be back to work.'

'She didn't mention it.'

It could've been Jordan who called from work, then.

'There's something else.' Summers nods to Flynn, who starts the engine. 'Liam said he called your mobile when he got to Scotland, to let you know he'd arrived, but there's no record of that call anywhere.'

The breath evaporates from my lungs. Why would he lie to the police? 'Did you ask him about it when you spoke to him this morning?'

'Yes. He said he didn't want to mention it last night in front of us because of your fragile state, but—'

'Fragile state?' I splutter. 'Anyone would be fragile who'd been through what I went through.'

'Those were his words, not mine,' he carries on calmly.

I fight to keep my breathing in check. In. Out. *Keep calm. Do not flip out and give them any excuse to believe you're crazy.*

'He told us that before he left to go to Scotland, you and he had an argument. You weren't speaking to him, so he decided it would be best not to call you. He said he wanted to give you time to calm down while he was away.'

'An argument?' I stare at him wide-eyed. 'What was it about?'

Summers clears his throat. 'Er . . . plates.'

'Excuse me?' I shake my head slightly, wondering if I'd heard him right.

'Liam said he brought you breakfast in bed before he left, and you accused him of using the wrong plate.'

I open my mouth. Close it. It doesn't make any sense. I wouldn't care what plate he put my breakfast on. It's something Liam would care about, not me. I scroll back through the memories I do know, searching for something that might explain what Liam said.

I can see it clearly. It's just after we got married. Everything was perfect. I was in our kitchen, humming to myself, dishing up a Thai curry for Liam, one of his favourite dishes that I'd been slaving over for hours. And then he started shouting at me, annoyed because the sauce spilt over the lip of the plate when he picked it up. It slopped down the front of his best work trousers, causing a stain that even the dry cleaner couldn't get out. Incensed with anger, he threw the plate across the room at the wall before storming out and heading for the pub. It took me ages to clean up the mess, and when he returned three hours later, he was full of apologies, smelling of alcohol and carrying a bunch of wilted flowers he'd bought at the all-night garage down the road.

I made sure I never gave him that plate again, but it didn't take long before he found something else to get angry about.

'He said you threw the plate at him and told him to get out.' Summers's voice brings me back to the present.

'I wouldn't argue about a plate,' I say with a forced steadiness. That's just not me. I don't like confrontation. I don't like having a bad atmosphere in the house. I'm not a violent person. 'And I would never throw something at him.'

I wouldn't. And if I didn't, that meant Liam was lying. If I did, it meant . . . what? That I was acting out of character? Having some kind of breakdown or episode again? Hallucinating?

Oh, God.

Despite the stiflingly hot car, I shiver and wrap my arms around myself.

Chapter Ten

'I thought I was going to die down there.' I wonder briefly who would care if I had. Sara would. I'm not so sure about Liam. My students might be a little sad, but they would get over it. I didn't want to think about Jordan. It was too complicated. 'All I could think about was doing anything to get out of there. To escape.'

'It must've been a horrific experience for you,' Dr Drew says, nodding at me in his calm, professional manner.

'But we couldn't find the place.' I tell him what happened with the police that morning. 'Nothing looked the same in the daylight. And . . .' I can just about summon up the energy to give him a defeated shrug. 'It wasn't like I was paying attention when I was running. I was just running for my life.'

'It's frustrating that you didn't recognise anything.'

'It was. The police said Sara and I called each other before I disappeared. They tried to phone her but couldn't get hold of her.' I fidget with my fingers, tight in their gauze, glancing around his office in the hospital. One wall houses a bookshelf stacked full with psychology books. The opposite wall holds various certificates in frames. Behind Dr Drew, the window looks out onto the hospital grounds. The sun's still shining, the sky squeezing out the last of the bright light.

Dr Drew picks up the phone on his desk, scattering a few sheets of paper. 'Do you want to try her again?'

'May I?'

'Be my guest.' He places it in front of me.

I press the numbers in, the motion sending a pain shooting up my finger. It rings and rings before finally cutting off. 'No answer.' I replace the receiver. 'I haven't spent much time with her lately. Just snatched cups of coffee for half an hour here or there when she's back in the UK, but if anyone is able to shed some light on what I was doing before I was taken, I'm sure it will be Sara.' I press my fingertips to my temples, ignoring the thumping pain filtering through my head. 'I just wish I could remember! If the memories are still in there somewhere, can't you just hypnotise me or something?'

'I'm afraid not. The use of hypnosis for dissociative disorders is considered controversial due to the risk of creating false memories.'

'False memories?' I blink rapidly.

'Although some sufferers of dissociative amnesia appear to spontaneously recover their memories, the brain can also create false memories, which the patient strongly believes but which don't actually reflect an accurate or real event from their past. Outside influences can affect or alter patient's memories for many reasons. For example, repetitive opinions by an authority figure, or information passed down through generations of certain cultures. Individuals with a heightened desire to please, to conform or get better, can also be easily influenced in those circumstances.'

'So if I do remember something, how will I know if it's true or false, then?'

'We have to be mindful of False Memory Syndrome. In my experience, it can become a serious problem if the patient strongly avoids confrontation with any evidence that might challenge the memory he or she believes to be true. Therefore, we must try to determine all the facts and seek evidence or corroboration from other people.' He scratches his head. 'We're all capable of creating false memories, not just people who suffer from amnesia. Sometimes, we don't remember an actual event but remember our thoughts or feelings associated with what happened instead. Or we recall it how we would have *liked* the event to take place. It's easy to reshape the details or lose them over the years.'

'Lie to yourself, you mean?'

'Not exactly. Although we're all capable of that, too. What I'm saying is that some of our memories are true, some are a mixture of fact and fantasy, and some are usually false.'

I glance out the window, unease sitting uncomfortably in the pit of my stomach.

'I've liaised with Dr Traynor, and he's happy to release you tomorrow since you have nothing much wrong with you physically. How do you feel about that?'

'Yesterday I just wanted to go home, but today . . .' I bite my lip, eyes watering. 'Today, I think maybe I'm safer here, surrounded by people all the time.'

'I'm sure the police are doing everything they can to find out what happened. As much as I'd like to keep you here for your own peace of mind, unfortunately the hospital is bursting at the seams. But being at home may trigger a memory that will give you more information. And I'd like to keep up a weekly appointment with you, if that's OK.'

'OK.'

'My secretary will set up an appointment for you before you're discharged. And you can call me anytime.' He hands me his card. 'My mobile number is there, too.'

'Thank you.' I take it and immediately bend the corners with my thumb. 'I'm not going mad, am I?' I lean forward, desperate for reassurance. 'I mean, you wouldn't release me if I were, would you?'

'I don't think you're going mad, dear. You're recovering from a traumatic event. Whether the Silepine itself caused the amnesia or the fact that the hallucinations it gave you were so distressful you've blocked them out, I still can't say for certain.'

I open my mouth to object, but there's no point. No one believes me. Maybe they're all right and I really did hallucinate the whole thing. 'So these memories I have of being held captive are definitely false?'

'The very definition of hallucination is experiencing something which does not exist.'

'But we all have a breaking point, don't we? What if I flipped? What if the grief and the incident with the antidepressants all took its toll, and *that* was my breaking point? If I started doing things that were out of character, wouldn't that be a sign I was going mad or having some kind of breakdown?'

'You're talking about the argument with Liam? Throwing the plate?'

I bite my thumbnail, afraid of his answer but at the same time desperate to hear it. 'Yes, and taking the sleeping tablets when I'd been advised not to take any more medication. Why would I do that?'

'I don't know. I can only make the assumption that you were having trouble sleeping and ignored medical advice.'

I feel the world teetering before my eyes, and I'm struggling to hold on tight before it completely tips me off. 'But that's the point, isn't it? It's an assumption. You see, I don't know what to think anymore. I don't know what the truth is.'

Chapter Eleven

Liam parks his black BMW 4×4 in our driveway and turns off the engine. I sit and stare at our house through the window. It's a three-bed detached in a quiet tree-lined cul-de-sac, newly built when Liam bought it five years ago, before he met me. It's never really felt like home, more like a show house you're not allowed to get messy because a potential buyer might walk in at any second. I prefer homes with character—period features, lots of wood, splashes of warm colour. Liam likes stark, white, crisp, and modern.

I look at it with the eyes of a stranger, scrutinizing as I search my brain for something to tell me what happened here before I lost my memory.

'Are you getting out?' Liam twists around to retrieve my bag from the back seat, then opens his door. He walks up the small path towards the bright red front door. It looks ominous all of a sudden. Like a blazing, bloody warning telling me to stay away.

I don't want to get out. I want to be back in the hospital, surrounded by nurses and doctors who will reassure me that I'm OK. Cocoon me in the stifling heat of the building and the protection of knowing someone is always around. Someone who would notice if a killer dragged me away kicking and screaming. But then, what did a killer look like? It wasn't as if such a person had the words tattooed on his forehead for easy recognition. Killers came in all shapes and sizes. What did the person who took me look like? Was he tall, short, ugly, spotty, attractive, fat, skinny? How would I even know? And despite what Dr Drew, Dr Traynor, and Liam think, the memory of being in that place is too real to be a hallucination.

I will my body to start working, and concentrate on putting one foot in front of the other until I'm inside the house.

'I'll put the kettle on,' Liam calls from the kitchen as I look around, trying to notice any subtle changes that might give me a clue.

The hallway leads through into the kitchen/diner. On my left, the door to the lounge is open. A bay window lets sunlight flood the room. The door to the dining room is closed. To my right is the white glossed banister and staircase with cream carpet. The downstairs has wood effect laminate floorboards throughout. The sterile white walls are impersonal, with only a few pictures dotted around. There's plenty of modern furniture—chrome and glass tables, black leather sofas with purple cushions, the only bit of colour Liam allowed me to add because he thinks I have no taste. It's horrible.

I go into the lounge. Everything is tidy. No magazines lying around. No used mugs littering the coffee table. Remote controls for the TV, DVD, and stereo all lined up neatly in a row as if Liam has spent hours setting them out with perfect precision.

I walk past the dining room door. We never use it to eat in, except when we have guests. Liam insists on holding dinner parties for his work colleagues, always trying to be the superior host who knows exactly which wine goes with which course. Who cares? As long as it tastes nice and you like it, it doesn't really matter if red wine doesn't go with fish. His finicky ways only put more pressure on me, since I'm an average cook. Even when I spend hours poring over fancy cookbook recipes, measuring ingredients precisely, timing things to within a second, I usually get something wrong. The soufflé sags in the middle, the chicken is tough and stringy, the vegetables not al dente enough. It doesn't help when Liam likes to make a big show of apologizing to our guests about the poor state of the food. He does it in a jokey, light-hearted way, saying we can't all be Nigella Lawson in the kitchen. Telling them he swore he told me not to leave it in the oven for so long. But it doesn't detract from the embarrassment when all eyes turn to me, and everyone's chuckling at my expense. And I know it's not a joke. At the end of the night, when I'm the one left with a table to clear, dishes to wash, and empty wine bottles to throw away, he'll tell me I'm not trying hard enough or not being a supportive wife, or that I've embarrassed him in front of his friends and ruined what's supposed to be a perfect night. The next day, I'll get the thick, oppressive silent treatment and the cold stares, and I'm forced to admit to myself what an idiot I am yet again because I can never get things right.

Hovering in the kitchen doorway now, I lean my forehead on the doorframe, watching Liam spooning coffee into a French press. Real coffee for him. Not the instant stuff. He looks smart in his business suit, self-assured and confident. He was wearing a suit the first time I met him at the nightclub. Liam was so different from the students I'd been used to hanging around with at Uni, whose uniform was just-got-out-of-bed hair; worn, faded jeans; and scuffed trainers. The only time Liam ever wears trainers is when he goes to the gym at work early in the morning before he starts his day.

All his colleagues think he's great. A great boss, a great delegator, a great squash partner, funny, witty. But people hide things in layers. No one *really* knows someone else—not until they live with the person.

'Here.' Liam hands me a mug of coffee, which probably isn't a good idea. I'm already jittery enough without caffeine, but Liam knows best, after all.

I reach out to take it, but they removed the gauze from my hands before I left the hospital, and the heat of the mug stings the tender scabs, making me drop it. The mug smashes on the floor, scalding hot coffee splashing up my legs.

I yelp and wipe at my leg with the back of my hand. When I look up at Liam, his eyes flash with anger for the briefest of moments before creasing at the corners as he smiles.

'That was my fault,' he says.

Wow. For once, it's not mine.

He sweeps up the shards of pottery carefully with a dustpan and brush, dumping it all into some newspaper, folding it over carefully so no pieces can escape. It jolts me enough to ask him about the argument with the plate. 'Summers said you told him we'd argued before you left for Scotland. About a plate. Is that right?'

He puts the newspaper in the bin under the sink. 'Yes, that's right. I didn't want to mention it in front of you because'—he swings round to face me, a concerned frown in place—'well, you've had a hard time lately. You've gone through a lot, and you're already fragile, darling.' He waves one hand casually through the air. 'Anyway, the argument wasn't important.'

I stare at him. Something's definitely not right. 'But I wouldn't smash a plate. I wouldn't throw something at you.' I don't mention that's his MO. 'So what did actually happen with this argument? I mean, did—'

'For God's sake, Chloe, just stop nagging about something so trivial. Why do you always have to make things so complicated?' His eyes flash with dark fury, and he bangs his fists down on the kitchen worktop so hard that it makes the kettle and toaster on top rattle.

Startled, a coldness shifts over me, as if all the air has been sucked out of the room.

Liam takes an exaggerated lungful of breath, trying to calm himself. He presses his fingers to his temples and closes his eyes for a moment. When he's composed again, he says, 'Like I said, it wasn't important. It doesn't matter now—let's just forget about it. The most important thing is trying to get you well again.'

But I'm not unwell. *I was kidnapped and left for dead. That's not exactly like a spot of flu I can recover from.* I bite my lip to keep the words I want to say locked deep inside.

'And Dr Traynor said it wouldn't do any good for you to blame yourself for things. It would only make you more agitated. *That's* why I didn't mention it in front of you.' He wipes up the spilt coffee from the floor with some paper towels and plonks those in the bin, too.

'What else did Dr Traynor say about me?' Inside I'm fuming that my doctor has been talking to Liam about me behind my back. *I'm* supposed to be the patient, not Liam.

'He's worried about you. We both are. He thinks you need some rest.' He pours a coffee for himself but doesn't offer me any more.

While he's occupied, I search the room for my handbag. It's not on the hook behind the kitchen door where I usually keep it, so I pull out a drawer and rummage around. It's not there either. I open more drawers, a twinge of tension forming between my shoulder blades.

'What are you doing?' He sighs.

'Looking for my handbag. My mobile phone would be in it, and my purse and keys.'

He mutters something that I can't hear under his breath and then says, 'They're not here. I already checked for you.'

I slump into a leather chair at the glass-topped kitchen table.

'I cancelled the bank cards and changed the locks, so there's no need to worry.'

I laugh then, even though nothing is remotely funny. 'No need to worry? That man might have them. And if he does, he'll know where I live.' My voice escalates.

Liam walks over to me and crouches down, resting on his haunches. He takes my hand in his and strokes it gently. 'Darling, nothing is going to happen. There is no man.'

'Why don't you believe me?' I shriek, pulling my hand away.

He stands upright, walks to the window, and looks out into the garden. 'Do you really want to know?'

'Yes! I can't remember anything that happened. I want to know what's going on. I have to know!'

He swings around and stares at me for a moment. The room is silent except for the clock ticking annoyingly in the background. Then he walks out of the room, and his heavy footsteps pound the stairs. When he comes back down, I'm pacing the floor, hands clutched to my elbows.

'Here.' He thrusts a piece of paper in my hand. 'This is why I don't believe you.'

I tentatively reach out and take it from him. It's a regular piece of A4 paper, the kind we use for printing things off the computer. It's got my handwriting on it, but it's an odd scrawl, as if I've written it in a hurry or I was drunk.

Or drugged.

Liam,
I can't go on like this anymore. I need to end it all.
I'm sorry.
Chloe

'It's a suicide letter, Chloe. I found it in the kitchen when I came back from Scotland.' His voice sounds weird to my ears, slowed down and distorted.

My knees buckle and I collapse to the floor, grasping the letter. I look up at him with a questioning gaze. 'I don't . . . I don't remember this.'

'You obviously intended to kill yourself while I was away. I think you tried to take an overdose of sleeping tablets and had another reaction to them before you could take enough to finish off the job. Depression runs in families, Chloe, and you're suffering from it, too. You're taking after your mum, don't you see? You were just hallucinating that you were kidnapped.'

No. No, no, no. I wouldn't do that. *Would I?* I press my hands over my ears to block out what he's saying. But Dr Drew said I was still grieving over the miscarriage. What if the grief escalated? What if I felt the only way to cope was to kill myself?

And I had thought of it before, after mum died and I was in the children's home.

At nine, I was still small for my age. I was shy, painfully so. Quiet, meek Chloe, who didn't like to speak anymore, even though her voice had returned. A perfect target for some of the bigger, older children who wanted to assert their authority. They bullied me mercilessly, and I blamed myself for everything. Thought it must be my fault the other kids didn't like me. It was my fault Mum did what she did. It was all something *I* was doing wrong.

Growing up, I learned to hate myself, and my self-esteem hit rock bottom. So, yes, I'd thought about suicide a few times over the years. Thought about jumping in front of a train or drowning myself or slitting my wrists. No one wanted me, and the world would just be better off without me.

I'm dizzy now. My chest tightens as I gasp for air.

Liam kneels next to me, pulling my hands away from my ears. He wraps his arms round me and rocks me gently. 'This is why I wanted you to stay in the hospital. You need to get some help.'

'But Dr Drew . . . Dr . . . Drew.' I fumble for some sort of coherent thought. 'He said . . . he said . . . I wasn't mad. Not going mad. No.'

'All right. Just take some deep breaths.' He cups my face in his hands and makes me look at him. 'Breathe slowly.'

I nod frantically. In. Out. In. Out. Tremors spread through every muscle.

'Come on now, calm down.' He strokes my hair.

The panic subsides, but the confusion remains, bright and burning in my head like a blinding light blocking out everything else.

'Did you tell Dr Drew you wanted to kill yourself?' Liam asks softly.

'No, because I *don't*. I don't feel suicidal. I don't want to kill myself.'

'Well, that's obviously why he thought you were safe to be released from hospital, then. Perhaps the amnesia and the things you've forgotten have made your urge to commit suicide disappear, too.'

'I don't . . .' I trail off. 'Did you tell Dr Drew about the letter?'

'Yes. I spoke with him before I saw you last night.'

'And what did he say?'

'That you weren't showing any signs of suicidal tendencies. The opposite, in fact—that you'd shown a will for survival.'

'Yes. He wouldn't have let me come out of hospital if he thought I'd harm myself, would he?' I say, trying to reassure myself.

'I'm not convinced Dr Drew is competent. Maybe we should get a different psychiatric opinion from someone else. Dr Traynor agrees with me and thinks everything that's happened while I've been away points to you trying to take your own life. He's also agreed with my concerns that depression and suicidal behaviour runs in families, and after what happened with your mother, it's likely you've inherited some kind of dysfunctional depressive gene.'

I close my eyes briefly. I don't want to open them again, but I do. 'And the police? Did you show them the letter?'

'Yes. DI Summers took a copy.'

'What did he say?'

'That this sheds a very different light on things and they would be winding up their enquiries.'

Oh, God. Oh, God. Oh, God. *What is happening to me? What has happened to me? Did I really fantasise the whole thing?*

I curl my fingers in the lapels of Liam's suit jacket, pulling him closer to me. My limbs are loose; my movements strangely slow, as if I'm wading through water. 'I need you to tell me everything that happened before you left for Scotland.'

Chapter Twelve

I sit at the kitchen table. Somewhere in my head, a pneumatic drill is going off, creating a steady drumming.

Liam opens a bottle of fruity white wine from the fridge and pours himself a large glass. I want one, too. After everything I've heard so far, I want to drink a whole bottle, maybe two, and then just sink into blissful oblivion and not have to think. Pull the duvet over my head and never get out of bed again. Have someone pamper me. Bring me hot chocolate and food, stroke my forehead, and tell me everything's going to be OK.

He sits down in front of me.

'I want one.' I stare at the condensation already surfacing on his glass.

'That's not a good idea.' He takes a sip and looks steadily at me over the rim.

'The last thing I remember is your party.' I tear my gaze away from him and stare at a thread pulled loose on my leggings. I twist it into a ball then untwist it again. Twist. Untwist. 'What happened after that?'

'Well, Jeremy and Alice stayed the night since neither of them wanted to drive back to Kent after having a drink. When they left the next morning, you presented me with a package wrapped up in gold paper. I thought it was another birthday present.' His lips curl into a smile, and his eyes light up. 'It was a pregnancy test. A positive one.'

I touch my hollow stomach with trembling hands. I had a life inside me. Our life. Ever since I was young, I knew I wanted children. Longed for them. A whole brood. Someone to love and nurture, as I never had been, growing up. Now I feel like my insides have been scooped out and left to rot. 'Were you happy about it?' I ask, dreading the answer.

The subject of children had come up before, of course. Liam made excuses because he was happy with it just being the two of us. At first, he wanted to wait until he got his promotion; then until the pressure of work lessened; then until we had more money, until we were more settled. It was never the right time for us to try, according to him.

And things changed between us. His moods, for one. The way he was so up and down. Volatile sometimes. Shouting at me if things weren't right. That was no environment in which to bring up a child. I thought maybe he was right. Perhaps it would never be a good time. But then it had happened by accident. I'd had a stomach bug—vomiting, diarrhoea—and I forgot to supplement my contraceptive pill with a condom like they always tell you to.

Liam takes my hand in his, gently tracing the cuts on my fingertips, dragging me back to the present. 'I was ecstatic.'

I release a breath caught tight inside.

'You thought you were about eight weeks pregnant when you told me, and you were feeling fine. No sickness or anything.'

A strangled cry escapes from my lips.

'In the early hours of the morning after you told me, you had the miscarriage. Then you started to get depressed. You were crying a lot and didn't want to get up in the mornings. Your sleep was erratic. You didn't want to talk. Couldn't be bothered to get dressed. You didn't even want to teach anymore. The doctor signed you off work and prescribed antidepressants and sleeping tablets, but a few days into taking the antidepressants you had some kind of reaction to them. That's when I came home and found you out in the garden.' His expression softens as he shakes his head. 'It was awful to see you like that.'

I try to imagine what I looked like then, scratching away at the path with wild eyes, screaming at the top of my lungs about people chasing me. Dying to get away. Dying inside. Losing Chloe and turning into a crazy woman. My mind disintegrating into paranoid delusion. I can't picture it at all.

'I called the doctor, and you were admitted to the psychiatric ward. Dr Drew treated you with antipsychotic drugs before they realised it must've been some kind of side effect of the antidepressants. So they stopped the antipsychotics and waited for the antidepressants to be purged from your system.'

'And when I came home?'

'You were coping better. You were functioning, getting dressed, making dinner, and you had an interest in certain things. But you were still very sad, understandably, and you couldn't sleep. You said the baby was haunting you at night.'

'Did I write a journal? Dr Drew said he encouraged me to write one to help with the grief.'

'A journal? No, not that I know of.'

I swallow past the golf ball–sized lump in my throat and lick my lips to bring back some moisture. 'Then what happened?'

'I was working hard, getting this new diabetes drug ready for production. I had to visit our manufacturing plant in Scotland, but you assured me you would be OK for the week I'd be away.'

'DI Summers mentioned that you didn't phone me when you were in Scotland, like you said you did.'

'Well, you were already very upset at the hospital. I didn't want to upset you more by telling you what really happened.'

'That's very considerate of you,' I say.

His eyebrow quirks up a fraction.

'What really happened with the argument before you left?' I grip his hand. 'I need to know.'

He lets go of my hand and lifts his glass to his mouth. Takes a sip. I watch his Adam's apple bob up and down, and it's as if he's delaying his answer, forming it in his head before he says it aloud. 'I brought you breakfast in bed before I left.'

'How thoughtful of you.' I smile. 'What did you make me?'

'Pardon?'

'What did you make me for breakfast?'

He shrugs dismissively. 'Tea and toast with marmalade.'

I bite my lip to stop myself speaking.

'Anyway, you just freaked out and started going mental on me. You said I'd given it to you on the wrong plate. That you never used the one I'd brought up to you, and it wasn't what you wanted. You were being irrational, angry. You knocked the plate out of my hand, and it smashed on the floor. Then you started crying. You curled up under the duvet and told me to get out—that you wanted some time on your own, and that I shouldn't call you while I was away.' He takes another swig of wine, his fingers tight against the glass. Any tighter and it might break. 'I thought it might agitate you more if I tried to calm you down, so I left to go up to Scotland.' He pauses for a moment. 'And that's all I know. When I left, you were upset and in bed. When I came back home after the hospital called, I found your suicide note.'

I stare at my feet, ignoring the queasiness lurching up in my throat. The thing is, I hate marmalade. Never touch the stuff. Can't stand the smell or the texture. He's never once given it to me in all the time we've been together because he knows how much I dislike it. He's just said the first thing that popped into his head, because he always has marmalade for breakfast.

And that's when I first suspect he's lying to me.

Chapter Thirteen

'Are you coming to bed?' Liam's voice echoes down the stairs.

I'm standing in the kitchen with the lights off, staring out into the dark garden. Right at the end, behind our own wooden fence and mature trees, is a three-and-a-half-metre chicken-wire fence that separates it from the Council tennis court behind. Our neighbours' houses on either side also have thick trees and bushes along their boundaries. The path that runs along the side of our house to the front driveway has a high wooden gate with a lock and a couple of bolts. So it would be hard for some unknown assailant to get into the garden. Hard, but not impossible.

Is he out there, the man who took me? Is he watching me now? I half-expect his face to loom up in front of the window like in a horror film.

'Did you hear me?' Liam shouts.

'I'll be up in a minute,' I call out.

'Don't wait too long.' His footsteps creak on the hallway as he enters our bedroom above the kitchen.

I open the fridge, grab the half-empty bottle of white wine and swallow it in big gulps. Then I put it back. Close the door, climb up the stairs, and get into bed. Liam reaches for me under the covers, pulling me into his arms so my head rests on his shoulder. If he feels me stiffen, he doesn't show it.

'I can't take any time off work at the moment to look after you. I'm swamped with all the stuff going on for this new drug.'

'I'm fine. Really. I'm fine. I'm not suicidal. You don't have to worry.'

'If anything happens, I want you to ring me. Or ring Dr Traynor or Dr Drew. OK? If you feel like hurting yourself, ring someone.'

'I won't hurt myself.'

He kisses my forehead. 'Good girl.' He turns over onto his side, facing away from me. Within minutes, his breath is deep and slow, and he's snoring softly.

I lie there, staring into the darkness, one thought chasing another. Round and round I go, my head in tortuous turmoil. I'm not going to hurt myself. The thought couldn't be further from the truth. But I wonder just who is trying to hurt me.

The letter makes it all easy. Makes it look like I've lost my mind. That I thought the only way out was to kill myself.

Did I really write it? It's my handwriting, even though it's messy. It could've been forged, I suppose, and it *sounds* like a suicide letter.

I go over what it said in my head: *Liam, I can't go on like this anymore. I need to end it all. I'm sorry. Chloe.*

But what if it wasn't me writing my last words? What if I meant I wanted to end our relationship instead? What if I was leaving him? And if I was, why? Why now? What had finally given me the courage to get away from him?

⌣

I pretend to be asleep when Liam gets up the next morning. I close my eyelids tight, slowing my breathing as the weight on the bed shifts. He pads to the en suite and takes his morning shower.

I need to think. Do something. Make phone calls. Search the house for clues of my disappearance. Because even though Dr Drew's been sympathetic and is the only one who seems to be on my side, he still concurs with Dr Traynor and Liam that I've taken sleeping tablets voluntarily and had another reaction to them. He still believes I've made up this whole thing and that there isn't a madman out there somewhere who could still be after me.

The police probably think I'm a raving lunatic, too, after what they've heard from Liam and from reading the letter I wrote. So, the only one who really believes me is me, and until I know the truth, my life is in danger.

Sometime later, Liam reappears in the bedroom. 'Chloe?' He nudges my shoulder. 'I've made you some tea.'

I open my eyes, stretch, sit up. I even give him a yawn for good measure. 'Thank you.'

He puts the mug on the bedside table and looks at me with concern. 'Will you really be OK?'

I feign a smile and say as convincingly as possible, 'Yes. I'll be fine.'

'I'll call you later from work to check up on you.' And the way he says it sounds like a threat.

I bring the mug to my lips so I don't have to speak.

When I hear the front door shutting, I pull the covers back and hastily grab the first thing I see in the wardrobe—a yellow sundress with red flowers. The early summer means the morning is already full of promising heat.

Downstairs, I make another cup of tea, strong and bitter. I pop two slices of toast in the toaster, and as I'm waiting for it to brown, I take butter from the fridge and grab a knife. I carry my breakfast to the kitchen table and take a bite, staring out into the garden. No one is there, but it doesn't make the fear go away. It oozes out of my pores like a cold sweat.

Trying to swallow the toast is like swallowing sandpaper. I wash it down with mouthfuls of tea so hot I burn my throat. I have to eat, though. It won't help me to collapse from weakness. I have to be strong. Have to be competent, methodical, in-control-of-my-life Chloe.

I finish the toast and leave the plate on the kitchen side. Liam would hate that. He can't stand clutter or mess. He'd want it put straight in the dishwasher, out of sight. Well, what he doesn't know won't hurt him. I leave it there in all its messy glory, pick up the phone from the base unit in the kitchen, and dial Sara's number as I pace up and down. It rings mockingly in my ear before cutting off. I try again. And again.

Where is she?

DI Summers. He might have got hold of her already. *What did I do with his card?*

It's then I realise Liam took it when Summers gave it to me. He put it in the pocket of his suit jacket, but I don't remember which one he was wearing. There was too much going on. Too many horrible skeletons jumping out of my closet.

I go into our bedroom and slide open the mirrored door to his side of the wardrobe. All his suits are lined up in a colour-coordinated fashion. Black ones to the left, charcoal next, then light grey, and blue. His shirts are the same. Ties hang neatly on a metal tie rack. His shoes are on a shelf at the bottom, all polished and shiny.

One by one, I check his pockets for the card until I touch something. I pull it out. It's a piece of paper. A credit card receipt in Liam's name. It's dated the twenty-first of March for a hotel in Welwyn. One double room. I stare at it until my eyes water, a cold shiver sliding up my spine.

So, two days before his birthday party, Liam had stayed in a hotel in a village a few miles away, but he'd told me he was going up to Scotland then. I distinctly remember, because I was worried he wouldn't make it back in time for the celebrations. He assured me he would, said it was only a quick overnight trip to sort out some problems that had cropped up with the diabetes drug. But he'd lied. Again. I wonder what else he's lied to me about.

I go through the other jacket pockets and find Summers's card in the last one, along with something else. Another receipt. This time for a white gold and diamond heart-shaped locket costing twelve hundred pounds. It's dated twenty-second of April. I finger the piece of paper. Who did he buy it for? Was it a gift for me to cheer me up, or was it for someone else?

I stride across the room to my dressing table. My jewellery box sits on top. It's one like those I'd always wanted as a child but never had, the kind with a ballerina that spins around to a melody when you open it. Liam bought it for me shortly after we first met, when I saw it in a department store.

I lift the lid and root through. There's some costume jewellery, the gold bracelet Liam bought me for our first wedding anniversary, and a ring with a stone missing. Odds and sods I've never got round to throwing away. The silver necklace with a turquoise pendant Liam bought me on our first Valentine's Day together, now broken, but I'd kept it anyway. After he gave it to me at the romantic restaurant he'd chosen, he expectantly waited for his gift, which I'd forgotten to buy. The longer the night went on, the more I could see him getting agitated. He demanded the bill before we even had coffee. When we got in the car on the way home, I tried to apologise that I'd been so busy with my new job, I'd forgotten to get him something. Gripping the steering wheel so tightly his knuckles turned white, he spat out, 'I spent ages choosing that necklace, and you couldn't even be bothered to get me anything to show how much you love me. Thanks a fucking lot!' He reached across and yanked the necklace from around my throat, sending it hurtling to the foot well.

I force myself back to the task at hand and lift up the top tray of the jewellery box, going through what's underneath. This is where

I keep my personal documents, and all I find is my passport and birth and marriage certificates. There's no white gold and diamond heart-shaped locket.

I suppose I could've been wearing it when I disappeared. It could've got lost. The chain could have been broken in a struggle with whoever took me. Or had I never been given it?

I search through the rest of Liam's wardrobe, looking for something else that might help me. I find nothing of any importance and take great care to rearrange everything as neatly as I found it. I swear he's got a photographic memory for minute details, and he'll know I've been looking through his stuff.

Next, I rummage through his bedside drawers. Maybe he's hidden the necklace in here and he's going to surprise me with it. I go through socks arranged in neat little bundles and boxers that look like they've been ironed, but the necklace definitely isn't there.

I head downstairs with Summers's card and make myself some more tea. Peppermint this time, to calm the rising and falling in my stomach. I take a sip, feeling like my life belongs to someone else, someone I no longer know. I pick up the phone from the kitchen table and dial Summers's number with a shaky hand.

'DI Summers,' he answers on the fifth ring.

'Hello, it's Chloe Benson.'

A pause. Then, 'Hello, Chloe. I heard the hospital released you. How are you feeling?'

'I'm OK. Just confused about everything still. Did you manage to get hold of Sara? I've tried lots of times, but she's still not answering.'

'No, I'm afraid not.' He clears his throat. 'Actually, I was going to call you today. Unfortunately, we have no leads and no clear lines of enquiry to follow up regarding your . . . incident. In view of your recent history, and our liaison with your doctors, we'll be putting the investigation on hold unless something new comes to light.'

My eyes well up, but I refuse to cry. I want to scream at him. Rant and rave, and tell him he doesn't have a clue what he's talking about, but of course that will just make me look unhinged. 'You read the letter I left Liam, didn't you?'

'He's very worried about your health, Chloe. So is Dr Traynor.'

'Liam's convinced you it was some kind of suicide letter.'

'Wasn't it? After reviewing everything, it seems the most likely theory, don't you agree?'

'It's not. I mean, I don't think—'

'But that's just it, Chloe, you don't *know* for certain because you can't remember.'

I couldn't argue with that. I wonder if I should tell him about the receipts I found, but what would I say? That Liam stayed in a hotel in Welwyn one night? That he bought a piece of jewellery I can't find? That he's lying about the argument we had, because I hate marmalade? It would only confirm what Summers already thinks, that I was crazy and paranoid.

No, the only way to get him to take me seriously is to find some kind of evidence of my abduction. Then he could protect me from the madman out there I can't yet identify. He'd do an investigation and arrest him. Put him in prison, and I'd be able to live again. But until I had proof, he wouldn't believe me. 'I'm not going mad,' I say, wondering if that's what all mad people say. If in doubt, just deny you're mad. Am I really just losing my grip on reality?

No. I know me. I know I'm not bloody losing it. I'm the sane one. It's everyone else who's the problem.

'I think we need to respect the advice of medical experts here. Look, if you remember something else, you can call me on this number,' he says in a bored tone that clearly means he doesn't want me to call him at all.

'Right.' I don't know what else to say.

'Take care of yourself, Chloe.'

I hang up and stare at the phone, wondering what to do next. Thoughts buzz around in my brain like wasps caught in a bottle. I'm utterly alone and utterly lost.

I go into the dining room and take a sheet of paper from the printer and a pen from the office desk in the corner. I take them back to the kitchen and think about finishing off that open bottle of wine. God knows I could do with it. Instead, I rummage around in the back of the cupboard under the sink and find an old packet of cigarettes left from before I gave up smoking.

Eleven remain, the white paper now tinged an orangey colour. A lighter with "I Love You" written on it is stuffed inside. A memento Liam picked up for me on a trip to London one day shortly after he said those words to me for the very first time. I remember the heart-soaring feeling I had every time he said it or wrote it on a note. Liam loved me—the girl who never thought anyone would.

I make a strong coffee, the next best thing to wine, and take everything out into the garden. My gaze flits to the trees at the end, to make sure no one is here but me. I'm alone. Completely alone, apart from two magpies and a squirrel.

I sit at the patio table and light the cigarette, inhaling deeply. The first rush of dizziness hits me. It's nice. Makes me lightheaded and relaxed for a moment. I take another drag, then a sip of coffee.

So, what do I really know for certain? What is only a possibility?

In between drinking and dragging on the cigarette, I write down everything I'm certain of in chronological order.

21 March
Liam stayed in the Royal Lodge Hotel, but said he was in Scotland.

23 March
Liam's party. Was going to tell him about the baby.

25 March
Had miscarriage in early hours of morning. Became depressed.

10 April
Went to GP. Was prescribed antidepressants and sleeping tablets.

13 April
I'm sectioned. Liam told doctors he found me clawing at garden path.
In psychiatric ward having treatment. (Dr Drew and Dr Traynor told me I was paranoid and hallucinating. I thought a man was chasing me, and I was trying to get away.)

20 April
Released from hospital. Still mildly depressed but otherwise OK.

22 April
Liam bought locket I can't find.

29 April
I phoned Sara and spoke for over an hour.

9 May
Rescued by a woman on the Great North Road. Ran through woods from an underground structure where I was being held. Lost memory of everything since the party.

I stare out at the garden path at which I was supposedly clawing. How did I get from point A to point B?

I don't know.

The only thing I do know is that I have to somehow retrace my recent past and find the parts that are missing. The answer is out there somewhere, the vital clue to prove I'm not making this all up.

The hotel, then. The first lie I remember Liam telling me. That's where I'll start.

PART THREE
LOOK BEHIND YOU

Chapter Fourteen

I check the kitchen clock and find it's 1:00 p.m. I've got plenty of time before Liam returns from work.

I put the makings of lunch on the worktop and prepare a ham and tomato sandwich with mayonnaise. I'm not hungry, but I need something to do with my hands. Need a distraction to keep me busy. And in some bizarre way, doing something mundane that I've done a million times before is comforting. It almost makes me feel normal for a moment.

I'm just about to take a bite when the phone rings. 'Hello?' I answer.

'Who were you talking to?' are the first words out of Liam's mouth.

'When?'

'Earlier. I tried to call you, but it was engaged.'

'Oh, it was just someone who had the wrong number,' I say. Liam's not the only one who can tell lies. 'How's work going?'

'Busy. What are you up to?'

'Nothing much. Just taking it easy like the doctors suggested. I'm just about to eat lunch.'

'What are you having?'

'A ham and tomato sandwich.'

'Don't make a mess, will you? You know how you always leave crumbs everywhere.'

I fight the urge to tell him I'm allowed to leave crumbs in my own house if I want to. I'm the one that has to clean them up, after all. But it would be futile. I'm not allowed to leave a mess. Even a stray crumb winds Liam up. 'No, I won't leave a mess,' I say breezily, and it sounds a little manic to my ears.

'Good girl. How about making something nice for dinner when I get home, hmm? That will give you something to do that's not too taxing.'

'Of course. Let me think of something.'

'In fact, I think you should reconsider my suggestion to give up work permanently. You know I earn in two hours what you can earn in a week. It would be much better for you to be at home where I can take care of you. We can take care of each other.'

Home waiting for your beck and call, you mean? I've heard that line so many times I barely bat an eyelid. 'I like working. I'm going to go back soon.'

'It would mean you'd have time to do all the stuff round the house that never gets done. It would be less pressure on you, darling. You know how fragile you are.'

'But—'

'We'll talk about it again. When you're feeling better.' He cuts me off in a tone that's not a request; it's a promise.

I stick two fingers up at the phone. Maybe it's childish, but it's my little bit of rebellion.

'I have to go now. I'll see you about seven o' clock.'

'OK, 'bye.' I press the "End Call" button before he can say anything else.

I chew the rest of my lunch automatically, totally preoccupied with the confusion of thoughts in my head.

A few minutes later, I look at the plate and wonder where the sandwich went. I rinse the plate, along with the one I left from breakfast, and stack them both in the dishwasher. Then I head upstairs and search out something I can use to disguise myself. After twisting my hair up into a bun, I pull on a big, floppy sunhat I bought for our honeymoon and never wore. Good—now it looks like my hair is short. Next, I put some big sunglasses on and survey myself in the mirror from all angles. I look nothing like me.

Liam hasn't given me a replacement front door key after the change of locks, so I take the new key from inside the kitchen door and step out into the back garden, shutting the door. It closes silently behind me. That's another pet peeve of Liam's, you see. Squeaking doors drive him mad. He's always oiling the hinges, just to make sure they don't make a sound.

I lock the door and put the key in an old handbag of mine, then walk along the gravel path that leads down the side of the house to the driveway. I've never learned how to drive. To be honest, the idea of it scares me. Being in control of a big hunk of metal is intimidating. So I make do with walking. I can walk to work in thirty minutes; walk to the main high street area in the opposite direction in twenty-five. Liam takes me food shopping when he's off work at the weekends. He moans about it, but really, I think he likes it. It means I'm more dependent on him. Maybe one day I'll learn how to drive myself.

I step out into the street and look both ways. No one is around, but as I walk out of my cul-de-sac towards the bus stop at the bottom of the hill, I have a horrible feeling I'm being watched. I turn round to see if anyone's following me, but there's only a young mum pushing a buggy. She's leaning over the handles, talking to her baby cocooned inside and doesn't even notice me. I scan the houses on either side of the street but don't see anyone in their gardens or looking through their windows at me.

I carry on walking, keeping a wary eye out for anyone who looks like a potential threat. It's scary being out here. Alone. Exposed.

When I get to the bus stop, I breathe a sigh of relief that other people are there. A teenage boy with angry red spots on his face is sitting on the bench. He's plugged into earphones, miming the words to a song. An elderly woman smiles at me and starts talking about how wonderful the weather's been lately. I don't want to talk to anyone. I just want to think, but I feel a bit safer amongst other people, so I humour her as best I can. At least no one can touch me in broad daylight with all these witnesses around.

I check the timetable. A bus is heading towards Welwyn Village in ten minutes. I shift from foot to foot and manage a few yeses and noes now and then as the woman speaks to me until my bus arrives.

It takes forty-five minutes to get to the stop nearest the hotel. I get off the bus and walk to the end of the road, then take a right. I glance behind me. No one else is around. I don't know if that's good or bad.

When I get to the car park at the front of the hotel, I have a weird sense of déjà vu. I've never stayed here, but I feel like I've been here before, standing in the same spot, staring at it and wondering what I'm about to find out. Maybe I've seen it advertised somewhere locally, a photo taken from this very spot, perhaps in the *Welwyn Gazette*. My heartbeat flutters inside my chest as I force myself to walk forward on shaky legs.

The building is sleek, bright and modern; exactly the kind of place Liam took me on our first romantic weekend away two weeks into our relationship. We stayed in York because Liam had never been and wanted to see it. We didn't actually get to see much, though. Instead, we spent most of the time tangled up in the sheets with each other, ordering room service if we were hungry.

When I'd finally got away from the children's home and escaped to Uni, where no one knew my past, I'd reinvented myself. The new Chloe was carefree, fun, and flirty, but I still wasn't confident enough to attract the boys. I seemed to lack some natural skill to find love that everyone else seemed to have, so I'd only ever slept with one person before Liam, and it had only been a brief fling. That's why I thought it was a miracle that Liam could love me at all—that anyone could. And even after such a short time together, I'd already known I felt the same way about him, too.

When we'd arrived at the hotel, he'd already organised for champagne and strawberries to be brought up to the room. He fed me the strawberries, dipped in champagne, and it was the most sophisticated and romantic thing anyone had ever done for me. Later, after the first time we made love, his gaze roamed my naked body, as if he was trying to commit every part of me to memory. 'You're so beautiful,' he said, his fingers sweeping over the curve of my breasts. 'Who cares if you have tiny boobs?'

His words crushed me, but I'd spent a long time trying to hide the pain of my past and my low self-esteem from everybody, so I laughed it off, trying to make it seem like I wasn't bothered by what he'd said. If he really knew exactly what damaged goods I was, he'd leave me in an instant. 'Isn't more than a handful supposed to be a waste?' I joked.

He just continued studying me as if he hadn't heard. 'Why don't I buy you some breast implants?'

It was only the first of many times he criticised my body, and I tried to ignore it for a while. When I couldn't ignore it any longer, I tried to minimise the times he saw me naked again.

I block out the memories. They're not the memories I want to remember. I want to find my lost ones instead.

As I walk into the reception, I take off my sunglasses. A young staff member in a smart uniform sits behind the counter, tapping away at his computer. He looks up as I approach and smiles. 'May I help you?'

I force a smile, but it sits uneasily on my face. 'Hi.' I pull out Liam's credit card receipt and place it on the counter, unfolding and smoothing it out. 'My husband has a credit card receipt from this hotel, and I wondered if you could tell me whether he stayed here with someone else.'

His friendly expression wavers, replaced by something that looks a lot like sympathy. Maybe I'm not the first woman to come here trying to find out if her husband is having an affair, although it doesn't look like the kind of place that rents rooms by the hour. He looks more closely at the receipt. 'I'm afraid we can't give out information about our guests. It's the hotel's privacy policy.'

'Yes, I understand that, but it's my husband's receipt. Surely you can tell me.'

'I'm sorry, madam, but I'm unable to help you. I did tell you that last time.'

My spine goes rigid. 'Last time?'

'Yes.' He turns to his computer again, looking bored now. 'You came in before asking the same question.'

'Did I?'

That jerks his gaze away from his screen. He frowns, probably wondering what kind of nutcase he's dealing with and whether he'll need to call security to remove me from the premises. 'Don't you remember? You were quite agitated when I said I couldn't tell you anything.'

'No, I . . .' My fingertips reach for the lump on the side of my head. 'I had an accident and can't remember anything.'

The frown gets bigger. 'I'm sorry to hear that, but I still can't help you.'

'When?'

'Pardon?'

'When did I come here before? Do you remember the date?'

He tilts his head, thinking. 'I'm not sure, exactly. Probably a little over two weeks ago.'

I calculate the days in my head. Today is the thirteenth of May, which would mean I came here sometime around the end of April, after I was released from the psychiatric ward.

'Now, I'm afraid I must get on,' he says, and I realise I'm staring at him open-mouthed.

I walk back along the road to the bus stop, lost in thought. I'd already visited the hotel, which means I must've suspected Liam was having an affair. It also means I must've found the receipts once before. What else did I find out?

Was it the discovery of my husband having an affair while I was pregnant that set off the miscarriage? Was I distraught enough to make me lose the baby?

No. That didn't work. My miscarriage was on the twenty-fifth of March. I didn't visit the hotel until the end of April, and I remember everything up until the party on the twenty-third of March. So I know for a fact that I couldn't have found out about Liam staying at the hotel until sometime after that.

And anyway, was he even having an affair, or was I just jumping to conclusions? Had I got muddled, thinking he'd said he was staying in Scotland when, in fact, he was staying here? Maybe there was some work conference on at the hotel.

But then, it was only a few miles from home. He would've just caught a cab back or driven, not stayed there. I know things aren't perfect between us, but both of us always vowed that marriage was for life. In fact, Liam's commitment to marriage and settling down was one of the things I'd found so attractive about him in the first place. In an era where more and more couples didn't want to get married, it was refreshing that Liam said he couldn't *wait* to marry me. We'd both had the same goals and ideas. We thought that whatever it took, whatever problems we went through, we should work at it. Stay together. And especially with a baby on the way. I didn't want any child of mine growing up the way I did. I wanted our child to know love from both parents, to feel safe and secure.

Except maybe I didn't feel safe and secure with Liam anymore. I'd ignored things for a long time. Accepted things. Put up with things. Until I didn't really know the Chloe I'd become. My personality had been eroded to make room for his. My dreams and wants had disappeared and became his needs and wants instead. But the baby. I remember now being so excited about telling him after the party.

I'd thought it was a sign. A brand new start for us to get things back on track. Maybe it would make Liam see *me* again and want to rekindle the loving relationship we'd had in the beginning. Last night he'd said he was happy when I'd told him I was pregnant, but had he really been? If he *was* having an affair, would it have been an inconvenience to him? A dent in his plans?

I shake my head. No, of course he wasn't having an affair. What was I thinking? I almost laugh aloud then. It's completely ridiculous. Maybe I am going mad.

But . . . what's the alternative? Why did I go to the hotel before to check up on him? I must've suspected something.

I'm so lost in thought that I don't realise I'm crossing the road in the path of an oncoming car. The driver's horn blares, bringing me quickly back to earth again, and I run across the road to avoid being hit. I take some deep breaths when I get to the other side, and wait at the bus stop.

When I get home, I retrieve my list from where I've hidden it at the back of the sink with the cigarettes and add this new revelation to it, wondering what else is out there waiting to hit me in the face.

Chapter Fifteen

'Have you been out today?' Liam breezes into the kitchen and puts his briefcase on the floor.

I'm just finishing off dinner. Chicken in a creamy tarragon sauce, green beans al dente, and crushed new potatoes. No mash for Liam. They have to be crushed ever so slightly with just the right amount of butter. Too much and they go greasy and oily. Too little and they're bland. His words again, not mine. Always his words, until they become my words, my thoughts, my actions, and I don't know who I am any more, except an extension of Liam.

'No.' I pull the chicken out of the oven and put it on the work-top. He walks up behind me and slides his hands round my waist, drawing me towards him so my head leans against his chest. He kisses my neck, and I tilt my head sideways to let him.

I close my eyes, and for a moment, I forget the fear and the suspicion. For a little while, I want to believe that everything is all right between us. That he's not lying to me or having an affair, and everything that's happened to me is all just some kind of horrific dream I've had. It would just be easier to believe Liam's version of events.

But I don't. And I can't.

'I called you earlier, and you didn't answer,' he says into my neck, his words vibrating on my skin.

'Oh, I must've been in the garden and didn't hear it. I fell asleep out there reading a book.' I give him what I hope is a vague look and wriggle away to drain the beans so he can't see the lie on my face. 'Did you have a good day?' I make my voice sound even and light and hope he can't see my jaw trembling.

'Yes, I managed to get a lot done.' He picks a bean out of the colander and takes a bite. 'They're soggy. You've cooked them for too long like you always do.'

'Sorry.' I turn away and dish up the dinner onto the plates Liam likes.

'What else did you do, apart from read?' He sits at the kitchen table and loosens his tie.

'Not much. Watched a bit of TV; made dinner.' I put the plate in front of him and sit opposite.

He forks in a mouthful of food and studies me carefully. 'I see the refuse collectors still haven't been. There are piles of rubbish sacks out on the street. They'll attract vermin soon. It's disgusting. How long are they going to be on strike for?'

I don't think he's expecting an answer from me, so I don't give him one. I don't give a shit about the refuse collectors. Don't even want to think about something so trivial right now. I push the food around on my plate, taking a mouthful here and there. He's right about the beans; they're too soft. But I like them that way.

He talks about how he won his squash game this morning before work against a colleague called Charles. Goes on about how Charles should just not bother playing, he's so useless, and how it's hardly a challenge for him when you've got someone as unfit for an opponent. I smile, nod, and make appropriate noises in the right places, to seem interested. When he finishes eating, he takes his plate to the draining board, rinses it methodically, and stacks it in the dishwasher. Then he pours himself a glass of red wine and says, 'I'm going on the computer for a while. I've got some reports to catch up on.'

'OK,' I say to his retreating back. 'I'll just clean up and have a shower. I'll probably get an early night.' I load up the dishwasher, wipe down the surfaces with cleaning spray until they're spotless, then trudge up the stairs to our bedroom.

I shower and wash my hair, the soap and shampoo stinging the cuts on my fingers. They're getting better now, but the scabs soften in the water. As I towel dry my hair in the bathroom, I see a pinkish tinge on the white fluffy fabric where they're oozing a little blood. Wiping the steam from the mirror, I stare at myself.

I don't recognise the woman who looks back at me. I've got dark rings under my haunted eyes, and my eyes are red and swollen. My skin and lips are pale, my cheeks hollow. I look like death, which is so ironic that I laugh at the woman in the mirror. Fading scratches lace my forehead and cheeks, a result of the branches slapping my face when I ran through the woods. I pull the hair back from the lump above my ear and examine it. The skin is a mixture of colours: jaundice yellow, rotten plum, mottled tomato.

Scratches. Yes, of course.

I lean closer to the mirror, touching them carefully with my fingertips. I can't hallucinate abrasions, can I? I can't magic them up from the depths of my imagination. They're real. They exist on my face, fingers, and wrists. No one can explain the lump on my head. If it were all something I'd concocted in my mind, I wouldn't have the evidence.

I stare at my reflection for a long time, as if this woman can help me find the answers somehow. In the end, I don't think she can. Maybe no one can. They'll just say I fell over and hit my head somewhere or make some other similar excuse.

I turn away and walk into the bedroom, where I slide the door to my side of the wardrobe open, looking for a clean T-shirt to wear in bed. My clothes aren't expensive or designer gear like Liam's. Only he's allowed that. They're cheap. High street brands that look acceptable but don't cost a fortune.

At first, I don't notice anything unusual. But as I slide the hangers from left to right, I see a few things are missing. My leather jacket. A pair of skinny jeans. My black boots with the wedged heel. A brown V-neck jumper. Some black leggings. A few T-shirts. A pair of ballet-style flats. I go through it all again, pushing things backwards and forwards, just to make sure they haven't got jumbled up in between other items somehow.

OK, so maybe the clothes are in the washing basket, but what about the boots and the shoes? I rummage around further and discover more things gone. A checked shirt, another pair of jeans. In the drawers underneath the clothes, my knickers appear to be sparser than usual. A polka-dot bra and some socks are missing.

I clutch my towel tighter around me and retrace my steps into the bathroom to check the washing basket. I tip everything out onto the floor. Liam's shirts, trousers, socks, boxers, one pair of my socks, and my pink cardigan. None of the missing items are in there.

I pull on a T-shirt and a pair of knickers and head downstairs, my bare feet silent on the carpet. The door to the dining room is half open, and I walk in. Liam is in the middle of sending an e-mail to someone.

E-mails. Of course! I should check my e-mails. Maybe I sent one to Sara that can shed some light on all of this.

When he hears me, he immediately clicks the mouse, and the screensaver pops up. It's a photo of a younger Liam with his cousin Jeremy when they were in their early twenties. They're at the top of Mount Snowdon, dressed in walking gear. Clouds hang like candy-floss in the bright blue sky behind. Liam is a head taller and has his arm flung around Jeremy's shoulder. They're both dark haired, with the same shaped angular jaws and regally straight noses. They each take after their mothers, who were identical twins.

'Yes? Is everything all right?' Liam swivels round in the brown leather office chair to face me.

'Some of my clothes seem to be missing.'

He gives me a reassuring smile. 'Don't you remember, darling, you had a bit of a clear-out before I went to Scotland?'

'Did I?'

'Yes. You thought it would be therapeutic to get rid of some things you never wear anymore that were just cluttering up your wardrobe. I took the old clothes to the charity shop for you; that's why you can't find them.'

'Right.' I nod vaguely, knowing full well I wouldn't have given those things away because they're either new or my favourites. And who in their right mind gives away used underwear?

He smiles and pats my hand. 'Is that all?'

'Er . . . yes.' I turn to leave and feel his gaze burning into my back, unease winding its way through every fibre of my body.

Hours later, I'm lying in bed, staring at the ceiling, wondering if I can come up with a rational explanation for all of this, but I can't. I keep circling back to the only conclusion that seems logical. I must've found the receipts and suspected Liam was having an affair. I went to the hotel to try to confirm it. Maybe I found some other evidence, too. Then I waited until he went to Scotland, before doing something about it so there would be no confrontation.

I'm certain now that the letter Liam showed me wasn't a suicide letter at all. I was leaving him. *That's* what the letter was about. He'd obviously found it and knew I'd left him. It would explain why my bag, phone, and some of my clothes are missing. I would've taken them with me. And if I did, Liam is lying to me *again* about me giving them to the charity shop. I wonder if he's trying to convince people I'm mad, or actually trying to make me go mad.

As I said to Dr Drew, everyone has a breaking point. Maybe that was mine. Perhaps I'd thought enough was enough and couldn't cope with Liam controlling me, criticizing everything, deciding what I should wear and what I should do. Maybe I'd realised there was more to life than the one I was living.

Jordan's face flashes into my head then, but I squash it back down.

But where did I go? Sara's would be the obvious choice. She's still away, and her flat would be empty. Summers said we'd called each other. Maybe it was to arrange for me to stay there. That's the only thing that makes sense.

So I went to Sara's, and then what? What happened next? What led to me being kidnapped and left somewhere underground in the woods? Was it someone I encountered after I left home who put me there? Or did Liam do it? Did he ply me with sleeping tablets, then bundle me in his car and leave me in that place? Was he really in Scotland at all? After all, he'd said he was going there before, when he'd stayed at the Royal Lodge Hotel. Who's to say he wasn't lying about being there this time, too? Does he hate me so much that he'd leave me for dead?

As Liam creeps into the darkened room and gets into bed, goose bumps rise on my flesh, and I wonder just who the hell I'm married to.

Chapter Sixteen

I mustn't let him suspect a thing. Must act normal. Well, as normal as I can, under the circumstances. So I get up the next morning with a bright smile on my face and make him toast and marmalade, even though just the smell of it makes me gag. It's on the kitchen table, ready and waiting for him when he comes down after his shower.

'Thanks.' His gaze slithers over me. 'Why are you wearing those tatty old jeans, darling?'

I glance down at them. The denim is soft and has faded over time. I love them. 'They're comfortable.'

'They make you look fat. Put that other pair on. The black ones. You know how I like you in those.'

'Hmm,' I mumble as I make tea for us both. 'I'll do it in a minute. It's not like I'm going out anywhere.' I pour milk into mugs, just the right amount. Stir. Put his in front of him and sit opposite.

'You really should start taking more care of your appearance,' he goes on. 'Your face looks awful.' He points at the scratches. 'Why don't you book yourself into the hair salon? You could do with a cut. It'll be a nice treat for you. It might make you feel more like your old self again. But make sure you don't go out in that state.' And just like that, he veils a criticism as something kind and caring.

Good old Liam—give you a compliment with one hand and take it away with the other.

But he's actually given me an idea, so I smile and nod. 'I think I will, actually—yes. Can I have a front door key? You haven't given me a new one yet.'

He pushes his empty plate away and stands up. Taking a set of keys from his pocket, he unclips one key from the key ring and puts it on the table. Then he takes his wallet from his other pocket and asks, 'How much money do you need for a haircut?'

'I'm not sure. Since I can't find my purse, I don't have any money until my new bank cards come through. Can you leave me fifty pounds?'

'Fifty! That's rather a lot, isn't it?'

'Well, I might stop at the supermarket to get a few bits, too.'

He puts thirty pounds on the table next to the key and eyes me suspiciously. 'Promise me you won't do anything stupid.'

'Of course not,' I say, although his idea of stupid and mine are probably vastly different now.

'Come straight back after the hairdresser's. You're probably still quite weak. You need to get plenty of rest.'

Weak. Yes. I've been weak for much too long.

I nod and smile to placate him. He kisses me on the cheek, picks up his briefcase, and leaves. I exhale a trembling breath and call Sara. I tried her at least fifty times yesterday, with no luck. Again, the phone just rings persistently in my ear, but she doesn't pick up.

I slam the phone back in the base unit and go into the dining room. Sitting at the computer desk, I switch on the laptop. It makes a whirring, beeping sound as it springs into action, and while I'm waiting, I search through the desk drawers. The first one holds folders of insurance documents, our mortgage details, instruction booklets, receipts, utility bills, bank statements. I rifle through the banks statements, looking for more credit card transactions from

Liam. I don't usually get to see these because Liam insists on dealing with everything financial.

'You'll only mess things up if you get involved,' he told me as soon as we were married, and he insisted I close my personal bank account and open a joint one with him. At first, I thought it was wonderful that he would deal with the responsibility of paying the mortgage and other bills, so I didn't have to, but now I have to tell him every penny I spend.

The statements go back two years, and for the last year there have been regular payments every month or so to the Royal Lodge Hotel. I don't find any more payments to jewellers. I put them back and go through the second drawer. It contains a couple of local phone directories and a Yellow Pages. Nothing much in the third drawer except packets of printing paper, envelopes, scotch tape, and a box of paper clips. On top of the desk, a blue ceramic pot holds pens. One of Liam's ex-girlfriends gave it to him a long time ago. What was her name? Katy, Katya, something like that. He told me she came to England from Moldova to work, but when she went back after a couple of years, he kept this memento from their relationship because he thought it was beautifully made.

He's right. It *is* beautiful. A kaleidoscope of indigo, turquoise, baby blue, and azure. It's like all the colours of the sea mixed together. I tip it upside down onto the desk. Five biros fall out, along with a small rubber and two paperclips, which I must've put in there because Liam would hate to get the paperclips mixed in with everything else. God forbid.

I don't even know exactly what I'm looking for. Something that proves my husband has tried to kill me? I open Google, bring up my e-mail account, and type in the e-mail address and password.

'Error. Password incorrect. Your account has been locked,' the screen flashes at me.

I frown and try again.

'Error. Password incorrect. Your account has been locked.'

What? I try again. Third time lucky, I'm hoping.

'Error. Password incorrect. Your account has been locked.'

I scroll down the page and read how to unlock my account.

'If you receive the above message, your password has been entered incorrectly three times, and your account has been locked for your security. To reinstate your account, fill in the details below:'

It asks for my alternative security word that I added when I set up the account. I type in Jordan's name and hit "Enter."

'We will now send a new password to the mobile phone number attached to this e-mail account.'

'Oh, for God's sake!' I throw my hands in the air. 'That would be great if I could bloody well find my mobile!' I jig my legs up and down in frustration, wondering what to do next. Chewing on my thumbnail, I click on the "History" tab at the top of the screen to see if that can give me any clues to what Liam or I have been looking at. It brings up a list of websites that have been browsed recently: my e-mail account, Liam's e-mail account, The Diamond Store, the Royal Lodge Hotel, our online banking account, Discount Wine Cellar, Amazon, Zolafaxine Side Effects, and Devon Pharmaceutical.

I click on the Zolafaxine page and read the list of side effects.

More common:
Hives
Inability to sit still
Itching
Restlessness
Rash

Less common:
Chills or fever
Joint or muscle pain

Rare:
Anxiety
Cold sweats
Confusion
Convulsions
Diarrhoea
Difficulty with concentration
Drowsiness
Dryness of the mouth
Excessive hunger
Fast or irregular heartbeat
Hallucinations
Headache
Increased sweating
Increased thirst
Lack of energy
Mood or behaviour changes
Overactive reflexes
Purple or red spots on the skin
Psychosis
Suicidal thoughts
Racing heartbeat
Shivering or shaking
Talking, feeling, and acting with excitement and activity you cannot control
Trouble with breathing

I click "Hallucinations," and it brings up another page of information:

The chemical in the brain that antidepressant medications like selective serotonin reuptake inhibitors (SSRIs) affect is the same brain chemical that LSD, PCP, and various psychedelic drugs mimic to create their hallucinogenic effects.

SSRIs prevent serotonin from being reabsorbed into the brain, which leaves behind an excess of serotonin. This allows continued stimulation of the brain and may produce depression, violent moods, suicidal thoughts, psychosis, and mania.

Jesus! How can they even prescribe this stuff? My skin grows clammy, and an icy shudder shoots up my spine when I reach the bottom of the page.

Manufactured by Devon Pharmaceutical.

I have to remind myself to breathe again, and I wipe my palms on my jeans as I think what this could mean. It could mean nothing, of course. It could be a gigantic coincidence. But Liam is responsible for manufacturing their drugs. He has unrestricted access to them. Yes, the information says hallucinogenic and psychosis-like reactions are possible, although rare, but maybe he had somehow tampered with them. Put something in them that would ensure I'd have psychosis-like symptoms.

The hair on the back of my neck prickles as I stare at the page with growing terror. I search the side effects of Silepine sleeping tablets and read through.

Common:
Blurred vision
Constipation
Dizziness
Double vision
Drooling or dry mouth
Drowsiness
Feeling restless or irritable
Loss of libido

Memory problems
Muscle weakness
Nausea
Skin rash
Slurred speech

Rare:
Agitation
Aggression
Amnesia/memory loss
Blackouts
Confusion
Decreased inhibitions/No fear of danger
Depression
Feeling like you might pass out
Hallucinations
Hostility
Hyperactivity
Muscle tremors
Psychosis
Seizures
Thoughts of suicide or hurting yourself
Unusual thoughts or behaviour
Weak or shallow breathing

The reasons why everyone thinks I tried to kill myself and then had some bizarre reaction to the Silepine are all there in black and white. I go to the next page, and it tells me a company called Ashe Pharma manufactures Silepine. Not Liam's company, then.

A loud banging at the front door makes me jump off my chair. I freeze, half-standing, half-crouching, heart pounding.

Bang, bang, bang!

Slowly, I inch my way out of the dining room and into the lounge at the front of the house. I stand along the back wall of the room and look through the net curtains out the bay window. There's a van parked in front of the house with *Flowers for All Occasions* written on the side.

I'm not opening the door. How do I know they're a genuine company? I can't be sure it's not some trap. This could have happened last time, for all I know. It would be a good ruse. Deliver flowers to some poor unsuspecting woman and then kidnap her when she opens the door.

I tremble as I watch a young man retreat down our path with a big bouquet of flowers in his hand. He gives one last look at the house before getting back in the van. I don't recognise him, but that's not saying much. I *could've* met him before and just don't remember.

As I turn to walk out of the room, a bookshelf in the corner, adorned with framed photos, catches my eye. I pick one up of Liam and me outside the register office. He wanted a simple, private wedding, just the two of us. We didn't even have any witnesses that we knew. He thought it would be fun and spontaneous to ask two people off the street.

The photo was taken by one of the witnesses, an elderly man who actually cried when he watched us get married, even though he'd never seen us before in his life. It's blurry and slightly wonky, but the smiles on our faces are blissful. My cheeks are pink, flushed with excitement and happiness. I don't look like that woman anymore. After it was taken, Liam held me close and whispered, 'You belong to me now. Don't ever leave me. I don't think I could bear it.' I thought it was romantic, that it showed a vulnerable side of him he didn't share with the rest of the world. Something reserved only for me because I was special. Because he loved me so much. Now I think it wasn't that at all. It was just an early warning sign.

I put it back down, and my gaze halts on another photo. My scalp tingles as I reach out and pick it up. It's a photo of Liam, encased in a silver frame. It looks recent. A huge banner in the background reads "Exalin." Devon Pharmaceutical is always hosting media events when the company is about to launch a new drug, and this one is for diabetes. It's what Liam's been working so hard on lately. Family members of employees aren't invited. It's purely for advertising purposes. The woman standing next to him with a wide smile is Julianne Day, Liam's boss. She's only a few years older than him, but you'd never guess. Her skin is smooth and youthful, no signs of wrinkles or crow's feet. She always looks exemplary. Hair perfectly sleek in a shiny, bouncy shoulder length bob. Makeup always looking like she's stepped out of a TV makeover programme. Eyebrows plucked in symmetrical arches. It's not strange, I suppose, for them to be photographed together at work. What is strange, though, is the jewellery hanging round her neck.

A white gold and diamond heart-shaped locket.

Chapter Seventeen

I should've known, or at least guessed. I remember at Liam's birthday party, I made a jokey comment to him that he was spending a lot of time with Julianne and neglecting his other guests. He pulled me very close and whispered in my ear, 'She's my boss, for fuck's sake! Of course, I'm going to be attentive. She signs my bonus cheques! Honestly, sometimes you're just so clueless. Half the time, I don't even know how you even managed to get a degree. You need to grow up and stop being so neurotic and jealous.'

It looked to anyone watching like he was cradling me in a loving hug, but I could feel the tension coming off him in waves, and I didn't want to make a scene in front of all his friends. I found myself wondering, *What the hell are you thinking, Chloe? This is crazy. You can't keep doing this.* But it was one rule for me and another for Liam; as soon as I talked to a man, he was by my side in an instant, and he watched me like a hawk.

But nothing was going to spoil my euphoric happiness about the baby. The little life inside me was all that mattered. Didn't Liam deserve the chance to change for the baby's sake?

So maybe deep down I did know, but at the same time, I denied it, as I've tried to deny many things. I'd put the photo back in exactly the same spot so it wouldn't look like I'd moved it.

I need to get out of the house. Get away from everything that's staring me in the face. The lounge feels impossibly small, as if it's squashing the life right out of me. I snatch the money and key from the table where Liam left them and head for the stairs, when I notice a card poking out of the letterbox. It's from the flower company, telling me they tried to deliver to the address and I should call the number listed on the front to rearrange another suitable time.

I find the Yellow Pages in the office drawer and look up Flowers for All Occasions. The telephone number on the card matches.

Liam couldn't have sent the flowers. He only gives me flowers after he's lost his temper about something, and he'd just bring them home with him, not have them delivered. Jordan? No. He wouldn't go that far. Sara wouldn't have sent them because she's not here. Which really only leaves Theresa, my boss.

I toss the card on the office desk and put on my disguise of sunglasses and sunhat. Then I rush out the front door, slamming it behind me. If Liam were here, he'd go mental at that. He hates the sound of slamming doors. But I don't care anymore. I want to kick the door, actually. Kick anything. Especially him.

I'm out of breath, hot, and sweaty by the time I've walked to the town centre, on high alert for any suspicious people following me. I swing open the door to the first hairdresser I find, and the smell of perm lotion hits the back of my throat.

'Hi, can I help you?' A chirpy young receptionist who has short, spiky blonde hair with streaks of purple in it smiles at me. When she notices the scratches on my face, her smile wavers a little.

'Yes.' I smile back, even though it's the last thing I feel like doing, but I want to appear normal. 'Do you have any appointments today?' I remove the sunglasses and hat and stuff them in my bag.

She chews on the end of her pen and looks up at my long, wavy dark hair that's now cascading over my shoulders. 'What do you want done?'

'Um . . .' I trail off, thinking. The thing is, even though it's obvious Liam has been having an affair, was he really the one who left me underground? After what I've found out so far, it seems possible, but what if he wasn't? What if the lies he's told me are all unconnected to what happened to me? In which case, whoever did take me knows what I look like. So I need to change. Drastically.

'I want it cut short and coloured. Something lighter.'

She taps the pen against her lips and looks down at a diary on the counter. 'Well, if you can wait half an hour, Denise will be able to do that.' She looks up expectantly.

'That's perfect, thank you.'

She swings an arm towards a rattan sofa behind me. 'Have a seat. Do you want a tea or coffee?'

I think about asking her for something stronger, but it's only 11:00 a.m. 'No, I'm fine, thank you.' I sit down, and the sofa squeaks under my weight. Two other women come in and sit opposite me. I avoid looking at them and pick up a celebrity magazine, flicking through it, but not seeing the pages. Everything's a blur, like the world is spinning and my vision can't keep up.

What to do, what to do?

I should just leave Liam. Now. Today. Except then I'll never know for sure if he's been trying to kill me or if it was someone else. But if I stay, my life could be in danger.

No. I need to stay in the house and see what other clues I can find. There must be something that will help me piece things together. Yes. I'll stay. Just until I can find out more and tell Summers.

The two women laugh to each other, and I look up. Their eyes are on me, and I realise I've been muttering my thoughts aloud like a crazy, homeless person.

I stare out the window to avoid them, watching ordinary people going about their daily lives making stupid, mundane plans— wondering what to cook for dinner tonight, what they're going to watch on TV, whether they remembered to feed the cat before they left for work, which dress they should buy in the sale, when the gas bill is due. They all seem so far removed from me now, in a different world a million miles away. They're all in the sunlight, and I've been abandoned in a dark place, trying to constantly kick my legs to keep my head above water before I drown.

I think about Liam and Julianne and wonder how long it's been going on and how I left him. Did I simply write that letter for him to say I was ending it all (our relationship, *not* my life!) when he went to Scotland, then pack a few things and move into Sara's? Or did we fight about it? Did he hit me? Knock me unconscious and try to get rid of the body? Did he drug me with sleeping pills and then hit me over the head?

No, of course not. What am I thinking? Liam isn't capable of doing something like that to me. Which can only mean my kidnapper is someone I don't know.

I wish I could remember, but all I feel is a scratching inside my head, as if maggots are gnawing on my brain. I'm so lost in thought I don't hear someone talking to me at first.

'. . . this way.'

I snap my head up, and a woman with a short, choppy, caramel-coloured bob is standing in front of me. 'Sorry?' I say.

'I'm ready for you now, if you'd like to come this way.' She walks past reception and stands behind a chair in the middle of a row along one wall. I sit down and stare at myself in the mirror.

I've lost more weight, even in the last few days. I look like a woman twice my age. I feel it, too. 'Are you OK?' She narrows her eyes at my scratches.

I make a mental note to wear some thick foundation the next time I go out. If people keep asking me whether I'm OK, I'll probably break down into a gibbering wreck. I muster up a convincing smile. 'Yes. I'm fine, thanks. I fell off my bicycle into a bush, that's all.'

She nods. 'So, you want a complete change, then?' She tilts her head, lifting up my hair. 'Shame. Your hair's gorgeous. In good condition, too. What do you fancy?'

I meet her gaze in the mirror. 'Can you do it like yours? A chin-length bob? And a lot lighter in colour.'

'Do you want it all coloured or just highlights? A whole head of colour will be quite drastic. Highlights will be more subtle.'

'A whole head, please.'

'No problem. And it's your lucky day.' She smiles. 'We've got a sale on at the moment. You get a free cut and blow dry with every colour.'

Lucky? That almost makes me laugh hysterically.

An hour and a half later, I don't recognise myself. I walk past the shop windows, catching glimpses of the new me as the air breathes on the back of my bare neck. Liam will hate it. He likes my hair long and kept down. Thinks it looks more feminine. Well, fuck him.

My stomach's shouting in hunger by the time I arrive home, but the thought of eating makes me nauseous. I open the fridge door. It's almost empty, and I only have five pounds left over from what Liam gave me to get some food. I close the door again and look at the fruit basket. A lone apple and two bananas stare back at me. I bite into the apple and ring Sara again. No answer. I wonder what she's doing. Knowing her, she's probably trekking in the mountains or white water rafting.

As I throw the apple core into the bin under the kitchen sink, I notice it's full. I tie the ends of the black bin liner together and heave it from the metal casing before going out the kitchen door and round the side path to the front of the house where the wheelie bin is. Since the refuse collectors still hasn't come, it's stuffed full, the lid pushed up and gaping half open, as if it's laughing at me. I put the bin bag on the ground next to it, and as I'm walking away, a thought strikes me. The plate that Liam told Summers we'd rowed about. The one he said I'd smashed. If that really happened, the remnants of broken crockery would be in one of these bin bags.

I pick up the bag I've just put down in one hand and take the top one from the wheelie bin in the other, carrying them both into the back garden. I retrieve the final two bags and deposit them next to the others. Then I hear a mangled, melodic sound, like a dying bird. Even though it's distorted, I know exactly what it is.

It's the ringtone from my missing mobile phone, and it's coming from inside one of the bags.

Chapter Eighteen

My fingers shake as I undo the knot on the first bag, the one I've just taken from the kitchen. The ringing has stopped now, so I don't know which one it's in. I dump the contents out onto the lawn and frantically pick through. If Summers could see me now, he'd definitely think I'd lost the plot. I let out a snort just thinking about it as I pick up soggy used tissues, kitchen waste, discarded post, empty shampoo and ketchup bottles, the mug I dropped that Liam wrapped up in newspaper, and the red dress I had on when I was found, which the hospital must've given to Liam. It's now ripped and torn, and I don't know why they thought I'd want it back.

Disgusting muck covers my hands when I finish putting the contents back in the bag and start on the next one.

That's where I find it.

The glass face of the phone is cracked so much I can't read the screen anymore, and filth covers it. It looks like it's been thrown or stamped on. Did I do that? Did Liam? I leave it on the grass and check through the rest of the bin bags for the remnants of the smashed plate. There's no sign of it, which means it never happened.

I'm not going mad. I didn't act out of character and throw the plate at him. It's yet another lie Liam's told that makes me look irrational and crazy. I replace all the rubbish back in the bin, then go into the kitchen. I wash my hands and wipe the phone repeatedly with antibacterial wipes until it's clean.

It's useless. I can't read a thing through the damaged screen. But it must be working if it was ringing, so maybe the SIM card will still be OK. I need to get another phone, so I can try it out. It's not likely I can buy a phone with five pounds, which means I'll have to get some more money from Liam. If I ask for more, he'll want to know what it's for, and he can't suspect I know things.

I'll steal it from his wallet then. Yes, that's it.

Another thought bursts into my head then. The sleeping tablets. I haven't noticed them in the house, and they certainly weren't in the bin. If I'd really taken them, they'd be somewhere around here. I search everywhere, starting in one of the kitchen cupboards where we keep a plastic container of medicine. I pull everything out, one by one: plasters, bandages, earwax removal drops, Optrex, ibuprofen, paracetamol, Anadin Extra, some out-of-date antibiotics Liam had for a tooth abscess, vitamin C tablets, laxatives. I search the bathroom cabinets and all the drawers in the bedroom.

No sleeping tablets.

'What the fuck have you done to your hair?' Liam's eyes widen when he walks into the kitchen. A red flush creeps up his neck, a sure sign he's getting angry. I know all the signs now. I've lived with them for too long. I don't want him to smash a hole in one of the doors or walls again, so I ignore the harsh tone of his voice. With a placid smile on my face, I stop stirring the spaghetti sauce I found in the freezer.

'I . . . I just fancied something different, that's all.' Instinctively, I reach a hand up to touch my hair, or lack of it.

'It looks bloody awful! You don't look anything like yourself anymore. Why on earth would you do that?' His hand goes to his hip. 'Honestly, Chloe, sometimes you're just so stupid. When I said get your hair cut, we agreed on a trim, but you're practically bald!'

'I just—'

'This is what I mean.' He points a finger at me, disapproval thick in his voice. 'You're just acting irrationally all the time. I'm going to ring Dr Drew tomorrow and express my concerns. *Again.*'

'How is cutting my hair irrational?' I dare to challenge him, suddenly brave.

'Because you don't usually do these kinds of things.' His tone is coaxing, as if he's trying to talk a child out of a tantrum.

'What things? Cut my hair? That's ridiculous!' I shake my head, but I know exactly what he means. He means I don't usually go against what *he* wants.

He strides towards me, picks up a tuft of hair, and tugs hard on the end.

'Ouch!' I reach for his hand. 'That hurts!'

'You've completely lost it, and you can't even see it.' He drops his hand, turns, and storms out of the room and up the stairs. When he's gone, I stick my tongue out at the space he's left. A pathetic gesture, I know, but I'm fighting now. Fighting for my sanity.

And I'm not stupid. If I were, I would never have managed to escape.

As I'm draining the pasta through a colander at the sink, the doorbell rings, scaring me senseless. I spill boiling water over my wrist and gasp.

I hear Liam opening the door and talking to a man. The door closes, and a few minutes later Liam walks into the kitchen with a bouquet of flowers in one hand and a small envelope that's been torn open in the other. He holds them out to me with an amused smile on his face. 'I thought you had a secret admirer at first, but they're just from Theresa.'

'Yes, I meant to tell you someone tried to deliver them earlier, but I didn't want to open the door. I arranged for the delivery man to come back when you'd be home.' I wipe my hands on a dishcloth and take the flowers.

They're lovely. Lush lilies and bright roses, all interspersed with green leaves and red ribbon. I slide out the card from the envelope that Liam's already opened.

Wishing you a speedy recovery.
Best Wishes,
Theresa (and all the staff at Downham College)

A speedy recovery? How do you recover from being kidnapped and left for dead? How do you recover from someone trying to make you go mad?

I wonder what Liam has told her and whether Summers has been to see her, asking questions. Did they both paint me as a lunatic who'd tried to kill herself? I risk a glance at Liam, who has a smug grin on his face.

'Shall I put them in water for you, darling?' He takes the bouquet from my hand and busies himself with finding a glass vase and filling it with water. I plate up the spaghetti and pour sauce on top neatly as Liam arranges the flowers.

We sit down at the table, but eating is almost impossible for me. I chew my food slowly and thoroughly to get it past my throat, which feels like it's closed up.

After I clear the dinner plates and clean the kitchen, Liam retreats to the dining room to use the computer. I pour a glass of red wine, then grab a cigarette and lighter and go out into the garden.

Hiding on the path round the side of the house, I light up and inhale, taking drags in between big gulps of alcohol. Both the cigarette and wine burn my throat, but it feels great. If I can feel pain, it means I'm still alive. When this is all over, I'll quit again. I don't care about getting lung cancer when my death could be imminent anyway.

I stub out the cigarette and throw it over the fence so Liam won't find it. Then I walk to the end of the garden and turn around, looking at the house that feels like a prison.

Liam's standing at our bedroom window, watching me, but I can't make out his expression from this far away. I exhale a weary, defeated sigh and head back into the house.

Quickly washing up the wine glass and putting it back in the cupboard, I chew on a polo mint to take away the smoky smell. As I finish cleaning the kitchen, Liam's coming down the stairs. I turn around and he's there, right behind me. He pulls me towards him, holding me gently, and I have to wrestle hard with myself to keep the scream deep inside.

'I'm sorry for moaning about your hair. It's just that I love you so much, I'm worried about you.' He strokes my back.

My muscles tense. 'You don't have to worry. I'm fine.' Or maybe that's what he's worried about, that I *am* actually fine and not either dead or in the loony bin, and he's not free to do whatever he wants.

'Everything you've been doing lately is so out of character. I think those drugs affected you more than we first thought. Something's happening to you.'

Shut up! You keep saying that! Is it me you're trying to convince, or yourself?

'I don't want to have the doctors intervene, but you must see that you're not acting like yourself.'

No. I don't see! I don't, I don't, I don't! You're trying to destroy me. Send me bloody insane!

I bite back what I really want to say. 'Cutting my hair doesn't mean I'm not acting like myself. I like it. It's more manageable this length.' I sniff into his shoulder.

He pulls back, blue eyes searching mine. 'Well, I suppose it will grow again,' he huffs. 'But don't cut it anymore.'

'No. I won't.'

'Good girl. Now, let me make you a cup of tea. You sit down and relax. This is all taking its toll on you, I can tell.' He kisses the top of my head and switches on the kettle, humming to himself. I watch his stiff back as I sit nervously at the table, wondering what he's going to do next. When he finishes the tea, he brings it over and sets it in front of me. 'There you are. When you've drunk that, we can watch a film together. Snuggle up on the sofa, eh?'

The thought makes my stomach bubble. 'That would be nice.' I smile, hoping he doesn't notice it wobble on my face, and bide my time.

Chapter Nineteen

I steal sixty-five pounds from Liam's wallet when he's having his morning shower and tuck it inside my pillowcase. I'm getting dressed in a black sundress he likes when he comes out of the bathroom, towel wrapped round his waist, hair still damp.

'Sleep well?' He tilts his head, a very slight smile on his face.

'Mmm, like a log.' It's a lie, of course. How can I sleep?

'Maybe that's what you need, just some good old rest.' He folds the used towel up and puts it on top of the dressing table, then pulls on some boxers he's already laid out neatly on the bed.

My gaze flicks to his body. A body I loved in the beginning.

Now I hate it.

I wonder how he'd feel if I criticised him. If I told him I could see the grey filtering through the blond at his temples. How the hard lines of his abs are filling out now with a slight paunch. How the definition of his jaw has changed, with the first appearance of loose skin, and there are puffy bags under his eyes.

He catches me looking and mistakes my expression for interest. 'I have a little time before I go to work.' He raises his eyebrows and walks towards me. He runs his fingertips down the side of my neck, over my collarbone, along the swell of my breast. I want to jerk away from him, but I clench the horrified shiver deep inside.

One corner of his lips lifts in a sultry smile as he undresses me slowly. I swallow back the repulsion, unsure of how I am actually holding it together without clawing at him. But I'm used to acting now, and this time it might save my life. So I roam my hands over his body as his piercing gaze holds mine.

He picks me up and carries me to the bed gently. I wrap my legs round his waist and angle my hips up to meet him, acting like I can't wait. A chill sinks into my bones, as if someone's just walked over my grave.

'No one will ever love you as much as me.' His hot breath fans across the shell of my ear when he thrusts inside me deeply. I bite back the cry of pain. He moves to his own rhythm, and I'm so convincing in my moans and groans of ecstasy that even I almost believe it.

After he leaves, I take a shower, trying to rid myself of his smell and touch on my skin. I scrub until the water runs cold, but I still don't feel clean.

I brush my teeth hard, making my gums bleed, then go downstairs and have a coffee and a cigarette, my hands shaking so hard I spill the coffee on the patio table. I rinse my cup and put it in the dishwasher, then put on my big sunglasses and study myself in the mirror. Everything looks different. I'm not Chloe Benson anymore. I don't know who I am.

I leave the house and walk towards town. The streets are eerily quiet, but I keep my eyes alert for anyone who might be suspicious. A feeling creeps chillingly up my spine that I'm not alone. It's as though someone's eyes are boring into my back.

Someone is behind me. I know it.

Every muscle tenses, and I force myself to look over my shoulder. A man's walking about twenty-five metres behind. He's big and bulky, wearing black jeans, trainers, and a baggy grey hoodie pulled over his head, casting a dark shadow so it's impossible to see his face properly.

My heartbeat slams in my chest as I increase my pace. I'm on a residential street, but I'm still terrified. Flynn said no one wants to get involved these days. A crime could be happening right in front of someone's nose, and the person would probably keep his head down and walk past.

His footsteps speed up.

I don't know whether to run. Or would that just let him know I'm scared and make him chase me? I cross to the other side of the road and keep walking, looking back to see where he is.

He turns his head towards me, but I still can't make out his face.

It could be him. The person who took me. But I don't know how he could possibly recognise me now.

I clamp my lips together to stop from screaming out and walk faster still. I can't hear his footsteps now over the sound of my heartbeat pounding in my ears. Fighting to keep my breathing calm, I wonder whether to stop at someone's house and ring their doorbell, but anyone could be inside, and all I can see in the windows are bright reflections of the street where the sunlight bounces off the glass.

Then I hear him again. Louder now, his footsteps close behind me, keeping in time with mine, and I'm pretty much power walking. Sweat trickles between my shoulder blades.

Someone shouts, 'Dave!' and I spin my head around once more.

The man in the hoodie has stopped, waiting for another man who jogs up to join him. They do some weird kind of handshake and stand there, talking.

I exhale a ragged breath of relief and carry on down the street, not letting up my pace, just in case. By the time I arrive in town, it feels like I'm about to have a heart attack, so I sit on a bench in the middle of town until the chaos in my head subsides. Then I square my shoulders and get up.

There are five mobile phone shops to choose from, but I go to the one that is my existing service provider. I push the door open, take off my sunglasses, and browse through the phones, looking for the cheapest pay-as-you-go. There's one for 20 pounds. That will do.

'Can I help you?' A salesman that looks about the same age as my students appears beside me.

'Yes, is this phone unlocked?'

'They're all unlocked here. You can use any SIM card in them. But you can't take photos on this one, and there's no Internet access.'

'That's OK. I'll take it.'

He gives me an odd look, as if I've just sprouted another head. 'Are you sure? We have a better model over here with the works on it.' He points to something bigger with a touch screen.

'No, this will be perfect.'

I pay quickly and rush home, my eyes scanning the streets for signs of possible danger. The ominous feeling I'm being watched makes my skin crawl, but the only people I see on the way home are two mums walking three noisy children down the street, an old man walking an even older-looking dog, and a woman getting out of a cab at the side of the road.

When I get inside, I tear at the phone's packaging, which I hide in the bottom of the kitchen bin. Then I insert the battery in the phone, plug it in, and let it charge. Sitting at the kitchen table, I watch the phone on the worktop as I rock back and forth, sliding my earring round and round in its pierced hole, waiting.

A ringing noise makes me jump, and at first, I think it's the mobile, but it's not.

'Hello?' I pick up the house phone, expecting it to be Liam checking up on me.

'Ah, is that Chloe? It's Dr Drew here.'

'Hello. I haven't missed our appointment, have I?' I panic, wondering if I've lost yet more time and don't remember. *What day is it, anyway?*

'No, that's not for another few days. The reason I'm ringing is that I've had a call from Liam this morning saying he's concerned about you, so I wanted to check in. How've you been?'

I scrunch up my face and rest my head in my free hand, then take a calming breath. 'I'm fine, Dr Drew, really. He . . .' I trail off. I wonder how much I should tell him. He seemed sympathetic before, even if he didn't believe me. But surely, if I explain what I've found out so far, he'll realise something strange is going on. 'Liam's telling me lies. And not just to me. He's telling lies to other people about me.'

'What kind of lies?'

'He's trying to convince people I'm going mad.' There, I've said it. And now that it's out in the open, the tension pulling me taut unravels a little.

'Why do you think that?'

'Because he's got things to hide. You know the antidepressants I was prescribed, Zola . . . something or other?'

'Zolafaxine.'

'Yes. Did you know they're made by the same company where Liam works?'

'Yes. In fact, Liam was very insistent about us filing the required reports with his company as soon as possible after your incident occurred.'

'I think he tampered with them somehow. Put something in them to make me go psychotic. I know it sounds far-fetched. Sounds ridiculous, even. But when you add everything together, it's the only answer.'

There's silence for a moment on the other end of the line. 'As both Dr Traynor and I told you, it *is* possible to suffer the side effects you did while taking that medication. It's been documented before. Although it's unusual, it does happen occasionally. And it's also entirely possible for you to have had a further reaction to the sleeping tablets you took, too, which, incidentally, are *not* made by Devon Pharmaceutical.'

'I didn't take them.'

'How can you be sure? You don't remember.'

'Why would I ignore advice not to take any more medication? It doesn't make any sense.'

'People ignore medical advice all the time.'

'But they're not here. They're not at the house. If I took them, they'd be here, wouldn't they?'

'You might have had them with you when you wandered off. You said your handbag was missing, so they could've been in there. And don't forget, you were still grieving. Liam said you were still having trouble sleeping, so that's obviously why you took them.'

'Yes, but Liam was having an affair. I've found proof of it.' I tell him about the hotel, the locket, and the photo of his boss, Julianne.

'That doesn't prove he was having an affair. Perhaps he was at a conference at the hotel that ended late in the evening, and he simply stayed there instead of disturbing you. The necklace could've been an innocent birthday gift for his boss, could it not?'

'Would you buy a twelve-hundred pound diamond and gold necklace as a birthday present for your boss?'

'My boss is a man, so I'm sure he wouldn't appreciate it very much.' He chuckles slightly. I want to reach my hand down the phone line and shake him hard. Shake some bloody sense into him.

'And my e-mail account was hacked. He must've been looking for something.'

'Do you know how many e-mail accounts are hacked into every day? It happened to me only a few months ago. Whoever did it managed to send an e-mail with a virus attached to all my contacts! It's very common, you know.'

'But when you consider everything else, it's all suspicious. He lied to me about that note I wrote being a suicide letter. He lied that I'd taken some of my clothes to the charity shop.'

'OK, OK, slow down. How do you know you didn't take your clothes to the charity shop? You may have wanted to clear out a few things. I've seen it many times before when people are getting over a traumatic event. They like to get rid of old, stagnant things in their life and make way for the clean and bright and new. It's actually a very therapeutic way to start dealing with life.'

'I wouldn't take used underwear to a charity shop. Would you?'

'Well, no, I can't say I would, but I'm sure it's been known. I bet they get all sorts of strange things donated. One person's rubbish is another person's gold, after all.'

'No, I just wouldn't do that.' My voice rises with hysteria. 'And then there's the place.'

'Which place?'

No, not the place. Wrong word. My brain feels fuzzy, like a gap is opening up inside. 'I mean the plate.'

'The plate?'

'Yes! The one Liam told you and the police I threw at him before he went to Scotland. There was no broken plate in the rubbish bin, so it couldn't have happened.'

I hear him sigh, and I don't know if it's with impatience or disbelief. 'Chloe, isn't it likely that the refuse collectors have already taken it away? It would've been a week ago now.'

'No, they're on strike. It's not possible at all,' I say triumphantly. And then I remember something Summers told me. 'Liam said he didn't phone me from Scotland because we'd rowed about the plate and I told him I didn't want to talk to him.'

'Yes.'

'But that's not right, because there *was* no plate. And Liam *always* phones me. Or texts me. Every day he'll ring to find out what I'm doing, where I am, what I'm thinking. Sometimes several times a day.'

'I'm not sure what you're getting at. It could be that—'

I cut him off with a loud sigh. 'Don't you see, though? He didn't call me from Scotland because my mobile phone was smashed and in the bin, so he knew I wouldn't be able to answer the phone. He knew because he put me in that place and left me to die!' My voice escalates.

'Calm down, dear. Take some deep breaths.'

I don't want to fucking calm down. I want someone to believe me!

'You don't know how your mobile phone came to be broken and in the bin. It could've happened before Liam left for Scotland, in which case he wouldn't call you, would he, if he knew about it?'

'He didn't call the house phone either, though. Summers told me.'

'Liam did mention how busy he's been with the new Exalin drug. It's possible he didn't get the chance to call.'

'But he *always* calls me. Always. Only not this time. It's suspicious. Very suspicious.'

'Have you asked Liam about all this?'

What was the point? I knew he'd just deny it. It was his word against mine, and everyone was on his side. 'No, I don't want to let him know I know yet.'

'All of these things you've mentioned have a rational explanation, but if you feel this way, then I think you should be talking to the police about it. They'll be able to put your mind at ease, I'm sure.' His voice is gentle but insistent.

'They won't believe me until I have some proof. Liam's managed to convince them I'm unstable. He said he showed you the letter I wrote. He told me it was my suicide letter, but it's not.' My right eye starts to twitch. I close it and press my finger against the lid, massaging it gently.

'I agree.'

'Hooray! That's first thing we've agreed on,' I snap. I know I should try to keep calm, but it's becoming increasingly difficult. I don't know why it isn't obvious to him after everything I've just said that Liam is somehow involved. Why isn't he listening to me?

But then I think about all the mentally unstable people he must see in his line of work. People who are delusional, who hear voices, who are paranoid and imagine things that aren't really happening. He must think I'm just like them.

He ignores my outburst and says in a calm voice, 'If I thought you were suicidal, I wouldn't have agreed to release you from hospital. On the contrary, I think you have a strong will for survival, which is the same thing I told Summers. Liam is convinced that you took the sleeping tablets in an attempt to overdose, which was thwarted when you had the reaction to it, and that's why he's so concerned about you.'

'Yes, he can be very convincing when he wants to be,' I mumble.

'I disagree with that theory, though. I simply think you took them to help you sleep. After everything you've told me, I believe you were very unhappy with your life and possibly became depressed again, which led to you not sleeping, just like the last time. But until you regain your memory, none of us knows for certain what led to you being found on that road at the edge of the woods. We can all make suppositions or look for things that seem suspicious, but the most plausible answer is that you willingly took some sleeping tablets, which set off another hallucinogenic and paranoid psychosis. Some people are just very sensitive to medication.'

'But what if you're wrong? What if Liam is trying to get rid of me?' My voice cracks then. I was so sure Liam was involved, but I don't know now. Can't be sure of anything. I don't know what's real and what my mind has distorted to fit what I *think* is real. Maybe I'm reading too much into all those things. They could all be just innocent little coincidences that have stacked up. Dr Drew has made them all sound as if they make perfect, rational sense. And he should know. He's the psychiatrist, after all. An expert of the human mind. I almost believe his reasoning myself.

Almost.

He pauses for a moment. 'Then, my dear, I think you should get out of the house and go somewhere safe.'

'I will. As soon as I know for sure. I can't prove anything yet, and that's the problem. I need to find out more first, because what if it *was* someone else? Someone I don't know about?'

'Wait a second—let me make sure I'm hearing this correctly. You've just tried to convince me Liam is trying to harm you, and yet now you suddenly think someone *other* than Liam is trying to harm you?' He pauses for a beat. 'Be careful, won't you, my dear? I don't want to see you back in the hospital again.' I can't tell if that's a warning or genuine concern on his part. 'If you need anything, just call me, OK? Day or night, it doesn't matter.'

'Thank you. I may just have to do that.'

We hang up, and I check the battery level on the mobile phone. It's still not charged enough to use. Damn.

I have too much nervous energy to sit here and wait. It really will make me go crazy. Every cell is buzzing, every muscle taut with tension. I grab my bag and let myself out of the house.

Chapter Twenty

When I arrive at Downham College, a distant memory is trying to niggle into my brain, but it hovers just on the edge of my periphery, as if I'm looking through a dirty mirror smudged with years' accumulation of grease and grime. I squeeze my eyes shut, trying to focus. It's something to do with one of my students, but I don't know what. I massage my forehead, hoping I can relax the thought back in somehow, but it's stuck behind an invisible brick wall.

I wander past the crowds of students milling around eating their lunch on the grass, taking advantage of the warm weather. The noise of their laughter and chatter penetrates my head, making it pound.

'Mrs Benson?' one of them calls as I pass a group throwing a rugby ball to each other.

I stop and turn around. Chris Barnes, one of my keener students, jogs towards me. Sweat plasters his messy hair to his forehead, and his face is flushed from exertion. He's dressed in baggy jeans and a blue T-shirt with some kind of logo on the front. He's a member of the college rugby team, stocky, and a lot taller than I am, so I have to look up at him as he stands in front of me, slightly out of breath.

'Hi, Chris, how are you?' I attempt a smile.

'I wasn't sure if that was you or not. You look different.' He wipes the sweaty hair off his forehead with the back of his hand. 'Yeah, I'm good, thanks. Sorry to hear you haven't been well. I've missed your classes.'

I wonder exactly what Theresa has told my students about why I've been off sick. 'Well, I hope you're as well behaved for your stand-in tutor as you are for me.'

He blushes. 'Of course. But it's not the same without you. When are you coming back?'

'Er . . . I'm not exactly sure yet. Soon, though.'

Another student I don't recognise shouts to Chris, telling him to get back and finish their game.

'OK . . . so . . . I'd better get back.' He smiles awkwardly. 'Hope to see you in class soon, then.' He jogs back off to join his friends, and I head up the front steps and along the corridor towards the offices.

I knock on the open doorway of Gillian's office, the college secretary. She's ancient and has been here since it opened in the sixties. She always reminds me of an old-fashioned Victorian schoolmistress, dressed in formal clothing that covers every part of her. Heavy skirts that swish against the floor as she walks and long-sleeved blouses, even in summer. But she's lovely.

She glances up at me, and it's as if she doesn't know me. Then her eyes light up in recognition. 'Chloe! How are you?' She stands and gives me a big hug. 'You've cut your hair! It makes you look really different.'

I rest my head on her shoulder and inhale the familiar lily of the valley—her signature perfume. I want to stay there all day, comforted in her warm arms. An adult woman hasn't held me since my mum, and for just a moment I feel like a little girl again.

All too soon, she releases me. 'How are you, dear?' She points to the scabs on my face. 'They look nasty.'

I touch them absentmindedly. 'Oh, that, um . . .' I hear Gillian talking and realise I've tuned out for a moment. 'Pardon?'

'I said, are you OK? Do you want to sit down? You look a bit peaky. Shouldn't you be at home, taking it easy?' She peers at me as if I'm a brittle piece of glass about to shatter right in front of her eyes.

'No, I'm OK.'

'Really?' She doesn't look convinced. 'We didn't expect you to rush back. I think Theresa was going to wait awhile before talking to you.'

'Talking to me?'

'Oh.' She blushes. 'It's probably best if you have a chat with her about things. Do you want to go in?' She tilts her head towards Theresa's office to her right. 'She's just eating her lunch.'

'Thanks.' I knock on Theresa's door.

'Come in,' she says in a clipped tone.

I open the door to find Theresa sitting behind her desk, swamped with paperwork, a sandwich in one hand, typing with the other. She looks Scandinavian. Tall, slim, with blonde hair tied up in a no-nonsense bun and pale green eyes that seem to stare right through you. She doesn't have a sense of humour, and to be honest, we've never really hit it off that well. She can be abrupt and abrasive most of the time. Theresa is all about budgets and efficiency, and saving money where she can, and she scares me a little.

'Chloe, how are you?' Theresa raises her eyebrows. 'We weren't expecting you back.'

'No, I know I'm still signed off sick, but I wanted to thank you for the flowers.'

'Flowers?' She tilts her head with a puzzled expression.

'You sent some flowers, wishing me a speedy recovery, didn't you?'

'Ah, yes, of course! Gillian sorted it out. I'm glad you liked them.' She pops the final piece of her sandwich in her mouth and chews slowly.

'Did the police come to see you about me?'

She waits a full minute while she finishes chewing and then takes a sip of water, avoiding looking at me. 'Yes. They said you'd been involved in some sort of accident and were suffering from amnesia.'

'Accident?'

'That's what they said.'

'It was more than an accident. I can't remember what happened in the last seven weeks. I was . . .' I trail off and look out of the window at Chris and his friends running along, playing rugby. I want to run, too. Run and run and never come back. Run somewhere no one knows me. Where no one could find me. Start a new life. Maybe change my name.

'They also said you'd had another allergic reaction to some sleeping tablets you were prescribed.' Her voice jerks me away from my daydream. 'Honestly, if I were you, I'd just avoid taking any drugs altogether. It seems like you're particularly sensitive to them.' She leans forward in her chair. 'Have you ever tried homeopathy? It's completely natural and works really well.'

I blink twice, trying to take in what she's saying. 'No, I've never tried it. Look, Theresa, the police didn't tell you exactly what happened to me, then?'

'They didn't go into detail; they just wanted to know if you'd been here since you came out of hospital after the problem you had with the antidepressants.' She says 'problem' in an accusing tone, as if somehow it's my fault I ended up in the psychiatric ward, acting like a lunatic.

'I was abducted and left somewhere underground. I escaped, but I can't remember what happened. The doctors aren't sure if the amnesia is from the drugs or some kind of trauma.'

Her face tightens in an expression of forced tolerance. 'Abducted?'

'I know it all sounds completely weird and far-fetched, but, yes, that's what happened. I'm trying to piece together what I did before I was taken, since I can't remember.'

'The police didn't mention abduction at all. Why wouldn't they tell me that?' she asks warily.

'I'm not sure.' I don't want to admit to her that the police don't believe me. 'Did we have a meeting at all recently, or did I come in and see you?'

'No.' She rests her forearms on the desk, as if she's preparing to interview me. 'As far as I knew, you were still recuperating from the reaction to the antidepressants. You weren't due to come back to work yet anyway, but a little while after that lovely detective inspector Summers came to see me, Liam called and told me . . .' She glances away briefly before looking at me again. 'Well, he said your depression was worse than they first thought and you'd tried to commit suicide with some sleeping tablets, but you'd had another reaction to them, so you didn't quite—your attempt wasn't successful. He said you were now under the care of a psychiatrist, and he hoped you'd be getting back to normal soon.'

'Commit suicide?' My mouth flaps open and closed like a fish. 'Is that what the police told you, too, that I tried to commit suicide?'

She shifts in her chair, looking uncomfortable. 'They didn't mention suicide; they just mentioned the reaction you'd had to some sleeping tablets and that you couldn't remember what happened. They told me you were found wandering along a road in the middle of the woods and asked if I could shed any light on anything.'

'Right. And what did you think when you heard that?' I rub at a tic under my right eye that's jumping and twitching in my line of vision.

'That we should of course send some flowers to cheer you up.' She gives me a beatific smile.

'You didn't think it all sounded odd?' I say, aware my voice is sounding harsh.

'Not after talking with Liam, no. He explained everything. He's such a compassionate and caring man. You're very lucky to have him.' She smiles. 'I was going to wait until you felt stronger to talk with you about your position at the college, but now you're here, it may be a good time.'

'My position? What do you mean?' I clasp and unclasp my hands repeatedly, unable to keep them still in my lap.

'If you're having difficulties like this, I'm afraid it's not very healthy for the students. We have a good reputation here, and we're up for the Standon Award for County Sixth Form College of the Year. We can't afford to jeopardise our chances by having tutors who are unstable or suffering from mental illness. Imagine the uproar if the parents found out! I discussed this at length with Liam the other day, and we both think it's in your best interests if you resign. It's the most sensible course of action all round.'

I clench my fists so tightly my fingernails dig into my palms. 'Why should I resign?'

She reaches a hand across the desk and clasps my wrist. 'So you can spend more time at home getting well, of course. This is for your benefit, you know. You've had a terribly difficult time with the miscarriage and depression. Everyone is thinking of your welfare— the doctors, the police, Liam, me. Once you get better, then we can talk again.'

Best course of action for them, maybe. Not for me. I want to howl at her, scream and shout at the top of my lungs, but that would just prove how unstable and unfit I was. So I bite back the anger igniting inside. 'Aren't I entitled to sick leave?'

'Yes, of course, but I don't feel that extended sick leave is an option here.' She pats my hand as if to reassure me it's all for the best then sits back in her chair. 'You must see it from my point of view. Our tutors have to set a good example to the students.'

'I didn't try to kill myself, Theresa,' I say with as much conviction as I can. I feel like I've become invisible. I'm talking, but no one is actually listening to what I'm saying. 'Liam is wrong, the police are wrong, and so are you.' I stand up, unable to contain my anger any longer. If I stay here, I'll probably say or do something I'll regret. 'What if I don't resign?' I lift my chin in the air and meet her unsympathetic gaze.

'Then I'm afraid we'll have to take other action.'

'Meaning?'

'Meaning we'll terminate your employment on medical grounds.'

'You can't do that. You can't just sack someone for being off sick. It's discrimination. I'll take it to an Industrial Tribunal if I have to. This job is all I have left.'

'Do you really want to go down that route in such a fragile state? Trust me; this is the best solution for everyone.' She picks up a stack of papers from her tray and shuffles them in front of her, signalling the meeting is over.

I storm out of her office without looking back, cheeks burning with anger. Fucking Liam, going behind my back and making out I've tried to kill myself! I want to kill him. Stab him through the heart, or set the house on fire with him in it, or . . . I don't know, something. Something painful. The amount of times he's tried to get me to give up working so he can keep me to himself, and now he's finally got what he wanted.

'I've worked hard to give you everything you need. Is it too much to ask you to look after me for a change?' is a favourite saying of his. Yes, this is the perfect solution for Liam.

I'm practically running down the front steps of the college when I hear someone calling my name behind me.

'Chloe?'

I swing around, and there's Jordan, hurrying in my direction. He's taller than Liam is, and leaner. But where Liam is blond and blue-eyed, Jordan is dark. His thick hair is cut short and shimmers in the sunlight. His eyes are an unusual hazel colour, like autumn leaves, and seem to change depending on his mood— sometimes green, sometimes golden or brown. He prefers casual clothes. Jeans, T-shirts, sweatshirts. I don't think I've ever seen him in a suit.

He's looking at me with such intense concern, I feel a shift inside, like my heart is clenching.

'It *is* you. I wasn't sure at first. Shit, I've been so worried. How are you?' Lines crinkle his forehead as he studies every part of my face.

'I've been better.' I try to laugh nonchalantly, but it comes out sounding more like a strangled cat.

'What's going on?' He reaches out and gently touches one of the scratches on my forehead with his thumb. 'How did you get those? Was it Liam? Did he hit you or something?' His eyes narrow. 'Are you OK?'

I don't really know where to start. The rational part of me thinks if I pour everything out to him, he'll believe I'm as nuts as everyone else does. But being here, with him so close, all the fear crumbles away. I feel my shoulders relaxing. Find it easier to breathe without the constant pain knotted in my stomach.

He puts a hand on my shoulder. 'Are you in trouble? Tell me what's going on.'

My eyes water, and I blink back the tears. 'Can we go somewhere and talk, or do you have a lesson?'

Jordan teaches A Level Maths, and it's not surprising the sixteen-to-eighteen-year-old female students swoon over him.

He doesn't hesitate. 'Yes. Yes, of course. I've got a class in an hour and a half. I was just going to mark some papers, but that can wait. Do you want to go to the canteen or somewhere off campus?'

'Definitely off campus.'

'Let's go to Kelly's Bistro.' He turns on his heels, and I swing into step beside him.

It takes us ten minutes to walk to the café, and from the corner of my eye, I catch him shooting worried glances at me, but he doesn't ask what's wrong.

'You've cut your hair. It makes you look really different,' he says finally, breaking the silence.

'Good.'

'Sorry?'

'I'll tell you about it when we get to the café.'

'OK. It really suits you.'

'Thank you.'

'Not that it didn't suit you before, of course.' He smiles, and despite everything, I find myself smiling back at him.

He buys me a cappuccino, and we sit in the corner of a little courtyard garden at the rear, away from the two other occupied tables. He waits patiently for me to talk, sipping his coffee slowly, watching me awkwardly over the cup.

'Oh, God, this is just so awful I don't know where to start.' I bury my head in my hands and want to leave it there forever.

His chair scrapes against the tiled floor as he drags it closer, so close his arm brushes against mine. 'Whatever's happened, you can tell me.'

I drop my hands, and they fall uselessly into my lap. 'What do you know about me being off sick?'

'Well, I know you were signed off with depression after your miscarriage.'

I think about my baby then, and a fresh wave of grief almost crushes me. Tears sting my eyes, and I blink rapidly to clear them. I'm sick of crying. Sick of my life. Sick of being Chloe Benson.

'And you had some kind of bad reaction to the antidepressants you were prescribed and ended up in hospital having treatment. When you came out, you were recuperating.'

I nod wearily.

'I called you,' he carries on.

'You did? When?' I lean forward, ears pricked.

'About ten days ago now, but you made it pretty clear you didn't want me to get involved.' He reaches across the table, about to touch my hand; then he seems to think better of it and lets it fall back onto his thigh. 'I've been so worried about you.'

I open my mouth to start. Close it again. Then I just decide to go for it. 'Involved in what? You see the thing is, I've lost part of my memory, and I don't remember what's happened.' I blurt it out before I can change my mind.

'What?'

I tell him the whole story, from what I remember about waking up in that underground place, to escaping and being discovered on the road in the middle of nowhere. Then I tell him what I've found out so far, about Liam having an affair, my missing clothes, the letter I wrote ending our relationship, my mobile phone smashed and left in the bin, Liam's lies.

He sits back in his chair, eyes wide. 'Shit. That's . . . bloody awful,' he says so loudly that an elderly man in the corner reading the paper looks over. He does take hold of my hand then. His touch is soft and subtle, and his skin is so warm against mine, I feel a kind of strength seeping into me. 'What are the police saying? Do they have any idea who could've abducted you?' he asks more quietly, and the man watching goes back to his paper.

I shrug. 'That's just it. They don't believe me either.'

'Surely they don't think you've made up something like that? How could they?' he asks incredulously.

'They all think I've had some sort of new psychotic reaction to a few sleeping pills that were in my system when they found me, and that I hallucinated the whole thing. It's what the doctors think, too. Most of them think I was still so depressed I apparently tried to kill myself.'

He shakes his head, too shocked to speak, so I fill the silence.

'But I didn't. I wouldn't try to kill myself; it would just feel like giving up.' I think about Mum then. Is that what she did? Just gave up on me, on herself? Or was her overdose really an accident? 'And I wouldn't take any sleeping tablets. I tried them once, and they made me feel so awful, I've never taken once since. Plus, the hospital told me not to take any more medication after what happened with the Zolafaxine. And I know it all sounds so weird and very similar to everything before, when I ended up sectioned, but I *know* what happened. I remember vividly being in that place underground. It couldn't have been a paranoid hallucination. It was real.' I shudder. 'Very real and very scary.'

Looking aghast, he squeezes my hand. 'I can't believe the police aren't doing anything. The person who took you is still out there somewhere, and you could be in real danger.'

'I'm scared.' My voice is so strange it doesn't sound like it belongs to me.

'I'm not surprised. What can I do to help?'

'I'm trying to piece together exactly what happened and how I ended up somewhere in the middle of those woods. I asked Theresa if she knew anything that might help, but she didn't. In fact, she's told me I have to resign.'

'What? Why would she do that?'

'Because she believes what Liam has told her. That I tried to kill myself because I was depressed, and now I'm apparently mentally unstable and not fit to be around the students.'

'She can't make you resign. It's discrimination.'

'No, maybe not, but she can make things very difficult for me. Anyway, I suppose that's the least of my problems at the moment. The most important thing is trying to stay alive.' I grip his hand tightly, and it feels like a lifeline. 'Maybe you might know something, since you phoned me shortly before I went missing. What did I say? What kind of state was I in?'

He removes his hand and runs both of them over his now pale face. 'God, I can't believe this.' He rests his jaw in his hand as he studies me for a moment. It looks like he's hoping I'm going to say this is all just one big joke. *Ha-ha, Jordan, not really—only kidding!* When I don't say a word, he shakes his head again slowly. 'You told me Liam was having an affair with his boss. You said you'd found out about him lying to you when he stayed in that hotel instead of going to Scotland, and about the locket he'd bought for Julianne. You said that was the last straw. You were going to leave him.' He bites his bottom lip, as if weighing up exactly what to say. 'Look, I know you've never told me exactly what he's done to you in the past, but I could guess there was something going on. I never saw any bruises on you, but . . .' He trails off and glances at the ground, his dark lashes casting shadows over his tanned skin. 'When you first started working here, you seemed so bubbly and lively. Then when you met Liam, something changed gradually, like a switch had been flipped off inside you. You made excuses not to go to work parties. If you were going to be late home because of a staff meeting, you panicked about the time. Your phone was going off all the time in the staff room when we had our breaks. Just little things like that made me wonder.'

'I knew Liam didn't deserve you, but that's something you had to work out on your own.' He gives me an uncertain smile. 'And it seemed like you finally had. When I spoke to you, you were going to call your friend Sara about moving into her place while she was away. You said you were going to leave while Liam was in Scotland, to avoid any problems.'

I stare at the sky and think about all the little things that add up, and before you know it, you're stuck. Trapped. Your confidence and self-esteem have withered away, but the very person you want to get away from is the one you rely on most. And you don't know when it happened. Can't pinpoint an exact day, week, or month, because it's a gradual, subtle process. It creeps up on you slowly. So slowly that you don't realise you're bending, breaking, and becoming a different person. A woman who's not happy, not living her own life, but the life her husband wants instead.

Sara once asked me why I stayed with him, and I didn't know how to answer. Maybe it was because I loved him, even if things weren't perfect. I tried to be what he wanted me to be, and the urge to please was like a cancerous disease ingrained deep in my soul. He wasn't all bad either. We'd had plenty of times in between when he was loving and caring. When we'd take long walks around the lakes, hand in hand, have romantic dinners out, or snuggle up in front of the TV with a film, share a bottle of wine in a candle-lit bath. Those moments made me think he'd change back to how he'd been in the beginning. And I thought it was my fault. I rubbed him up the wrong way. He was too stressed with work. I wasn't trying hard enough.

Why does anyone stay in a relationship that deep down they know isn't right? You don't know why until it happens to you. It's easy to fool yourself. To stuff things under the surface where they can't hurt you. To persuade yourself it's all just normal. Make excuses.

There's a fine line between craziness and love.

If he'd been violent, maybe I would've left the first time he hit me. But he wasn't. Unlike bruises and broken bones, it was something invisible. And Liam always filled the calm after the storm with flowers and sweet attentiveness. If he was happy, he rewarded me with love and affection, until the bad days eventually outweighed the good.

No, I couldn't really put a name to what he was. How do you sum it up in just one word? As I say, it's just the little things. And a lot of pressure and time to get to the point where you finally blow.

In the beginning, I used to complain to Sara about what Liam would do, but eventually I stopped telling her stuff, which made me even lonelier. There was no point in moaning. She couldn't change things; only I could, and I was obviously too weak to try. So I hid it from her. From everyone—or so I thought. Because I'd always seen myself as failure and didn't want everyone to know I was failing at my marriage, too.

In the end, though, it looked like I'd finally stood up for myself. But then what had happened? Had I made it to Sara's? Had I actually left Liam? Had he found me? Or was it someone else?

'It happened with my mum and dad,' Jordan carries on. 'My dad was an alcoholic. He was a mean bastard. He never hit her, but who needs fists when words can slice through you like a scalpel? Physical wounds can heal, can't they? But it takes a long time to recover from having your self-confidence and self-esteem crushed to nothing. I watched him smother the life right out of her, day by day.'

'I'm sorry.' I touch his arm gently. 'What happened to her?'

'She left him in the end. She took my sister and me and ran away one day when he was passed out drunk. She worked three jobs to support us. Eventually, she got strong again. And there was never another argument in the house. We didn't have to walk round on eggshells all the time. There was no more trying to anticipate his moods that controlled the whole family. I think my childhood really began the day we moved out.'

'She sounds brave.'

'She is. It's just such a shame it took her so long to realise it.' He looks straight into my eyes, and I get the feeling he's not just talking about his mum.

I glance away for a moment. 'So what else did I say? When you phoned me?'

'I wanted to help you to move some of your stuff to Sara's, since you don't drive and I have lots of room in the campervan, but you said you wanted to do it on your own. You said you didn't need me pressuring you and not to call because you had to get your head sorted out.' He looks at me, a wistful expression on his face.

'Did you pressure me?'

'No, of course not.' His gaze flits away for a second before settling back on my face. 'But I told you how I felt about you. I couldn't keep it a secret any more. When you first started working here, I thought something might happen between us.' He shakes his head. 'No, that's not quite right. I *wanted* something to happen. But I was seeing Holly, even though I knew I could never see myself settling down with her, and then by the time I ended things with her and plucked up the courage to ask you out, you'd met Liam.'

A warm feeling bursts into life deep inside my core, spreading to my extremities. My brain doesn't remember him saying it, but my body seems to. 'What else did I say?'

'That was pretty much it. You've been through so much lately, and I respected what you said, so I didn't call you again. I wanted to—God, did I want to, but I had to give you space to get over things. I was just hoping that when you were ready, we might . . .' He trails off and gives me a self-conscious shrug. 'You know, just that I'm still here for you as a friend, like always.'

I knew he liked me. Knew from the moment I started working with him. I'd catch him stealing looks at me in the staff room or at meetings when he thought I wasn't looking. It made me uncomfortable, but not in a bad way. In a way that made me won-der what it would be like to run my fingers through his thick dark hair. What his lips would feel like on my skin. But he was seeing a long-term girlfriend at the time, and then Liam had come along, and, well, whatever attraction there was between us was just bad timing.

'I . . . I don't know what to say. I . . .'

'Then don't say anything. But the offer still stands. I'm here for you as a friend if you need anything.' He holds my gaze, and this time I can't tear it away. 'Maybe I can help you try and piece things together, and from what you've said, you could definitely do with someone on your side.'

'Thank you. I might just have to take you up on that.'

'I want you to, because this sounds like a very dangerous situa-tion you're in. I mean, do you think Liam really tampered with your drugs in the first place? It all seems like too much of a coincidence, doesn't it? And trying to paint you as suicidal would be very conve-nient to get you out of the way.'

'Very convenient, indeed. But I wasn't suicidal. I know I wasn't.'

'When I spoke to you, you definitely weren't thinking of harm-ing yourself. You seemed really positive and determined to get away from him and start over again. You sounded stronger than I'd ever heard you.'

I breathe a sigh of relief, because hearing him say all this is the first actual proof I've had that Liam is trying to . . . trying to what? Manipulate me into believing I'm falling apart? Convince me I'm going mad? Get me sectioned again so he can carry on his affair? Prove I'm suicidal so he could kill me and make it look like I'd done it to myself? All of the above? I shudder at the sudden chill claw-ing at my insides. 'It's obvious Liam has been up to something, but would he really kidnap me and leave me for dead? It just sounds too . . . too . . .' I can't think of a word for what it is.

'Evil?' Jordan's eyes widen.

'Yes, I suppose. And I know he's not perfect, but surely that would mean he was mad, and I don't think he is.'

'Plenty of people who've killed lead normal lives. They have families, hold down good jobs, and function just like you or me. It doesn't mean they're mad.'

'I need to know what happened after I took some of my clothes and left him. How did my phone end up in the bin? Surely, I wouldn't have left it voluntarily. So did I actually get away, or did he stop me and throw me underground, waiting for me to die?' I lean forward, arms across my stomach. 'I just seem to be going round in circles. And I really need you to believe me, because no one else does.' I struggle to stop the tears welling up.

'Of course I believe you! Why wouldn't I?' He takes hold of my hand again and squeezes it gently.

And for once, I don't see disbelief from someone. I see sadness and horror. 'Because it sounds absolutely crazy, doesn't it?'

'You're right. It is crazy. And improbable and horrific. But is it any crazier or more improbable than having two psychotic reactions to different drugs in less than a month?' He doesn't say anything for a while, just stares into the distance as if he's lost in thought. Then he turns back to me. 'Have you heard of Occam's Razor?'

'No.'

'It's a line of reasoning that detectives use to solve crimes. Doctors use it, too, to diagnose illnesses. It's also used by computer programmers and scientists—even mathematicians. I'll save you the big explanation behind it, but basically, it's a theory that given two possible answers for the same thing, the simpler one is usually correct. Some people swear by it for working out a problem, but personally, I'm sceptical. For one thing, how do you determine whether something is simple or not? It's all subjective. And for another, I don't believe the idea that simplicity equals truth.'

I blink rapidly. 'I'm lost. I mean, I understand the principle of the simplest explanation usually being the right one, but how does that relate to me?'

'Well, the police and doctors don't believe you, because the simplest answer for them is that since you were found with sleeping tablets in your system, you took them yourself and had a psychotic reaction, because that's what happened before with the antidepressants.'

'Yes.'

'But that doesn't mean it's the right answer. So the other answer, the one that can prove what you're saying is true, is to find out *how* the sleeping tablets really did get in your system in the first place. You said you wouldn't have taken them, because they made you feel bad before. You also wouldn't have taken them, because the doctors advised you not to, which means someone must've given them to you, and if you can prove that, they'll have to believe you.'

'How do I prove I didn't take them myself? That I wasn't trying to commit suicide?'

'I don't know yet.'

'I didn't find them at my house, which I thought was odd, but now I know I left and went to Sara's; maybe I'll find them there.'

'And if they're not there, then it would be very suspicious, wouldn't it? Because if you took them to help you sleep or to commit suicide, like they all think, you'd do it at Sara's house. That's how you might be able to prove it.'

'Dr Drew thinks they may have been in my bag when I wandered off in a supposedly psychotic state, and they were lost when I was hallucinating.'

'There's only one way to check, and that's get into Sara's house and see if you left them there. And I'd say go there as soon as you can, because if Liam is involved, you're not safe at home. If he's not involved, maybe you're still not safe since you don't know where you encountered whoever abducted you. Do you want to stay at my place?'

I meet his gaze. It sounds like the perfect answer. I want to trust him. My body obviously does, and I get a safe feeling whenever I'm with him, but my mind . . . well, I don't know for sure *he's* not involved somehow. Jordan's already admitted he likes me, cares about me. I don't know whether to be flattered or scared to death. I've never seen a hint of anger in him. Never seen him get flustered or lose his temper, even when a bunch of sixteen-year-old boys were playing up. But maybe he was obsessed with me somehow. He could've stalked me, and when he couldn't have me, maybe he decided to kidnap me. It sounds equally as farfetched as everything else does, but it could happen, couldn't it?

'Thank you, but I . . . I think I need to do this on my own.'

'Yes, but that's what you said last time, and look what happened.'

Chapter Twenty-One

As Jordan walks me out of the coffee shop, I suddenly don't want to go. I want to take him up on his offer. Want to feel safe, like no one is breathing down the back of my neck, waiting to harm me. Or kill me. I want to more than anything, but I don't. I'm close to finding out the next piece of the puzzle, and I think my phone and Sara's house might hold the key.

It's getting on to 5:00 p.m. when I arrive home. The first thing I do is retrieve my list from behind the kitchen sink and write down everything else I've discovered. Then I check to see whether the mobile phone has charged, and insert the SIM card from my old phone. Success. It's working.

I unplug it from the charger, which I hide in an old shoebox at the back of my bedroom wardrobe. I'm sitting on the bed, scrolling back through the list of phone calls on it, when Liam's voice shouts to me from downstairs. He's early, and I haven't even heard the front door open.

'Chloe? Where are you?'

I quickly turn off the phone and slide it underneath my side of the mattress. Standing up, I take a deep breath, plaster a smile on my face, and head downstairs. Liam is peering into the fridge when I walk into the kitchen.

'Hi,' I say brightly.

Inside I'm thinking, *You bastard. You bastard. You fucking bastard! What are you trying to do to me?* It feels like I'm living right in the middle of that film *Sleeping with the Enemy.*

'Hi, darling.' He leans over with a bottle of wine in his hand and kisses my forehead. 'How are you feeling?'

'Good, thank you.'

He gives me a questioning look. 'Are you sure?'

'Yes. Positive. How was your day?' *Tried to kill anyone lately?*

'Very productive.' He gives me a smug grin. 'Dr Drew said he was going to check up on you today after I called and expressed my concern. Did he phone you?'

'Yes. He said I was fine. I wish you'd just believe me.'

'Well, that's pretty hard to do, isn't it, after everything that's happened.' He grabs a wine glass from the cupboard and pours himself a hefty measure of Pinot grigio. Leaning his hip against the worktop, he crosses one ankle casually over the other and takes a sip while watching me closely.

'But Dr Drew agrees I'm OK, so please, can we just—'

'What? Can we just what?' His eyes flash with cold challenge.

Don't push it. The last thing you need is for him to get angry. I can be compliant, spineless Chloe if that's what it takes. After all, I have been for long enough. I don't even have to act that much. 'Nothing. I'm sorry.'

'Good girl,' he says, and it makes me want to scream.

I'm not a girl—I'm a woman! A woman with choices. A woman who's not bloody crazy!

'Haven't you started on dinner yet? What have you been doing all day?' There's a hint of accusation in his tone, but he says it with a bright smile.

'I've just been taking it easy.'

'Really? Then why didn't you answer the phone when I called you earlier?'

I want to slap myself then. I really must start checking caller ID if I go out. 'Oh, I went for a walk. I wanted to get some fresh air.'

'A walk?' He says it as if I've just suggested I took a walk in the Alps.

'Mmm, a walk,' I say evenly.

'Where?'

'Just for a walk. Nowhere special.' I wave my hand casually.

'You know I get worried if I can't get hold of you.' He puts his glass of wine on the worktop and pulls me towards him, wrapping his arms round me. It takes all my strength not to push him away. 'You need to have a new mobile phone.'

'Pardon?' My heart starts to race. Does he know something about how my phone ended up broken in the rubbish bin?

'You can't find yours, can you? You must've lost it when you had the episode with the sleeping tablets and wandered off. I'll get you a new one at the weekend,' he murmurs into my hair. 'So I can make sure you're safe when you're not with me.'

'Good idea,' I agree, even though he's not worried about my safety. It's so he can keep tabs on me and find out where I am, what I'm doing, who I'm talking to, when I'll be home.

'I'm full of them.' He pulls back, cups my cheeks in his hands, and stares into my eyes. I don't like what I see there. 'You know how much I love you, don't you?'

Not trusting myself to speak, I just nod and give him the smile I've practised perfectly over the years.

He kisses me hard on the lips before releasing me and picking up his wine glass. 'Now, what are you going to do for dinner?'

'I'll make an omelette.' I grab some mushrooms and peppers from the fridge and start chopping them.

'I'm going to send some e-mails while you're doing that.'

I look over my shoulder at his retreating back and want more than anything to stab him in it.

⌣

After dinner, I fake a headache and tell Liam I'm going to lie down. He's gone back to the computer, and I'm itching to get my hands on my mobile phone and see what clues it can tell me. I scroll through the phone logs first and find a call from Jordan to me on the twenty-ninth of April, just as he said. It lasted a little over five minutes. A few minutes later, I called Sara's number and spoke to her for sixty-five minutes. I picture myself telling her I'd found out about Liam's affair. She would call him a wanker and then offer for me to stay at her place before I even asked her if it was OK.

On the day Liam went to Scotland, there was a call from Sara to me that I didn't answer. Was she seeing if I was still going to her place? Making sure I hadn't changed my mind? Checking that I hadn't been murdered in my sleep by my psychopathic husband?

The last call is the one from yesterday, when I heard my phone ringing in the bin. It's from the college number. Theresa didn't mention phoning me to see if I was OK, and I wonder if it was from Jordan. There are no more calls, so I check my texts, expecting some between Sara and me, but there aren't any. Odd. We usually texted a few times a week, more when she was away on her travels. Did I delete them so Liam wouldn't find them? Or had I not texted her before I disappeared because I'd already spoken to her on the phone? There's just one text from my e-mail provider, sending a code for me to enter when I log back into my account.

I still can't work out how my phone ended up in the rubbish bin. Had I left it in the house accidentally when I moved out? Had Liam found it and smashed it to pieces in anger when he discovered I'd gone? That seemed the most likely scenario. I would be in a blind panic and not thinking straight. Just taking a few clothes and escaping while he was firmly out of the way four hundred odd miles from here. I'd already been on the Internet looking up side effects of the antidepressants, so I would've discovered Liam's company made them. I was probably already suspecting what I suspect now, that he was trying to make me go crazy. How easy it would be for him to get me out of the way. What could be better than having his wife sectioned in the loony bin?

A dead wife. That would be even better. No one could argue with that. He didn't succeed in having me permanently locked up, so he goes to Plan B. Kidnap me and leave me for dead. I had no actual proof that Liam really did go to Scotland. I don't know if DI Summers even checked that out. Probably not, if he believed what Liam had told him.

I hear footsteps coming up the stairs and turn off the phone. My heart races as I slide it under the mattress again and close my eyes, forcing myself to breathe deeply so Liam thinks I'm fast asleep.

The night drags on forever. I toss and turn, unable to switch off, horrible thoughts swimming around in my head so fast I'm scared I might drown in them. I think about getting up in the early hours and making a cup of chamomile tea, but I don't want to get out of bed. Can't risk Liam finding the phone I've hidden. No, I have to guard it, although the idea that I'm guarding a mobile phone is so completely ridiculous that it almost makes me laugh. Instead, I lie there thinking about death and dying, and wait for morning.

Chapter Twenty-Two

When Liam's in the shower, I slide my hands under the mattress, retrieve the phone, and go downstairs, hiding it at the back of the cupboard under the sink. Then I make him tea and toast with marmalade and leave it on the kitchen table, ready and waiting for him like the good Stepford wife I am. I can't eat. My stomach is on an out-of-control rollercoaster ride, leaping and swirling all over the place.

'Not hungry?' Liam chews thoughtfully on a bite of toast.

Hungry? I want to vomit. 'Not at the moment.' I cradle my mug of tea. 'I'll have something later.'

'Maybe that's a good thing. You must admit you've been getting a bit chubby lately. You need to be careful.' He grins playfully, but I know he didn't mean it in jest.

When I was in my early teens and my body started filling out, some of the boys in the children's home taunted me for being fat. It was a slippery slope from being completely self-conscious of what I ate and counting calories manically to binge eating. Stuffing down as much as I could to fill up the hunger that never disappeared, then purging it by sticking my fingers down my throat. I told Liam about it one day at the beginning of our relationship, and in true Liam style, he likes to bring it up sometimes, using my insecurities against me.

'Yes, maybe you're right,' I agree, because it's just easier to go along with him.

'I usually am.' He pats my hand and takes his plate to the dishwasher. 'Well, I'm off. I'll probably be late tonight.'

'OK,' I say, even though I don't care in the least. I'm not going to be here.

When he leaves, I quickly check my e-mails, but there are no recent ones except some spam trying to sell me a penis extension. I pack a small suitcase with some essential clothes, underwear, and toiletries. In a short while, I'm going to be free of Liam, but I wonder what else I am walking into. I don't know which is the lesser of two evils. What if Liam is only guilty of having an affair? What if he genuinely is concerned about me being mentally unstable again and is trying to protect me? What if he didn't tamper with the drugs, and it's all my ridiculous imagination? What if he didn't try to kill me?

What if, what if?

I don't know for certain. Maybe I'll never know, and the thought fills me with such dread I have to push it away before I unravel into a gibbering wreck cowering in the corner of the room. All I know is, I can't stay here any longer. For my sanity and my safety, I have to leave. The only problem is, my new bank cards still haven't arrived, so I have no money. Maybe I'll call Jordan and see if can lend me some. Just until I get sorted out.

I see Jordan's face in my head, and it makes me smile. At some point in the future, in my heart I see something happening between us. Maybe it's because I need some hope. Some light at the end of the tunnel. The idea that I *will* have a future after all this. That I will still be alive. Or maybe it's more than that.

I can't afford to think about any of that now, though. At this moment, I can only think of survival. All I have to do is stay alive long enough to fight back.

I sit at the office desk, pull out a sheet of printer paper from the drawer, and grab a pen to write my second letter to Liam, telling him I'm leaving.

Tapping the end of the pen against my teeth, I stare at the page, which is as blank as my mind. What do you write in these kinds of circumstances?

God knows.

I put the pen to the paper. Stop. Lift it up again. Stop. I don't have a clue how to sum up my life and how I came to be here like this right now. I think about the letter I wrote the last time: *I can't go on like this anymore. I need to end it all. I'm sorry.* Even though it was so ambiguous that it could be used against me, I can't think of anything truer. But this time I'll make sure no one can misinterpret it.

> *Liam,*
> *Our relationship is over.*
> *I don't want to see you or talk to you. You won't be able to change my mind.*
> *Please stay away from me.*
> *Chloe*

There. I can't make it much clearer than that. Short and to the point. Some things just can't be put into words.

I leave it propped up in front of the kettle and put on my sunglasses. I exit the house and head towards Sara's as I wheel the suitcase behind me. It would be easier to catch a cab, but it could be what I did last time. You hear about dodgy cab drivers preying on women sometimes, and I can't take the risk, so I ignore my aching arm and carry on.

The spare key I kept for Sara in case of emergencies wasn't in the drawer at home and must've been lost along with my other house keys, but I know there's one hidden in her garden. Hopefully, it's still there. I don't fancy the thought of having to break a window to get in.

There's a rockery at the front of her house. I say 'rockery,' but there are no plants in it. Since Sara is away a lot, she's made the garden as maintenance-free as possible. This rockery just consists of different sizes, colours, and texture of stone. The big granite lump is the one I want. I bend down, lift it up, and there's the key.

As I open her front door, the first thing I notice is the smell. Stale, musty, and unlived in. The next thing I notice are my black wedged boots and ballet flats by the radiator in the hall. I close the door and lean against it, shutting my eyes for a moment to let things sink in.

So I did make it here. I really did leave Liam. I've followed my footsteps to the next place I went, but I don't know what else I'm going to discover. I already feel a heightened sense of freedom, as if I've shed a dirty skin that's been suffocating me. Finally, I've taken back control of my life. Not sure how long I'll have a life, though, if my abductor finds me again, but at least for this precious moment it's all mine.

I step over a pile of post that's been pushed through the letterbox, put my suitcase next to my boots, and head into her small lounge. It's stuffed with books and colourful throws in bright oranges, reds, and yellows. Turkish rugs, African wooden carvings, shells, a didgeridoo painted with bright tribal markings, Chinese scriptures. Things she's brought back over the years from her travels. It radiates warmth and happiness like a proper home should. Somewhere the owner has left the mark of her existence, instead of the soulless shell of bricks and mortar I shared with Liam.

The red light on her answerphone blinks wildly at me, so I listen to the messages. 'Hi, it's me.' Sara's voice. 'Hope you're settling in

OK. I lost my bloody phone in a market this morning and had to get another one, so I've got a new number now.' She rattles off the number. So that's why I haven't been able to get hold of her. 'Call me on this one and let me know you're all right. Forgot to tell you the instructions on how to get the boiler working. It can be a bit temperamental sometimes, especially if it's been turned off. Help yourself to whatever. Just treat the place like home. I'm so glad you woke up and got away from that controlling wanker.'

She left the message on the sixth of May, the day Liam went to Scotland. The day I would've left him.

The machine bleeps and starts the next message. Sara again. 'Hey, where are you? Out having fun for a change, I bloody hope! I'm going to be on a yoga retreat for the next ten days, so you won't be able to get hold of me. No modern technology allowed here!' She laughs. 'Give me a ring when I get out. Ha-ha—that sounds like I'm going to prison, doesn't it? Anyway, hope you managed to work the boiler. Speak soon. Hugs.'

The date on the second message is the eighth of May. Today is the fifteenth, so she won't be back from her retreat yet. I'll have to wait a bit longer to see if she can fill in any more missing pieces of my life.

I go upstairs and open her bedroom door. No sheets are on the bed, and the room has an abandoned feel. In the spare bedroom, I find evidence of my existence. The duvet is turned back and the sheets in disarray, hanging half off the bed, as if I slept fitfully and got up in a hurry. My polka-dot bra, leather jacket, and brown V-neck jumper hang over a director's chair by the window. I don't see any sleeping tablets on the small bedside table—just a red biro and a glass of water with dust floating on the surface. A plastic carrier bag sits by the side of the bed, with some of my knickers inside it. Maybe I used it to transport my clothes here before.

There's one toothbrush in the bathroom, with a new tube of toothpaste I must've bought. Above the sink is a wooden cabinet with a mirror. I open the door and look through. Inside, I find a box of paracetamol, a bottle of cough medicine, a plastic container of cotton buds, an unopened tube of toothpaste, some Vick's VapoRub, and a mostly empty box of Tampax.

I head downstairs and check all the windows and the back door that leads from the kitchen out into the postage stamp–sized garden. There's no sign of forced entry or a struggle anywhere in the house.

I peer into the fridge to see if Sara's left any bottled or tinned food that's still edible. I don't feel much like going food shopping at the moment, but I'm going to have to eat. I find a carton of long-life semi-skimmed milk, a block of cheddar, six eggs, a packet of rocket, a few tomatoes, an onion, a bottle of sparkling white wine, butter, and a sliced loaf of wholemeal bread. The packet of rocket is out of date, the green leaves soggy and yellowing behind the plastic, but everything else is still edible, so I must've been shopping after I arrived the last time.

I'm just reaching for a glass from the cupboard above the cooker to get a drink of water when I spy my handbag on top of the microwave in the corner of the room. I put the glass down and rummage around inside it. My purse is there, complete with the bank cards Liam has now cancelled. The good news is I have two hundred and thirty-three pounds and fifty-four pence to my name now. That will keep me going for a bit.

The only other things in my bag are a packet of tissues, a biro, a broken toothpick, a can of deodorant, and a lot of fluff. The sleeping tablets aren't inside, which doesn't make sense. If they're nowhere to be found, I couldn't possibly have taken them. Yes, I could've lost them if I was having some kind of weird reaction, but if I didn't have my bag with me, where would I put them? When I escaped from that place, all I had on was a thin red dress with no pockets. It's unlikely I would've just had them in my hand. My keys aren't there, either, and it gets me thinking. If my bag is here but the keys aren't, I must've gone out somewhere. Somewhere close by I could walk to. Somewhere I didn't think I'd need any money. But where?

Sod the water. I need alcohol now. I pour myself some icy cold wine and swallow, feeling an instant hit of mellowness hit my empty stomach. It's probably not a good idea under the circumstances. I need to keep my wits about me. But I'm having a hard time keeping the fear at bay, and mellowness is exactly what I need.

After rummaging around in the cupboards, I find a packet of dried pasta, so I put together a veggie dish with the tomatoes and onion and some dried herbs, topping it with a thick grating of cheese. In between mouthfuls of food and wine, I think about what I should do next. Liam will guess I'm here, even though I've kept my ongoing friendship with Sara hidden from him as best I can. Where else could I possibly be? Maybe I should check into a hotel. But I don't have many funds and won't be able to stay there indefinitely.

Or maybe I should ask Jordan if I can stay with him, after all. I trust him. At least I think I do. But . . . well, you never *really* know someone. Especially if you can't remember things. I thought I knew Liam, and look how that's turned out.

If I stay here, though, anything could happen.

After finishing my food and drink, I wash my plate and glass, and leave it on the draining board. Then I phone the bank on my new mobile and go through an annoying automated system, pressing one key, then another, until I finally get to talk to a real person and not a robot.

'Hi, my husband cancelled my debit card the other day because I lost my purse, and I just wanted to update you with a new address to send it to instead.'

The woman on the other end asks for my name and my previous address, then for my telephone banking PIN. I hear her tapping away and fiddle with my earring as I wait.

'Oh, it looks like you've already updated us with that address, Mrs Benson.'

'Really?' I gasp. 'When?'

'On the sixth of May.'

The same day I left Liam and came here.

'We don't have any record of your husband cancelling your bank cards, and even if he did call, we couldn't have cancelled them because they're in your name. Although it's a joint account, we always need to talk to the card holder for security reasons.'

Well, well, well, Liam's lies were just stacking up on top of each other. I couldn't trust anything that came out of his mouth. 'You're absolutely sure he didn't call you?'

'Yes, definitely.'

I'm speechless. If he didn't cancel them like he'd claimed, why not? I'd told him my bag and purse were missing, and surely he wouldn't have wanted anyone to find them and use them. I can come up with only two possible scenarios: One, he knew where my purse was all along. Here, safe and sound in Sara's house. Which would mean he'd already been here and found me once before. Or two, he genuinely thought I'd made up the whole thing about being abducted and didn't believe they were really missing at all.

I think back to one Saturday about six months ago. Liam was taking me food shopping, and I couldn't find my handbag. He got increasingly annoyed with me as I searched the house for it, opening drawers, checking in the cupboards, and even under the bed. I looked everywhere and still couldn't find it.

'For fuck's sake, I'm not waiting any longer. You can bloody well meet me at the supermarket. I'm not messing around on my day off because you've got a brain like a sieve.' He stormed out of the house and drove off.

By the time I walked the twenty minutes to the supermarket, I was flustered, trying hard to keep the hurt in check. I saw him in the café at the front, having a Danish pastry and a latte and calmly reading the newspaper.

The next day, when I was vacuuming, I found my bag behind the small gap between the wall and the sofa. God knows how it had got there, and I could've sworn I'd already checked.

The woman's voice jolts me back to earth. 'Is there anything else I can do for you today, Mrs Benson?'

Yes. Find out who's trying to kill me.

'Er . . . no, thank you.' I hang up and stare at my mobile. If I phoned them on the day I left Liam and came here, what did I do next?

Something flashes in my head. A blurred picture. A distant memory. Something about my mobile phone. I try to hang onto it, but it's gone, retreating just out of reach. I know I didn't call them from my old phone, because it was smashed in the bin at home, and when I checked the call log on the SIM card, the last call was from Sara to me. So that means I must've used Sara's landline to call the bank. Perhaps I made some other calls, too. I go into her lounge, pick up her receiver, and press the "Call" button. It rings in my ear before I get my bank's automated system again. Damn. Now I have no way of knowing whether I called someone else, since it only stores the last number dialled.

I'm replacing the phone back into the base unit when the memory hits me fully . . .

I was rushing along the upstairs hallway in my house, clothes clutched in my hands, mobile phone tucked under my arm, preparing to leave. Liam had already left to go to Scotland. At the top of the stairs, my phone rang. The sudden loud sound in my panicked state made me jump and drop it with fright. The phone bounced down each step until it reached the bottom with a clattering smash. When I picked it up and examined it, the screen was cracked and completely unreadable. But I thought maybe it was a good thing. I didn't want Liam to be able to call me anyway. I threw it in the kitchen bin and quickly scribbled the letter to him, which I left on the kitchen worktop. Then I shoved my few clothes in a heavy-duty plastic bag and rushed out of the front door.

My breath comes in hard pants. It's the first memory that's come back to me, and it's vivid and sharp until I get to the door, where it fades away into blankness. I drop onto the sofa, forcing my brain to think. It's useless, though. My mind is a black hole once more.

But this could mean there's hope I'll eventually remember the rest.

I wrap my arms around myself, shaking, as I piece all the little bits I know together. I physically walked out of my house and came here. I called the bank to give them Sara's address. I obviously went to the supermarket. To Waitrose, by the labels on the food. Then I came back and did . . . what?

I go to the kitchen, get the notes I've written out of my bag, along with a biro, and update them.

21 March
Liam stayed in the Royal Lodge Hotel, but said he was in Scotland.

23 March
Liam's party. Was going to tell him about the baby.

25 March
Had miscarriage in early hours of morning. Became depressed.

10 April
Went to GP. Was prescribed antidepressants and sleeping tablets.

13 April
I'm sectioned. Liam told doctors he found me clawing at garden path. In psychiatric ward having treatment. (Dr Drew and Dr Traynor told me I was paranoid and hallucinating. I thought a man was chasing me, and I was trying to get away.)

20 April
Released from hospital. Still mildly depressed but otherwise OK.

22 April
Liam bought locket that Julianne is wearing in the photo taken at the launch party for Exalin drug.

Around 26 April
I went to the Royal Lodge Hotel to check up on whether Liam stayed there with someone.

29 April
Jordan phoned me to see how I was. I told him about Liam's affair with Julianne and said I was going to ask Sara if I could stay at her house.
I phoned Sara and we spoke for over an hour.

6 May
Liam left for Scotland? (Did he really go there?)
Dropped and smashed mobile phone. Left it in the kitchen bin.
I packed clothes and left note for Liam.
Went to Sara's house.
I phoned the bank from Sara's and told them of my new address.

Bought food from Waitrose.
Spent the night at Sara's? (Her spare room was slept in, and my missing clothes were there).
Sara called me at her flat and left an answerphone message. Did I call her back?

8 May
Sara left another message on her answerphone, saying she was on a yoga retreat and had a new phone number. (Most likely, I was already missing by then if Dr Traynor thought I hadn't drunk for one or two days.)

9 May
Rescued by a woman on the Great North Road. Ran through woods from an underground structure where I was being held. Lost memory of everything since the party.
Blood test showed I'd taken Silepine sleeping tablets. Dr Drew and Dr Traynor thought I'd had another reaction to them that made me hallucinate things.

I chew on the end of the pen, staring at the notes. Sometime between the sixth and eighth of May is when I went missing.

Something's niggling at me, but I can't work out what. The more I think, the more my brain feels blurry, and my memories are more unreachable. I make myself a coffee, pour in a splash of milk from a carton that I must've bought before, and take it back into the lounge. Curling up on the sofa, I stare at the floorboards.

Come on, Chloe—think logically!

So far, everything is pointing to Liam being involved in my abduction, but I wonder if there was any way he couldn't have done it.

If Liam really did think the letter I left him was a suicide letter, that would mean he didn't know I'd left him. If things had happened as *he* said they did, he went to Scotland on the sixth of May and didn't phone me because we'd had a fight. Then, on the ninth of May, he gets a call from the hospital saying I'd been admitted and had lost my memory. He then flew back to see me.

Is it possible he was in Scotland all that time and really didn't know I'd gone at all? That he genuinely believed I was having some kind of breakdown or allergic reaction again?

But that doesn't make sense for a few reasons. His version that we'd had an argument about the plate and I'd thrown it at him, for starters. I didn't believe that for a second, and there was no evidence of a smashed plate in the bin. It would be a perfect reason to give to the police as an excuse why he hadn't contacted me while he'd been away, but in all the time we've been together, there hasn't been a single day when he hasn't called me. Not one. That points to him knowing my phone was already smashed and in the bin, or he knew I couldn't answer the phone because he'd already abducted me. In which case, he must've really been here when he was supposed to be in Scotland.

He was also having an affair and had lied to me about taking clothes to the charity shop and cancelling my bank cards. He was head of manufacturing where the Zolafaxine was made, so he had plenty of opportunity to tamper with those drugs.

There's only one way to find out for certain if Liam is involved. Rummaging through my suitcase that I packed this morning, I find Summers's card among my meagre clothes, and punch in his number.

'DI Summers,' he answers after a long time.

'Hi, it's Chloe Benson.'

'Chloe. How are you?' He sounds polite but bored.

I hesitate for a second, wondering how to answer that. In the end, I don't bother. 'I've been trying to find out what happened, and I really need to check some things urgently.'

'Did you recover your memory?'

'No. Not exactly. Are you free?' I ask breathlessly, worried he'll make up some excuse—and I need to know. Need to know right now.

A pause. Then, 'Do you want to come to the station? I can be free in an hour.'

'Yes. Thank you. I'll be there.'

Chapter Twenty-Three

After I finish talking, I hand Summers the page of my scribbled notes. He reads it with an impatient roll of his eyes that he thinks I don't see. I fidget in my chair opposite him in his office, trying to distract myself by picking at the crusty scabs left on my fingertips. Eventually, he looks up at me, and I can't read the expression on his face. Sympathy, perhaps, or disbelief.

On the way to the police station, I mentally rehearse what to say over and over again so it will sound the least insane. Judging by Summers's expression, though, it doesn't work.

He leans forward and rests his forearms on the table, clasping his hands together. 'So, let me get this straight. You left Liam on the day he went to Scotland because he was having an affair, and you moved into Sara's house?'

'Yes. So you see, it proves the letter he told you was a suicide letter couldn't have been, could it? It was a letter I wrote telling Liam I was leaving him, that's all. He also told you he didn't phone me from Scotland because we had a row about a plate, but we couldn't have because there was no evidence of a smashed plate in the bin.' The words come out in a rush, and I know I'm babbling, but I don't care. I'm desperate.

'You went through the rubbish bin?'

'Yes.'

'How do you know the refuse collectors hadn't removed it already? It would've been nine days ago by now.'

'Because they're on strike, aren't they? We had four bags of rubbish, and I went through all of it. No plate. And since he didn't phone me from Scotland, there are only two possible reasons why. One, he knew that my mobile phone was already smashed and in the bin, or two, he was the one who abducted me and knew I couldn't answer. Both of those reasons mean he had to have come back from Scotland.'

Summers looks at me with a puzzled expression. 'Don't you think it's possible that he just didn't call you because he was busy at work?'

I shake my head so hard I hear a vertebra click. 'No. He *always* phones me when we're not together. And if I miss a call, I have to call him straight back.'

'Even if you've had an argument?'

'Especially then! He also lied to me about taking my clothes to the charity shop, didn't he?'

Summers shifts uncomfortably in his chair, having a hard time trying to be patient. 'How do you know you didn't take some clothes to the charity shop?'

'Because I took them to Sara's instead.'

'You're sure you couldn't have taken a few other things to the charity shop as well? Have you ever donated old clothes before?'

'Well, yes, a few times, but—'

'So, it's possible you could've done so this time, too?'

I think about the few items that weren't in my wardrobes or drawers that I found at Sara's. Was anything else missing? I didn't think so, but it was possible there were some clothes I didn't remember. 'I'm pretty sure everything that was missing from my house was at Sara's.'

'Pretty sure?'

'Yes. Then there's the fact that the company he works for makes the Zolafaxine. How do I know he didn't tamper with it to make me have some kind of reaction?'

Summers's eyes widen. 'You think your husband was trying to poison you?'

I swallow hard, knowing what it's going to sound like. Knowing Summers will just think it's my warped imagination again. 'Not poison, no.'

He looks relieved.

'I think he was trying to kill me.'

Summers studies my face for a moment, then sits back in his chair slowly. His mouth falls open a little. 'You think he was trying to kill you?' He enunciates every syllable slowly.

'Well, it makes sense, doesn't it?'

'Does it?'

'Yes!' I fight the urge to bang my head repeatedly against the desk.

'Why?'

I count to six before I speak. I know they always say you should count to ten, but I couldn't possibly make it that far. 'Because of everything I've just said.'

'Chloe, there are perfectly plausible reasons for all of the things you've mentioned. For—'

'Occam's Razor,' I mutter.

'Pardon?' He looks at me as if I've just spoken Japanese.

'Occam's Razor. It's a theory used by police and doctors. It means the simplest explanation is usually the right one. But it *isn't* always the right one, is it? I know how this looks when you take things individually, but if you add everything up together, it all points to Liam. If the letter wasn't a suicide letter, I wasn't trying to kill myself, so why would I take the sleeping tablets against medical advice? If Liam wasn't really in Scotland, he'd know my phone was in the bin, which is the real reason he didn't call me. If he lied about me taking the clothes to the charity shop, then he knew I'd already taken them somewhere else because I'd left him. See? It all makes perfect sense.'

Summers's eyes narrow slightly as he weighs everything up.

'The sleeping tablets are the key to this. If I really did take them willingly, where are they? Yours and the doctors' theory that I took them either to help me sleep or kill myself can't be right, can it? I couldn't find them at my house and they're not at Sara's, either.'

'Yes, but that doesn't mean—'

'Wait. I'm not finished.' I hold my hand up to cut him off. 'If you were going to take sleeping tablets, where would you put them?'

He presses his lips together for a moment, thinking, or maybe trying to hatch an excuse to get rid of me. 'Probably in my medicine cabinet or by the bed.'

'Exactly! But they're nowhere to be found. So your theory is impossible now, isn't it? If I took the sleeping tablets to help me sleep, or even to commit suicide, I would've taken them at Sara's house after I moved out.' I almost want to say 'Ta-da!' and do an elaborate, triumphant hand gesture.

Summers just stares at me.

'So I need to know if you checked whether Liam really was in Scotland when he said he was. He lied to me about going there before, you see.'

'When he stayed in the . . .' He picks up my notes and reads again before his gaze goes back to me. 'The Royal Lodge Hotel?'

'Yes. Several times, apparently.'

He taps his fingertips against the desk, eyeing me. 'Do you want something to drink? Tea or coffee?'

'No, thank you. I just want to find out what you know.'

'We made a request to the Scottish police to carry out some enquiries after I spoke to you in the hospital. Liam flew from

Stansted to Aberdeen on the sixth of May, as he said he did, and checked into the Murray Inn. Our Scottish counterparts confirmed that during the time he was in Aberdeen, there was only a maximum of eight hours when he wasn't accounted for. He was either seen by hotel staff or staff at the Devon Pharmaceutical plant.'

'Yes, but what about those eight hours in between? Couldn't he have flown back and found me?'

'We checked the passenger lists for all flights from Scotland. His name wasn't on any of them until the tenth of May, when he flew back to Stansted, so he couldn't have come back in between that time.'

'Well, maybe he hired a car and drove down.'

'It takes about eight and a half hours to drive one way alone. There's not enough time unaccounted for where he could drive here and back again.'

'Couldn't he have hired a really fast car, though?'

'Have you ever hired a car before?'

'No, I can't drive.'

'Of course. Well, when you hire a car, they want to see annoying bits of information, like driving licences and proof of address. They can't risk someone taking it and not returning it, which means they do plenty of checks to be sure. So, no, he couldn't have hired a car, whether it was a Ferrari or a Smart Car.'

'OK, what about a train, then. They'd be quicker, wouldn't they?'

'We checked the train times, too. The fastest train from London to Aberdeen takes seven hours and five minutes, and he'd have to get from London to here and then back again.'

'Yes, but . . . but . . .' But what, I wonder? 'Couldn't the witnesses who saw him be lying?'

Summers makes a noise that sounds like a cross between a cough and a snort. 'All nine of them? No, I'm afraid it's just not possible in any way, shape, or form, for Liam to have travelled back here.'

His words hit me like an icy wind blowing in my face. Not possible. Not possible.

I thought Liam was lying to me. Trying to make me go mad. Trying to kill me. But this means he couldn't have known I'd left him, so he genuinely thought the letter I'd written was a suicide letter when he found it on his return from Scotland after the hospital rang him. *That's* why he was so concerned about me. And if he didn't lie about that, then maybe he didn't lie about the other things either. Maybe I did really take a few clothes to the charity shop that I haven't even noticed are gone. Maybe he really didn't phone me from Scotland because he was busy. Or maybe we did have a row about a plate but it didn't actually smash. I've been so preoccupied with thinking it was Liam that maybe I've ignored the obvious.

Right then, I don't know which is worse, thinking my husband was involved in kidnapping me or finding out he's not. Because now I really don't have any clue who could've done this to me. It means someone is still out there, lurking in the shadows. Someone who could take me again and I wouldn't even recognise them.

A gurgled sound hits my ears, and I realise it's coming from me. I want to cry. Want to let out all the frustration, fear, and terror, but I'm afraid if I do, I'll never be able to stop again.

Must stay calm. Must try harder. Must think clearly!

'Look, I'll get you a coffee with some sugar in it, OK? You look a bit ill.' Summers stands and exits the room.

I rub my stomach, trying to stop the queasy feeling. *It wasn't Liam. It wasn't Liam. It wasn't Liam.*

So who the hell was it?

A few minutes later, he returns with a lukewarm coffee from a vending machine. He puts it on the desk in front of me, and my gaze meets his. This time I think I see pity. I grasp the cup and hold it to my chest for comfort. 'So . . . so if Liam didn't do it, who did?' My voice wobbles.

'Chloe,' he says calmly and patiently. 'I liaised with Dr Traynor and Dr Drew before, and they both thought it was another kind of reaction you were having to the sleeping tablets. You were hallucinating and wandered off into the woods somewhere, ending up on the road where you were picked up by the motorist.'

'I know that! But they're not right! Dr Drew would've told you I was perfectly sane.'

He pauses for a moment. 'Dr Drew also explained to me about False Memory Syndrome. You could be—'

'These aren't false memories! I spoke to Jordan on the phone and told him I was leaving Liam. I found my stuff at Sara's, but no sleeping tablets. That's evidence and corroboration, isn't it?' Tears well up in my eyes. I close them and press my fingers against the lids until I see white lights, hoping to push the tears back inside.

'It shows you moved out of your house, nothing more.' He leans forward. 'We had to look at all the evidence available at the time, and that evidence pointed to a medical issue rather than a criminal issue. You couldn't give us any further information to go on, so we had to make a professional decision based on the facts in front of us.'

'But it's not true. Something happened. Yes, I can't remember what, but it *did* happen. I woke up underground, where someone left me for dead!' I'm yelling now, unable to control myself any longer. I've been trying to keep calm, trying to fight the hysteria curling like a serpent in my guts, but it's too late now. All the pent up feelings are unleashed. 'If something happens to me, it will be on your head. If I disappear again, or you find me dead, then you'll know I was telling the truth, won't you?' I glare at him, my eyes feeling like they're about to pop out of my sockets. 'And then it will be too late!'

He recoils then, as if I've slapped him. 'OK, OK. Don't get yourself upset, now.'

'How can I not? Don't you get it? Someone tried to kill me!' I'm fully prepared to take this further, to go over his head if necessary, but this seems to spur him into action finally.

He breathes in slowly, studying me with a look of concentration on his face. 'After what you've told me today, I admit there are some questions.'

'So, you believe me now that I was abducted?'

'I think it's odd you can't find the sleeping tablets.'

I notice he doesn't answer my question, but it's a start. 'Exactly.'

'But since you obviously did take them, because traces were found in your system, it's still possible you had some kind of hallucinogenic allergic reaction to them and *imagined* you were being held captive. Or perhaps during this hallucinogenic state, you took the tablets with you somewhere and lost them.'

'No, it's not possible.'

'Why not? It happened before.'

'Because if I can't find them at Sara's, someone must've given them to me somehow. They must've used them to knock me out so they could abduct me and leave me underground in that place. Even if I took them voluntarily, how did I end up miles away on a road in the middle of nowhere? Someone must've seen me if I was wandering around *hallucinating all over the place!*'

He doesn't look convinced. 'The things is, though, that you don't remember what happened after you got to Sara's. You could've gone to stay somewhere else. Maybe to another friend's house? You could've taken the tablets at another location, and that's where we'll find them. We're just going round in circles here.' He glances at his watch.

'But I didn't have anywhere else to go.'

He gives a reluctant sigh, as if he's just humouring the crazy woman so he can get rid of her. 'Did you find anything at Sara's that might help discover what you did next?'

I shake my head forcefully. 'Not really. I rang the bank, which is the last call from her landline. I went to Waitrose at some point and came back with food. I slept there at least one night, because my stuff is in the bedroom and the bedclothes are rumpled.' I suck in a breath and hold it as I try to formulate things in my mind. 'Dr Traynor said my level of dehydration pointed to not drinking for no more than two days.'

'Were there any signs of a struggle or break-in at Sara's?'

'No, I checked. The doors and windows were all locked and secured, and there were no signs of a fight or struggle.'

'OK, so let's work out a timeline of the missing days.' He slides my notes closer to him and glances at them. 'You were found on the road on the ninth of May. On the sixth, you went to Sara's and probably stayed the night if the bedclothes were slept in. So whatever happened occurred somewhere between the seventh and ninth. Do you agree?'

'Yes.'

'Let's have a hypothetical question, then.' He taps his finger on the desk thoughtfully. 'Instinctively, you already seem to be repeating what you did before. You've found out about Liam's affair, and you've moved to Sara's house. You've phoned the bank to change your address. So, what would you do next? Where would you go? Who would you talk to?'

'I've thought about that so much, and nothing can point me in one direction or another. It's all just a dead end after that.'

'Think about it again, then,' he says calmly. 'Sara isn't due to come home for another few months, so you could've stayed there for a while. Is that what you would've done, or would you have looked for a place of your own?'

'I . . . I don't know. I mean, Liam would've most likely known where I'd be, and I wouldn't have wanted him to try to find me and change my mind. I probably would've looked for somewhere else to live. Somewhere he didn't know about.'

'Right, that's a start. And you were still signed off work, so you wouldn't have gone back there? Theresa said she hadn't seen you, but would you have gone to speak to any of your other colleagues?'

Jordan is the only one I would've wanted to see, but he didn't mention it. In fact, he said he wanted to call me but stopped himself because I'd told him that's what I wanted. 'I don't think so.' I bite my lip and stare at the ceiling, as if it somehow it has all the answers I need.

'You'd already been food shopping, so you didn't need immediate supplies.'

'That's right.'

'What about your mobile phone? You said you broke it when you were leaving home. Would you have gone to buy another one?'

'Maybe. It's a possibility, but I didn't see a new phone at Sara's house.'

'Did you find any receipts? Or anything else?'

'I was only really looking for the sleeping tablets, and I was in a rush to talk to you, so I don't know. There could be something there.'

'I think we should go back to Sara's and have a good look around.' He stands up just as his mobile phone goes off. 'DI Summers,' he answers, listening for a few moments. 'Actually, I'm with Chloe at the moment.' He looks at me. 'I'll be there soon. I'll bring her with me. OK, see you then.' He hangs up. 'That was Theresa. She says something has come to light I need to be aware of. She wants to show me something, and it might help if you're there, too.'

Chapter Twenty-Four

Summers drives his police issue car to the college and parks next to Jordan's classic VW camper that he restored himself. As I get out, I look around for Jordan, hoping to catch a glimpse of him, but he's nowhere to be seen. I lead the way to Theresa's office, and Gillian blushes, acting tongue-tied in front of Summers. That's how anxious I felt around the police only a few days ago. Now, I just think Summers doesn't have a clue what he's doing.

A pile of paperwork surrounds Theresa, and her reading glasses are perched on the end of her nose, when we enter her office. She glances up and rises, extending her hand to Summers before giving me an embarrassed nod. 'How are you?' she asks me, her pinched lips quirking up a fraction. It's the closest thing I've seen to a smile on her face in years.

'Not that great, actually.'

She avoids looking at me and turns to Summers. 'Thank you for coming.' She waves us into the two seats opposite her. 'When you came to see me initially to ask about Chloe being off sick, you didn't go into specific details about what had happened to her.' She gives him a stern look, and I pity the poor students sent to her office for a telling off.

Summers shifts in his chair and has the good grace to look chastised. 'We weren't exactly sure what we were dealing with initially, but some further things have come to light.'

'Yes.' She glances briefly at me before turning to him again. 'When I spoke to Chloe yesterday, she told me a rather shocking version of events.'

I don't point out that she didn't believe me and practically ordered me to resign.

'This morning, when I had a routine staff meeting with Chloe's stand-in tutor and informed her what Chloe had told me, she went as white as a sheet and immediately alerted me to this.' She picks up a few pieces of paper stapled together from her desk and hands it to Summers. 'You should read it.'

I want to read it over Summers's shoulder or, better yet, rip it out of his hands. What is it, and how does it relate to me? I give Theresa a questioning look, but her gaze darts immediately back to Summers, watching him while he reads. I squirm in my seat the whole time.

When he finishes, he looks solemn and hands it to me.

It's a creative writing assignment I gave my students just before I went on sick leave after the miscarriage. I set them the title "Darkness," and instructed them to write a short story with that theme. The name of the student who's written the story is at the top of the page: Chris Barnes.

The opening paragraphs describe a man who's secretly stalking a woman. He watches her in her house, follows her when she goes out, notices things about her she probably doesn't even see herself, like the way she fiddles with her small hooped earrings, turning them round and round absentmindedly. This man has pursued other women before, looking for the perfect one he thinks will love him back.

He waits for the right moment. She's alone in the house. Her husband is away working. The stalker is an expert in picking locks and enters the house through the kitchen door. She's asleep in bed and doesn't hear a thing. He strikes her on the head with a small baton he brought with him. It knocks her unconscious, and he binds her hands and feet with rope and gags her before bundling her into his car parked on the driveway, the number plates already exchanged for fake ones. It's the early hours of the morning, and the street is quiet. Everyone's sleeping. No one sees anything. He takes her to his house in the middle of nowhere and leaves her in the basement.

The next few pages follow the stalker's state of mind. He hasn't decided what to do with the woman yet. Part of him wants to kill her straightaway. The other part wants to keep her there forever, to worship her and show her just how much he loves her. He's in turmoil. The first woman he took didn't deserve to live. She whined and moaned, always begging him for her life, so he got sick of her quickly and killed her. The second one cracked immediately. Said she'd do anything to stay alive. Anything, if he promised he wouldn't kill her. The third . . . well, the third is the woman in the basement.

He starts drinking whisky, and the more he drinks, the more confused he becomes, eventually falling into a drunken sleep. When he wakes up, she's gone. Somehow, she's managed to escape. Or was it all just a drunken fantasy?

As I read the last word on the page, the walls get narrower, closing in on me. I fall off the chair, and the floor rushes up to meet me.

Chapter Twenty-Five

'Chloe? Chloe, are you OK?' a voice says. Someone taps my hand lightly. 'Can you hear me?'

My eyelids flutter open. I'm lying on the floor, Theresa kneeling beside me, holding my hand.

'You went down with a hell of a bang. Are you OK?'

I reach up and touch the back of my head. It's throbbing. 'Ouch.'

'You hit your head on the floor when you fell off the chair.'

I try to sit up, but she guides me back down again with one hand on my back.

'No, stay there. Don't move yet. I want to get you checked out by the nurse first.'

She's probably only worried about being sued for an industrial injury. 'I'm OK. Really.' I blink once, twice, to clear my vision.

'I want to make sure you haven't got concussion. Are you cold? Do you want a blanket?'

'Honestly, I'm fine. I feel much better now.'

The nurse, Elaine Waters, enters the room then. She's in her early fifties, with kind eyes. 'Oh, dear.' She kneels on the other side of me. 'How are you feeling?'

I'm sick of people asking me that lately. I want to scream at them all to shut up, but that would be ungrateful and mean. 'I'm fine. There's absolutely no need to make a fuss. I just fainted, that's all.'

'She hit her head, I think,' Theresa says to Elaine.

'But I'm *fine*,' I insist, trying to sit up again.

'You're not feeling dizzy or sick?' Elaine helps me up because she can tell I'm not just going to lie there.

'No. I know what concussion feels like, and I'm OK. Honestly.' I attempt a smile.

Elaine slips a hand under my right arm while Theresa takes my left, and they help me up into the chair. 'Did you have anything to eat today?' Elaine peers at me with concern.

'Yes. I had a big bowl of pasta.'

'You look like you're wasting away, Chloe.' Elaine rubs her hand up and down my arm. 'This must be an incredibly stressful time for you.'

Theresa gives Elaine the same stern look she gave Summers earlier, which reminds me that he isn't in the room.

'Where's Summers?' I don't have time for sympathetic chitchat. I need to find out what's going on.

'He's gone to speak to Chris.'

I want to rub the back of my head, soothe out the throbbing there, but I daren't risk them trying to keep me here any longer. I stand up, steadying myself on the edge of Theresa's desk. 'I need to find out what's going on. I mean his assignment . . .' I shiver. 'It's so similar to what happened to me.'

Elaine guides me gently into the seat again. 'Chloe, this is for the police to deal with. Now, let me get you some sweet tea and a biscuit.'

I know she's just trying to be nice and helpful, but it's not helpful at all. This is my life we're talking about here. I can't just sit helplessly and wait. Sweet tea and a bloody stupid biscuit aren't going to help.

'If you start feeling unwell, make sure you call me.' Elaine smiles before exiting the office.

Theresa and I sit in silence. When she catches my eye, she looks away. I still don't think she believes me. She's just covering her arse by getting Summers involved now.

When Elaine returns, she sets a cup and saucer, along with a plate of chocolate digestives, on Theresa's desk in front of me before disappearing again. I take the saucer, but my hand shakes and the tea spills, leaving a brown moat of liquid around the bottom of the cup.

Theresa pulls out a wad of tissues from a box on her desk and passes them to me. 'Here, use these.'

I put the saucer back on her desk, fold up the tissues, and place them under the cup. 'Thanks.' And then I burst into tears. Shoulder-shaking sobs wrack my whole body as I wrap my arms around myself and rock back and forth. It's comforting, calming.

'I don't know what to say.' A red flush creeps up Theresa's neck to her cheeks.

I don't, either. Yes, Chris is a big lad. He plays rugby and is stocky and powerful, but he's only seventeen! He's never given me a reason to think he'd harm me. In fact, he's always been polite and friendly in class, and conscientious with his work. Helpful, even. Always the first to volunteer when I ask for someone's help. I suspected some kind of schoolboy crush, but kidnapping me? Surely, he couldn't be capable of that.

So, no, I don't know what to say. Don't know what to think. Can only cry at this point. So much has happened in the gap of memories missing from my head, I don't even know how to process it all. I'm drained. Exhausted. I want to sleep for a hundred years.

Or sleep and never wake up. That would probably be better. Then I wouldn't have to deal with it. I wouldn't have to think at all.

Summers comes back in the room a little while later. Before he can even say anything, I ask, 'What happened? Did he admit to kidnapping me? Do you think it was him? Have you arrested him?'

He takes in my puffy eyes and tear-stained face before saying, 'Chris was very shocked and visibility upset when I informed him that his story was incredibly similar to details you'd given us. He said you were one of his favourite teachers, and he was really sorry something bad had happened to you.'

'Yes, but he would say that, wouldn't he! If it were him, he'd deny it! And this can't be just a coincidence, can it?'

Summers takes a breath. 'He says he has an alibi for the time period you were—well, for the time period we're missing.'

I notice he still won't admit my abduction. He still isn't convinced I didn't just wander off somewhere in a drug-induced state, but I'm too agitated to make a fuss right now. 'What alibi?'

'Chris said he was away camping with his dad. His parents have shared custody, and since Chris wasn't in college on that Monday, he and his dad decided to go away for a long weekend. They were apparently in the Peak District on a hiking trip.'

'Do you believe him?'

He hesitates for a second. 'At the moment, yes. Flynn's taken him to the police station, where we'll wait for his father to arrive and confirm or deny it. In the meantime, are you up to going back to Sara's house and looking around?'

I stand up too quickly, and the room spins. I blink for a few seconds. 'Yes. I can't just sit here and do nothing.'

As we head to his car, my scalp tingles with fear as if it's on fire. Is it another dead end, or is Chris lying?

Chapter Twenty-Six

Summers opens Sara's front door with her key and steps over the post. An eerie déjà vu hits me again, but I know that's because I've already done this once today.

'What are we looking for, exactly?' I follow him into the lounge.

He looks around. 'I don't know. Some kind of evidence you were here before, and what you did or where you might have gone. You didn't get time to answer my question back at the station.'

'Which question?'

'The hypothetical one. Right here, right now, what would you instinctively do next?'

I shake my head. 'I don't know.'

'Think about it. It's the only kind of trail we have to follow at the moment.'

'My bag was left in the kitchen.'

'OK. Let's start there, then.'

I lead the way.

Summers opens the fridge and peers inside. 'These are the things you bought?'

'They must be. They're fairly fresh.'

'Where's the receipt for them?' His gaze wanders round the kitchen. He opens the bottom cupboards until he finds a plastic bin with a swing lid underneath the one next to the sink. He pulls on some latex gloves from his pocket and removes the bin lid, putting it on the lino floor and wrinkling up his nose. He lifts out an empty pizza box, Waitrose's own brand. Next comes the plastic base it would've sat on and a plastic wrapper with the remains of congealed tomato sauce and cheese.

'Meat feast pizza,' I say automatically.

'Did you eat that?'

I shrug. 'I must've done if it's here. I never got to eat pizza with Liam; he hated it. Maybe I was trying to give myself a treat.'

His hand disappears in the bin again and retrieves a piece of paper screwed up into a ball. He unfolds it. 'Receipt from Waitrose. Paid in cash.' He shows it to me.

'That makes sense.'

'That's it. There's nothing else apart from two Waitrose carrier bags.' He puts the food cartons back in the bin, pulls off his gloves, turning them inside out with a loud snap, and throws them in, too. Then he puts the lid back on and washes his hands. He's wiping them on a kitchen towel when he says, 'The food was bought on the sixth, so it's all pointing to something happening to you the next day. I'll get a team to make some door-to-door enquiries with Sara's neighbours. See if they saw you or noticed anyone suspicious hanging around.'

'OK.' I lift my shoulders slightly. At least he's *doing* something now. At least he believes me. Sort of.

We look around the rest of the downstairs but don't find any other clues. We're just about to go upstairs when I spy the post again. 'Maybe there's something in here addressed to me. If I told the bank about Sara's address, maybe I told someone else, too.' I pick it up and rummage through, but it's either bills or junk mail in Sara's name, so I put it all on the bottom stair and we head to the bathroom. On top of one corner of the bath are bottles of shampoo, conditioner, and shower gel. They're not the brand I use, so it's probably safe to say they're Sara's.

Summers opens the whitewashed wooden cabinet with a mirror on it, above the sink. He picks things up, examining the items I've already checked as I stand next to him, tapping my foot. He gives the room one last look over, but there's nowhere else in here the sleeping tablets could be.

'This is Sara's room.' I open the door, and we go in. There are two white wooden drawers either side of the bed. Summers goes through them, and I feel sorry for Sara. It's bad enough having my life examined under a microscope, but poor Sara is just an innocent party in all this. He pulls things out and puts them on the top. Some lavender essential oil, a pen, old earplugs in a clear plastic container, a *Lonely Planet* guide of Australia. I cringe when he finds some furry handcuffs, a shiny silver vibrator, and a well-used tube of KY Jelly. Other than a few crumpled scraps of paper with phone numbers and names written on them, there's nothing else, so he turns his attention to the drawer underneath. A few pairs of knickers and socks, a suspender belt, stockings.

The drawers on the other side have nothing that could help, either. No sleeping tablets, no X marks the spot, no "CLUE" written in conveniently big letters.

There's a plastic washing basket in the corner of the room. Summers lifts the lid but only finds a lone black sock inside. I briefly wonder where the other sock is, but who cares? It's not important. He opens the doors to Sara's wardrobe, sliding sparse hangers of clothes across the rail from one side to the other. At the bottom of the wardrobe are a couple of shoeboxes, both empty. He heads out of the door, and I follow him into the spare room.

'See.' I point to the rumpled sheets. 'I must've slept in it.' I swing my arm around to my clothes. 'These are mine, too.'

He nods, his gaze taking everything in. Apart from the bed and small table next to it, there's only the director's chair in the corner. No drawers or wardrobe to store anything. On top of the table are piles of travel books: *How To Drop Everything and Travel Around the World, A is for Africa, Zanzibar to Timbuktu, A Guide to Machu Picchu, Lonely Planet Turkey, Adventures on the East Coast of Australia, Trekking in the Himalaya.*

Summers picks up the books and leafs through them. 'Are these Sara's or yours?'

'Well . . . Sara's, I suppose.'

'You've never thought about travelling before?'

'Only for holidays.' I pick up the Australia book and flick through, wondering why the pages look so familiar. I put it back down again and wave my hand round the room. 'There are no sleeping tablets anywhere, just like I said.'

He walks to the opposite side of the bed, where there's a small gap between it and the wall. He bends down, and when he stands back up again he's holding a newspaper left open to the classified page. 'It's the local one,' he says. 'Dated the fifth of May.'

I look over his shoulder as I skim the page. Amongst several ads for driving lessons, logs for sale, kittens, puppies and hamsters, and ironing services with free collection and delivery, a few flats for rent are circled in red pen.

'So you probably were looking for somewhere to rent.'

I shrug uselessly. 'I suppose I must've been. I wouldn't have wanted to deal with Liam banging on the door and trying to convince me to come back. I was probably hoping just to avoid him forever. Or at least until I was feeling stronger.'

'Is that what you think he'll do? Bang on the door? Cause trouble?'

I bite my lip and nod.

Something like concern flashes in his eyes. It makes him look almost sympathetic for a change. 'Has he ever hit you?'

'No. But . . .' I trail off, avoiding his gaze because I feel weak and pathetic. Maybe Liam was right after all. I am stupid. Stupid for staying so long.

'But what?'

'Words and actions can bruise deeper than any fist. Scars aren't always on the outside, are they?'

He studies me for a moment. 'Not always, no.'

I can't talk about this yet. Can't deal with it. When I find out who took me, *then* I can fall apart and cry for what should've been but never was. For the woman who lost herself. For what she thought was real love but was only something toxic and warped.

But not now. Now I need to find out who abducted me. 'It doesn't matter now,' I say dismissively. 'I left him. Twice. I'm going to get on with my life and be OK. If this unknown person doesn't kill me first, of course.' I shoot him a grave look.

'Do you have anywhere else you can go? I don't think it's safe for you to stay here while we make further enquiries. Even if Liam doesn't try to see you, we still don't know what happened here and whether you left of your own free will. The sleeping tablets, or lack of them, are bothering me.'

'I could go to Jordan's,' I say immediately. He's the only person I know well enough, and there's no one else to turn to.

'Who's Jordan?'

'A . . . a colleague.' A hot flush creeps into my cheeks.

'Call him and see if it's possible.'

I go to where I left my mobile phone, find his number from the last time he called, and hit "Redial."

'Chloe! I've just got out of class and heard something about Chris being questioned. I was just about to call you. What's going on? Are you all right?' He's breathless, like he's walking fast. I hear a cacophony of teenage voices laughing and shouting in the background.

'Yes. I'm OK.' I glance at Summers. 'I'm with the police.'

'Good. As long as you're safe. But, Chris? I mean, do they really think he's involved in this? He's in my class. I never would've—'

'They think he has an alibi,' I cut in. 'Look, Jordan. You know you said to call if you could help? Well, I need a favour.'

'Of course. What do you need?'

'Can I stay at your place? Just for a few days maybe, until I get something else sorted.'

'Absolutely,' he says with no hesitation. 'You can stay as long as you like. I've got a spare room.'

'Thank you.'

'Do you want me to pick you up from somewhere?'

'No, it's OK. I can walk. Or get a lift from DI Summers.'

'OK, well, I've finished for the day, so I'll be home in about twenty minutes. I can meet you at home.'

'That would be great. I'll see you there.' I hang up. I don't ask for his address since I already know it. He had a moving-in party there, back when I first started working at the college. It seems so long ago now. So far away. 'Ninety-five Curzon Street,' I tell Summers. 'That's where I'll be. And, please, don't tell Liam.'

'It will be completely confidential.' He writes the address down in his notepad and then waits until I've gathered my meagre belongings together before walking me outside. 'Do you trust this Jordan?'

Trust. Five small letters that can have such a big effect on your life. I want to tell Summers I don't trust *him*. He didn't believe me in the first place. He tossed me aside, abandoned me to my fate, even if he is making amends now. I don't know he won't do it again. I also trusted Liam, and look where that got me.

Do I trust Jordan? My heart does, even if my head doesn't know what to think. 'I have to trust someone, don't I?' I say. 'At least if I disappear again, you'll know where to look for the last place I was.'

Chapter Twenty-Seven

When Jordan opens the door, he's got that worried frown of concern on his face. We stand there, staring at each other, and it's as if a whole silent conversation passes between us. He lifts his arms up, making me think he's about to reach out and pull me close to him. I want that. Want to feel protected and cared about for once. I know I'll feel safe with him wrapped around me. But the moment vanishes when he notices Summers sitting in his car parked at the kerb.

I turn, give Summers a small wave, and he drives off. Jordan steps back to let me inside, and I can't help looking around. They say you can tell a lot about a person by their home.

His house is a small two-bedroom cottage, all original sanded floorboards, wooden beams, and uneven plasterwork. I take a quick glance through the open door to the lounge, which has an old-fashioned log burner and a comfy-looking, sagging sofa. Scenic photos and throws provide splashes of bright colour.

He leads me into the sunny kitchen, painted a yellow that reminds me of daffodils, at the back of the house. The kitchen units look handmade, with rustic barn door type cupboards and battered iron handles. There's a Range cooker on the back wall where a large brick open fireplace once stood. It's small, but warm and cosy, like Sara's, and it fits him perfectly.

'Have a seat.' Jordan waves at a distressed wooden kitchen table in the centre of the room. It looks like it's seen a lot of use. Plate and cup rings are burned into the surface, scratches and scrapes that tell a history and only add to its charm. Liam would hate it. 'Do you want a tea or coffee?' He leans his hip against the worktop.

'Actually, do you have something stronger?' I sit on what looks like part of an old wooden church pew and put the small suitcase with all my worldly belongings in it on the floor, along with my handbag, 'I could really do with it.'

He raises his eyebrows casually. 'Sure. I've got beer or wine or . . .' He bends down and rummages around in a cupboard. His black T-shirt clings to his broad back and shoulders, and I wonder again what it would feel like to have his arms wrapped around me. 'Vodka?' He holds up a bottle and catches me looking.

Heat floods my cheeks.

He smiles, and my stomach flips. 'Might have some rum some-where as well.'

For the first time in what feels like years, I smile, too. 'Beer is good.'

He puts the vodka back and stands up. 'Beer it is, then.' He grabs two bottles from the fridge, twists the caps off, and throws them in the bin before handing me one.

I take a sip. I never knew beer could taste so good. Or maybe it's the company.

'We can go into the lounge if you want.'

'No, this is OK. Unless you want to?'

'No. This is fine.' He takes a swig of beer, his gaze on me. Today his eyes look more of a warm honey-brown colour, and I wonder why I'm even noticing that in the midst of everything going on. I don't feel uncomfortable under his gaze as I do with Liam. I'm not watching and waiting for something to happen. Now I just feel . . . safe.

We sit in silence for a moment. I look out the kitchen window to the small courtyard garden outside. A tall, whitewashed wall surrounds it, with wildflowers around the borders and a completely private decked patio area. 'You have a nice house. You've done a lot to it since your party.'

'Thanks. When I moved in, it was a bit of a state. I renovated it myself.'

I'm not surprised. Jordan seems like the kind of guy who's hands-on.

'Have the police found out any more about Chris?'

'I'm still waiting to hear. Chris said he was away with his dad when I was taken.'

He scrunches up his face. 'Well, I couldn't believe it when I heard what had happened. If he does have an alibi, it's a bit of a coincidence, isn't it? His story being almost exactly like what happened to you?'

I think about all the coincidences that made me think Liam was involved, and yet he couldn't have possibly been. 'Coincidences seem to be following me around everywhere, but maybe it really is just another one.' I pick at the label on the bottle, then realise what I'm doing and stop abruptly. I don't want to make a mess. 'Sorry.' I smooth down the label so none of it falls off onto the table.

'Hey, no problem. Treat this place like your own while you're here. If you want to pull off beer labels, be my guest.' He grins. 'It might be a good kind of stress relief.'

I laugh, and it sounds so foreign to my ears. 'Summers is going to call me when they've spoken to Chris's dad. And they're going to do some house-to-house enquiries at Sara's.' I tell him everything I've found out since I last saw him.

'So you know for certain now you *did* actually leave Liam, then?'

'Yes. But Liam didn't know. He was still in Scotland when I was kidnapped, so he must've really thought I'd tried to kill myself because of the letter he found when he got back and the sleeping tablets in my system.'

'What do you think he'll do when he finds out you've left now?'

'Luckily, he doesn't know I've got a new phone, or he'd be ringing me constantly. He'd start off being all kind and caring and apologetic, telling me how much he loves me, then rapidly turn into an angry drunk, and everything would be my fault. He'd be shouting, swearing, calling me all the names under the sun, wondering how I could dare to leave him. How meek and mild Chloe could ever stick up for herself.' I take another swig of beer. 'I can't deal with him at the moment. I just want to be left alone to figure things out before this person comes back.'

Jordan nods in agreement, but I detect a note of sadness in his eyes, and I don't know if that sadness is for me, for him, for bad timing.

'The police haven't been very helpful, but at least Summers does believe something strange happened now.' I attempt to change the subject from getting too personal. It's too much, too soon. 'He thinks it's weird that the sleeping tablets aren't anywhere to be found.'

'So do I. Which must mean someone gave them to you, mustn't it? They must've used them to knock you out so they could abduct you.'

'Summers said I could've found somewhere else to stay, and maybe that's where I took them. In Sara's spare bedroom, we found last week's local paper, and I'd circled some flats for rent. Do you have a copy? Because Summers took it, and I want to have a look and see if it rings any bells. I have to prove to him somehow

217

I didn't take those sleeping pills. Then I can negate his theory that I hallucinated the whole abduction thing, and he'll have to believe something more sinister happened.'

'I don't think I've thrown it out yet. Hang on.' As he wanders out of the room, I watch his retreating back. He's relaxed, unhurried, always cool and calm, even in a crisis. 'Got it!' He returns a few minutes later and sits down again.

I spread it out on the table and flip to the classified page.

'If you had found somewhere else to live, wouldn't you have taken your stuff that was at Sara's?'

'Yes, and that's why I'm positive I didn't move out of her house. Have you got a pen?'

He swivels in his chair to the drawer behind him, opens it, and grabs a biro. 'One pen, madam.' He presents it as if he's showing me an expensive bottle of wine.

I laugh again. Wow, that's twice in about five minutes. I hope with all my heart this was a good idea coming here. I've made enough mistakes in my life; I don't want to live to regret this.

If I live.

But Jordan's my only friend right now, so I don't have an alternative. I put a red circle round the ones I'd marked before and swing the paper round to show him. 'Apparently, I marked these three.'

'Do you want to call them? See if you went there to check them out?'

'Summers said he was going to do that, but I just feel so helpless, waiting for someone else to take control of my life. I've had enough of that already. *I* need to be in control for a change.'

'I'll get the phone. It won't hurt to call them.' He disappears out of the room again.

A loud slamming noise comes from the kitchen door, which makes me jump so hard I bite my tongue. I snap my head round in that direction and see it's only a small black cat that's charged through the cat flap. It sits in the middle of the floor, looking up at me as if wondering whether I'm friend or foe. Deciding on the former, the cat winds itself around my legs.

'So you've met John, then. He's my other roommate.' Jordan sits back down.

'John!' I chuckle, reaching down to pick John up and put him on my lap. He treats me to a loud purr as he nudges his head against my hand. 'How can you call a cat 'John'?'

'I don't know.' His lips curve into a smile. 'He looks like a John, don't you think?'

I raise an eyebrow. 'How can a cat look like a John? Fluffy or Tiddles or Blacky, or something, but he definitely doesn't look like John.'

Jordan shrugs. 'So what should I call him, then? You choose.'

'You can't just rename him!'

'Why? He won't know the difference, will he?'

'But don't you call him when you want him to come in? He'll just get confused when you give him another name.'

'No, he pretty much comes and goes as he wants. That's what I like about cats. They're independent, and they come to you because they choose to, not because you make them.' He smiles, and once again I sense his words have a deeper meaning than the subject we're talking about.

A jolt of heat flushes through my cheeks. I lean over and kiss John on the head so Jordan doesn't notice.

'Another beer?' He nods to my bottle that I didn't realise was empty.

'Yes, please.'

Jordan grabs two more from the fridge and places them on the table, then waves the phone at me. 'Do you want to call these numbers, then?'

I take a swig of beer for courage, wondering what I'm going to find out. It feels like I'm a voyeur in my own life, investigating myself when I know I haven't done anything wrong. What will these people tell me? There's only one way to find out, so I punch in the first number and listen to it ringing.

'Hello?' a deep voice answers. In the background, booming bass music plays, and a fruit machine is going off.

'Oh, hi, yes, my name's Chloe Benson, and I'm ringing about the flat.'

'What, again?' he shouts over the noise.

'Did I call before?' My gaze flicks to Jordan, who's looking at me with brows raised.

'Yeah, but when I told you it was above the pub, you didn't want it. Have you changed your mind, then? It's still vacant.'

'Um . . . no, thank you. Sorry to bother you.' I hang up and dial the next number I'd marked. 'Above a pub. I didn't want it,' I say to Jordan.

'Hello? Can I help you?' a male with an Indian accent answers.

'Hi, my name's Chloe Benson, and I'm ringing about the flat advertised in the paper.'

'I'm sorry, it's been rented.'

'OK, but . . . um . . . do you remember whether I called before?'

'I'm sorry, I don't remember. I spoke to a lot of people on the phone.'

'Right. So do you remember if I came over and looked at it, then?'

'No, you couldn't have done. The first person who looked took it.'

'OK. Well, thanks for your help.' I hang up and sigh. 'Third time lucky,' I say to Jordan and ring the last number I'd circled.

'Yeah?' a woman answers the phone. I think she's chewing gum, judging by the lip-smacking sound.

'Oh, hi, I'm ringing about the flat for rent.'

'Yeah, it's taken, I'm afraid. Someone rented it the day before the advert came out in the local. Sorry, it was too late to stop it.'

'Right. Well, thanks for your help.'

'No problem.'

I lean back in the chair, shoulders slumping. John rubs his head under my chin for another stroke, and I oblige.

'No luck, then?' Jordan says. 'You didn't go and see any of them?'

'No.'

'Don't worry, Chloe.' He lays a hand on mine with a tenderness that makes my throat clench. As soon as he touches me, his warmth spreads over my chilled skin. 'We'll figure it out. You've gone through some terrible things, but whatever happened, we can find out together. I just want to help you.'

The air suddenly feels charged, heavy with all the words he's not saying. The things I know he feels for me. And I don't know if I can do this. I don't know if I can handle someone being so nice to me right now. It might make me fall apart, and I have to stay strong.

Chapter Twenty-Eight

Jordan is chopping onions, mushrooms, peppers, and garlic. He bites his lower lip as he concentrates, a clean tea towel hanging casually out the back pocket of his jeans, looking completely at home in the kitchen. Stealing a glance over his shoulder, he catches me watching him. 'What?' His lips quirk up.

'You cook.'

'Yes.'

'You cook, and you own a cat.'

He laughs. It's deep and throaty and carefree. The sounds ripples through me, and I realise I want to hear more of it. 'Is there a law that says a man can't cook *and* own a cat?' He waves the knife he's been using at me, but it's not threatening. Not when his eyes sparkle with laugher like that.

I'm about to tell him that it's nice. It's . . . refreshing. Liam wouldn't cook a meal; that was my job. And he'd probably kick a cat if he saw it. He hated how they'd always use our garden as a toilet. He even put cayenne pepper all over the grass and borders once to try to get rid of them. He was livid when a sudden breeze blew some of it in his eye as he was dispersing it. It didn't deter the cats anyway.

'It's sweet,' I say.

'I'm not sure whether being called "sweet" is an insult to my manliness.' He raises an amused eyebrow.

'Trust me. Sweet is good.' I stare deep into his eyes, and my skin tingles. Abruptly, I look away, and the moment is lost.

By the time Jordan puts a plate of beef curry and basmati rice garnished with freshly chopped coriander in front of me, my stomach's rumbling. I've eaten very little recently, and I'm suddenly famished.

I pick up my fork. 'It looks delicious.'

'If you don't like it, I can make something else.'

I take a bite, and it's the best thing I've ever tasted. 'You're a good cook.'

'Just one of my many talents.' He looks pleased, and we eat in silence for a while until he asks, 'So, what's the plan?'

'Tomorrow I have a follow-up appointment with Dr Drew. And I'll have to wait to hear from Summers and see what he's found out. After that . . .' I shrug. 'I don't know.' I glance at the terracotta wall clock, wondering what's taking Summers so long to get back to me. Surely, he would've got hold of Chris's dad by now, who'd confirm Chris was lying. With that story he wrote, it *had* to be him. Summers would break through his alibi and lock him up where he belonged, and then I'd be able to breathe again. But until that happened, I had to do something to take my mind off this waiting game. 'Look, tonight can we just not talk about things? For just one night, I want to forget everything. If I think about it anymore, it's going to send me round the bend. Can we just do something normal, like watch a film or listen to music or'—I raise my bottle of beer—'have another drink.'

He puts his knife and fork down and clinks his bottle against mine. 'Then that's exactly what we'll do.'

We finish eating, and he doesn't let me clear up. Doesn't let me lift a finger, in fact.

'Red or white wine?' He holds up a bottle in each hand.

'White, please.' I probably shouldn't. I need to keep focused. Keep my wits about me. But I'm enjoying the soft-around-the-edges fuzzy feeling, and I don't want it ever to go away.

He puts the red bottle down, grabs two glasses from a cupboard, and ambles barefoot into the lounge. I sit on one side of the soft sofa and tuck my legs up beside me. After pouring me a glass of wine, Jordan sits in front of the reclaimed wooden TV cabinet and opens a drawer filled with DVDs. He pulls out a pile and reads the titles aloud.

'*The Mechanic, Alpha Papa, Snatch, Harry Potter and the Goblet of Fire, The Lucky One, Mississippi Burning.* Or *The Notebook.*'

I don't want anything romantic that will remind me of Liam in the early days—or make me think of possibilities with Jordan. I don't want horror or action, where people are being killed, because it's too close for comfort right now. So I ask for something I wouldn't normally watch. Something I can just lose myself in for a few hours. '*Harry Potter.*'

He wiggles the cover at me. 'Good choice.' He slides it in the DVD player, flicks on the TV, and sits next to me on the sofa. It dips under his weight, pushing us closer together. He smells of outdoors and spicy aftershave. It's familiar and comforting as I concentrate on fantasy, monsters, and wizards, and for a time I don't have to think about anything. It's heaven.

A loud banging noise wakes me some time later. I jerk up on the sofa, disoriented for a moment, my heart beating so loudly that my chest feels like it's about to explode.

'It's OK. You fell asleep.' Jordan gets up to answer the door.

'It might be Liam.' I pull my knees up towards me, wrapping my arms around them.

'I'm sure it's not. He doesn't know where I live,' he says over his shoulder.

'You'd be surprised,' I say sadly. 'I wouldn't put it past him to know all sorts of things.'

'Don't worry. I'll be back in a moment.'

I hear the door open. Raised voices. My gaze darts round the room, looking for somewhere to hide if necessary. As the voices get closer, I realise it's Summers. I press a hand to my cheek and breathe deeply. I get up as he enters the room, closely followed by Jordan.

'What did you find out?' I ask urgently. 'You've been ages!'

'Yes, it ended up being a little more complicated than we thought, trying to verify things. We spoke with Chris's dad, and Chris *was* with him in the Peak District during the time you can't remember, so there's no way he could've been involved in anything untoward.'

'How do you know for sure? I mean, how do you know his dad hasn't made up some kind of alibi to protect his son?' I wring my hands together.

'Well, that's what was taking so long. Since they were camping in the middle of nowhere, off the beaten track instead of on a registered site, we had to wait for our colleagues in the Peak District to make a few enquiries.'

'And what did they find out?' Jordan asks.

'They were spotted on CCTV in a local garage and also in the nearest village's café several times. There was also the farmer whose land they were on, who saw them there. Chris wouldn't have had time to get back here and do anything untoward.'

I shake my head with disbelief, pacing up and down. 'But . . . how can that be? You read his story, didn't you? It was identical to what happened to me.'

Summers purses his lips and just looks at me for a moment. 'Have you ever received e-mails in the past from students about the coursework you gave them?'

'Well, yes, sometimes. Their coursework makes up part of their final A Level, so I always tell them to e-mail me if they have a problem or something they're not sure about. Why?' A cold, tingling sensation breaks out on my scalp.

'Because Chris said he e-mailed you a copy of the first draft of his story while you were off sick, so you could answer a couple of questions for him.'

I stare at him blankly, unable even to blink.

'So, it's entirely possible the story is almost identical because it's stuck in your memory from when you read it before. Isn't it?'

I open my mouth to speak, but my voice has disappeared for a moment with confusion and shock.

Luckily, Jordan speaks for me then. 'Chloe's e-mail account was hacked, so she has no way of checking if that's true. Did you look at Chris's e-mail account to see if it was in his sent folder?'

'We made him check it at the station, but unfortunately, his account doesn't autosave sent messages, and he forgot to do that before he sent it. But I can't see why he'd make that up, and, as I say, he has a confirmed alibi anyway.'

I rest my hands against my cheeks and stare at the floor. Is that really what happened? I read Chris's story when I was off sick after coming home from the psychiatric ward, and it's somehow been lodged in my brain? And if so, then does it mean I really have hallucinated someone kidnapping me, as they all think? 'So he's . . . he's definitely not guilty, then?'

'The only thing he's guilty of is having a good imagination. And I'm sure one day he'll make an excellent crime author.'

I flop back down on the sofa. After what I'd read, I was sure it was him.

'You're absolutely sure?' I say.

'Positive. So, we're no further along, I'm afraid. We carried out house-to-house enquiries in Sara's street, but no one remembers

seeing anyone matching your description or anything suspicious.'
Summers sits down next to me.

I stare at the floor. A dull ache starts in the back of my eyes.
I don't know if it's from the alcohol wearing off or just weariness and
too much adrenaline flooding through me permanently.

'What's next, then?' Jordan sits on the floor.

'We'll contact those numbers you circled in the paper. See if
they have any information for us.'

'I already did that.' My gaze flicks up to Summers, and I tell
him what happened when I called them earlier.

He sighs, puts his hands on his knees, and stands wearily.
'Unless you can remember anything else, then I'm not sure what
enquiries we can pursue next.'

'What, so that's it?' Jordan says. 'You're not going to do anything else?'

Summers hesitates for a while, as if he's making up his mind
exactly which excuse to use. 'What can we do? Usually, there are
procedures we can follow—talking to witnesses, doing house-to-
house enquiries, some of which we've done, but Chloe has no
memory of what happened. She could've gone anywhere and done
anything on the day she went missing. How can we realistically
investigate something we have no idea of? It's not just looking for a
needle in a haystack. We need to find the haystack first.'

I rub at my right eye, which has started twitching now. I almost
want to laugh.

'If you remember or discover something else, phone me and
we'll check it out, but in the meantime, we have nowhere to go with
this. I'm sorry, but I'm still not satisfied a crime has even been com-
mitted, and since we have no independent witnesses to verify the
events you've described . . .' He leaves his words dangling in the air
like a shrug, giving me one last expressionless look before heading
out of the room.

Jordan follows him, and I hear mumbled voices before the front door clicks shut. I jig my right leg up and down, trying to work off the raw energy accumulating inside. My skin feels tight against my muscles, my clothes irritating and scratchy.

When Jordan comes back in, he stands in the doorway. And now even he's got a shadow of wary doubt in his eyes as he looks at me. 'So . . . um . . . what do you want to do next?' He rubs a hand over his hair.

I avert my gaze, unable to face the possibility of losing my one and only ally. 'What *can* I do?'

Chapter Twenty-Nine

I sleep in the spare room sandwiched between the bathroom and Jordan's bedroom. He's made up the bed for me with clean, pine-scented sheets and left a folded towel at the end of it with an unopened packet of soap. I touch the soap and smile at his thoughtfulness.

The floorboards upstairs creak under my weight, and I think that's a good thing. An early alarm system. But it still doesn't make me feel completely safe, so I turn the key in the bedroom door and position a wooden chair under the handle. If someone comes to get me in the middle of the night, at least I'll hear it. I undress and pull on a T-shirt from my bag. I should've brought more things with me from home. Tomorrow I'll go back and get some when Liam's at work.

Liam. What's he doing now? Getting drunk and angry and blaming me for everything? Or consoling himself in the arms of Julianne? Well, at least they can be together now without me standing in the way. Good luck to her—that's all I can say.

I turn off the bedside lamp and get into bed, listening to the unfamiliar sounds of the house: the hot water pipes ticking, the fridge downstairs humming, and an owl hooting outside on the roof. Jordan's footsteps go into the bathroom. The light clicks on, then the toilet flushes. The floorboards creak outside my door, and I know he's standing just on the other side. I clutch the duvet around me and listen. Part of me wants to open the door and see that smile of his for reassurance. Part of me is terrified.

Seconds pass. His weight shifts. Then his footsteps disappear up the hall, and his bedroom door closes. I close my eyes, expecting to have trouble sleeping, but I'm so exhausted I fall asleep straight away. It's not restful sleep, though. I dream I'm back there again, running through the woods.

There's no moon this time, and it's so dark I can hardly see. An owl chases me. I can hear it calling close behind, feel the cold air against my back as its wings flap. Any minute its claws will dig into my head and attack.

But the owl isn't the only thing out there. Even though I can't see anyone watching me, can't hear the sound of footsteps behind me, I know he's there.

Branches tear into my face as I run through the trees, ripping away the skin until no flesh is left and I'm just sinew and bone. They slice through my eyes, too, and I'm completely blind now.

A howling noise deafens me, reverberating through my ears. And then I hear nothing. I'm running and running, but I can't see and I can't hear. All I know is something's chasing after me.

Then I fall into somewhere deep, dark. A bottomless pit. I'm falling and falling, and no one is out there who can drag me back to the surface.

I sit bolt upright in bed, bathed in cold sweat, panting hard. I blink in the darkness, eyes adjusting to the unfamiliar shapes that loom towards me. A chair under the door. A chest of drawers in the corner. A single wardrobe. And then I remember I'm in Jordan's bedroom.

It's just a nightmare. It can't hurt me. I'm safe!

Except it's not a nightmare. Not really. It's chillingly real. And I wonder if I will ever really be safe again. Because even if Summers and the doctors don't believe me, even if it all points to me imagining this whole thing, even if *I* don't know whether to believe me half the time anymore, what about the sleeping tablets? If I really took them willingly, where the hell are they? Something isn't right about this.

I throw back the covers, swing my legs over the side of the bed, and lean forward, head resting in my hands, until my breathing goes back to normal. I go over to the window and pull back the curtains, staring out at the view to try to drag my thoughts away from roaming the dark pathways in my head. The frustration and uncertainty of waiting for some madman to come back and kill me will drive me insane before he can finish off the job.

A fox stealthily creeps across the lawn. The moon is clear and vibrant, the stars glittering back at me.

Getting back into bed, I stare into the darkness, too afraid to close my eyes and sleep again. Summers's question keeps revolving in my head. *What would you do next?* But all I can think is, *Why Me? Why did he pick me?* I could've been stalked before I was taken. Or maybe it was a chance sighting. Did I know the person? Had I seen him before? Spoken to him, maybe? Did I walk past him to work every day, unaware? How long would I have until he found me again?

I give up at 5:00 a.m., no closer to finding the answer. Some thread must connect everything together, but I have no memory of it. Nothing in my head can help me now. Maybe it's better not to know anything. To not see it coming.

At that moment, I have an irrational wish for my kidnapper just to get it over with quickly. To come and get me right now and kill me. I can't stand this torture, trying so hard to think of some kind of clue but trying desperately not to think at the same time.

The constant fear is a burning hole in my chest as I blindly wait for something dreadful and painful to happen. I'm driving myself mad with it. I want it to be over.

My face aches with the pressure of unshed tears, but I won't cry anymore. Crying won't help me stay alive. I get dressed and go into the bathroom. After splashing cold water on my face, I look at my reflection in the mirror. My pupils are huge, my hair wild, my skin pale and waxy. I brush my teeth, go downstairs, and make a cup of tea. Sitting out on the kitchen step, I chain-smoke until the sun rises over the garden.

Butterflies and bees flutter around flowers, stopping every now and then on one that takes their fancy. Birds sing their morning chorus. Clouds glide through the air. I don't know how everything can look so normal yet be so far removed from it.

Jordan finds me awhile later. He's wearing faded jeans and an old T-shirt, his hair rumpled from sleep. He runs a hand over it as he walks into the kitchen, humming a tune I don't recognise. He stops when he sees me and breaks into a smile, his whole face lighting up. 'Oh, hi. Didn't see you there.'

I find myself smiling back, drinking in the sight of him. 'Hi.'

'Did you sleep OK?'

For some reason, I can't help laughing. It sounds shrill, a noise that could split me in two. No, not shrill; it sounds mad. I am actually going round the bend now. I can feel it. 'Not really.'

'No, I don't suppose you did.' His smile drops and he looks serious, his eyes gentle. 'I admire your courage, you know.'

'I'm not courageous at all. I'm scared to death. I always have been.' I jump up and change the subject to dilute the fear. 'Are you hungry? Let me make you breakfast. It's the least I can do.'

He waves me back down. 'Sit. I'll do it.'

'But you've been kind enough to let me stay here, so I should do it.'

'You're a guest. And guests don't have to lift a finger. Besides, you've been through a lot. You deserve a bit of pampering.'

My cheeks flush then, but I don't know if it's with gratitude or something else.

'So.' He peers in the fridge. 'What do you fancy? Poached eggs on toast? Cereal? Or I can do a mean bacon sandwich.'

'A bacon sandwich sounds perfect.'

He puts toast in the toaster and bacon under the grill, and we talk about how good the weather is this year for May, the last book we read, the fox I saw in the garden that Jordan's nicknamed Foxy (as original as the cat's name). Nothing important or heavy. I like that he doesn't force me to talk about what's going on in my head. It's nice to be distracted with normalcy for a while. And as he works, it feels like this *is* the most normal thing in the world. Like we're an old married couple used to the rhythms of each other. It's easy and relaxing, something I only had with Liam in the very beginning.

John clatters through the cat flap as Jordan dishes up the bacon sandwiches. 'Yeah, thought you might be back when you smelled this!' Jordan says to him, cutting off some crispy fat and putting it in John's bowl. John wolfs it down and purrs loudly, looking up expectantly for more.

'What's on the agenda for today, then?' Jordan asks as he hands me a plate.

'I've got an appointment with Dr Drew this morning. I also need to go back to my house and pick up some more of my stuff.'

'I have classes this morning, but I can go with you this afternoon to your house if you like?' He takes a bite of sandwich.

'Are you sure? I don't want to put you to any trouble.'

He swallows. 'It's no trouble. We can get a lot more in the camper. And besides, until we find out what happened, this psycho could still be after you. I just want to make sure you're safe.'

Tears of appreciation prick at my eyes. The promise I made myself in the dead of night not to cry is hard to keep up in the cold light of day. But I have to hold it together. My survival depends on it. 'I feel safe here.'

'I'm glad about that, but if you go anywhere without me, text or phone me so I know where you are. That way, if something happens, I'll be able to find you.'

'Thanks.'

'You don't have to thank me.' He shrugs casually, but a note of vulnerability filters through his voice. 'It's what friends do, isn't it?'

'I've left Liam,' I tell Dr Drew.

He raises his eyebrows slightly. 'And how do you feel about that?'

'I don't know. I haven't had much time to process it, really.'

'Do you want to think about it now? We have time.'

I stare over his shoulder out the window. 'It feels like I've been living in the middle of a volcano for years. I've been drowning underneath molten lava that's bubbling away, threatening to erupt at any moment. Now the volcano's gone off, and my life's just exploded.'

'Volcanoes are destructive. But they also create fertility and life. A natural cycle of growth.'

'Yes.' I nod. 'I feel sad, of course, but I just feel this overwhelming relief, too. And I've got a little spark of hope. A flicker of excitement that there are new possibilities out there. My life doesn't have to be controlled anymore. I can do what I want, say what I want, go where I want. I feel free.'

'Then that's a good thing. And you certainly look physically better than when I last saw you, so something must agree with you.'

'But then there's the other problem, isn't there? The person still out there that I don't know about. I mean, it's weird, isn't it? I left Liam before, and I don't even remember. I must've gone through the same thoughts before, done the same things, and I can't bloody remember it. And that's the key, isn't it? If I'm naturally retracing my footsteps, what would I have done next?'

'Only you can answer that.'

'But I don't *know* the answer!' I gnaw on my lip. 'I remembered a little bit about dropping my phone at home before I left him. If I remember that, why can't I remember anything else? Anything useful.'

'Maybe you're thinking about it too much. Sometimes if we stop thinking about a problem, the answer becomes obvious.'

'How can I *not* think about it?'

'I know it's hard, but stressing and worrying will only make things worse.'

'That's always easy for people to say when it's not their problem. I'm in limbo. Waiting for something to happen and watching for someone I don't even know exists.'

'Do you want to go over the things you've told me and see if we can find the answer together about where you might have gone?'

I sit up in my seat. 'Yes. If it might help.'

'All right, let's see.' Dr Drew clasps his hands together over his stomach. 'You left Liam and went to Sara's.'

'Yes.'

'You bought some food and supplies.'

I nod.

'Then you spent the night in her spare room, and the following day you went missing.' Deep in thought, he steeples his fingers. 'You'd circled some flats to rent because you didn't want Liam to know where you were and cause trouble when he found out you'd gone.'

'That's right.'

'You called the first number you marked, but it was above a pub, and you didn't like the idea of that. The second and third flats were already taken.'

'Yes.'

'Then you presumably left Sara's house without your purse or bag.'

'Why wouldn't I take my purse with me?'

Dr Drew tilts his head. 'You couldn't have been going shopping without any money, so that's ruled out. You could've been just visiting a friend. You could've gone back to your house to collect more items. You could've gone for a walk.'

'I don't think I would've gone for a walk.'

'Why not?'

'I don't walk to clear my head or get perspective on things like some people do. Going for a walk wouldn't really achieve anything.'

'Could you have gone to the college? To see your boss or a colleague?'

I know now I didn't go to see Theresa, but Jordan . . . would I have gone to see him? To tell him I'd left Liam? No, he would've mentioned it, wouldn't he? And I told him I needed time to get my head together. 'I doubt it. I would've wanted to get on with things. Arrange things. Start organizing my new life without Liam.'

'Exactly!' He holds a finger up. 'From what I see, I think you want to take control of your life. You made the decision to leave Liam, and your first instinct was to go to Sara's for some breathing space. The next instinct was to phone your bank and give them her address so you could have some sort of financial security without Liam knowing. *Then* you looked at flats to rent.'

I frown. 'Yes, but that still doesn't help me, because I've now hit a brick wall.'

'I think you already have the answer in here, my dear.' He taps the side of his head. 'Would you have given up looking for somewhere to live just because those rental properties weren't an option?'

I think about it. 'No, I suppose not.'

He smiles. 'So that would be your logical next step. You were actively seeking somewhere to live.'

'But where? Where would I have gone?' I lift my hands in the air in a questioning gesture.

'Where can you find a multitude of places to rent in one place?'

'An estate agent.'

'Exactly. That's where you should start. Would you have wanted to stay in the area or move somewhere else?'

'I'd want to stay here. It's closer to work, and I know the area.' I think of the town centre. Loads of estate agents are there.

'Then that's the next step. You just have to see where it leads you.'

Chapter Thirty

I think about phoning Summers and telling him about the estate agents but decide against it. It's not as if I have concrete proof of a crime happening yet, so he'd just fob me off anyway. He isn't going to save me, and he can do nothing that I can't. No, it's simply a matter of seeing if someone remembers me.

When Jordan comes back from college, we walk into town. He offers to drive, but I would've been walking before, so I want to relive it as accurately as possible in case it sparks off a memory. We hit the town centre from the same end I would've arrived at from Sara's. Two shops down on the left is the first estate agent. Jordan opens the door, and we step inside.

The place has four desks, all empty. As we close the door, a suited man in his early twenties, who smells as if he's poured half a bottle of aftershave over himself, appears through a doorway at the back, chewing something.

'You caught me eating my lunch!' He grins sheepishly. 'We've got two people off sick with this flu bug that's been going around, so I'm trying to do everything.' He shakes first Jordan's hand, then mine. 'I'm Guy. How can I help?' His gaze lingers on my face for a moment longer than necessary. I've covered my skin in concealer and foundation to try to hide the scratches, so I don't know if that's what he's looking at or whether he recognises me.

'I was wondering if you remember me coming in here nine days ago?' I ask. 'I was probably looking for a place to rent.'

'Probably?' He tilts his head, seemingly unable to tear his gaze away from my face. 'Don't you know?' He laughs.

'No, I had an accident, and I can't remember. I looked different, though. My hair was long and dark.'

'Oh, sorry to hear that.' He looks awkward then. 'Um . . . I don't remember you, but you could've seen one of the other members of staff. As I said, they're off sick this week. You can come back another time if you like, and ask them.'

'It's pretty urgent that I find out.'

'Let me just check our database and see if any of them added you to our mailing list.' He leans over a computer screen at one of the empty desks and types in a few things. 'What did you say your name was?'

'Chloe Benson.'

'Right.' More tapping. 'Well, I can't see your name on here, so you probably didn't come in. We do try and get everyone on the database so we can send out details as soon as any property comes in.'

'Could you possibly ring them at home for me, just to double-check? Maybe they forgot to add me to the list for some reason.' I give him a pleading smile.

He gives me a strange look. 'Wow, you're really desperate for a rental, aren't you?' He shrugs. 'I suppose there's no harm in phoning them.' He waves a hand at a couple of chairs in front of the desk. 'Have a seat.'

I chew on the skin at the side of my finger while we wait, listening to Guy as he tries to explain to his colleagues what I've told him and then give a description of me.

Ten minutes later, we're back on the street. No one remembers me.

Jordan points to another estate agent across the road. 'Let's try in there.'

Two women sit behind desks. An older woman with severely cut short hair and glasses is on the phone. The other one, with a black ponytail and heavy makeup, gets up and greets us with a smile. 'Can I help you?'

'Yes. Do you remember if I was in here nine days ago looking for a place to rent?'

She scrutinises my face for a moment. 'Which property were you interested in? Or did you just want to go on our mailing list?'

'I don't know. I don't know if I definitely did come in. Do you remember me? My hair was different, though.' I smooth a hand over my head. 'It was long and dark and wavy.'

She glances at Jordan questioningly before dragging her gaze back to me. 'You don't remember?'

I sigh impatiently, sick to death of explaining. 'I've lost my memory. I had a head injury, so I can't remember whether I came in here or not. That's why I'm asking if you recognise me.'

'Oh. God.' She tilts her head, appraising me again. 'Um . . . I don't think I recognise you.' Her colleague puts the phone down then, and she turns back to her. 'Sheila, do you remember this lady coming in about nine days ago, looking for a place to rent?'

Sheila looks up at me.

'My hair was different,' I say. 'Long and dark and wavy.'

A light of recognition sparks in her face. 'Oh, yes. Yes, I do remember. Your name's Chloe?'

'Yes, how did you remember that?'

'My daughter's name is Chloe. It's hard to forget.' She smiles. 'Did you want to go and look at it again?'

'What did I look at?'

Sheila's colleague sits behind her desk again and watches me with interest. 'This lady's had an accident and lost her memory. She doesn't remember what happened,' she tells her with a gossipy glint in her eye.

'Oh, that's awful,' Sheila gasps. 'Are you OK?'

'Yes,' I say quickly. No time for small talk. 'So what happened? Did you show me a place?'

'I did. Hang on a sec; let me get the details.' She walks to a metal filing cabinet behind her desk and pulls open a drawer, sliding folders along until she finds the one she wants. She puts it on her desk, then flicks through and hands me a sheet of paper with details of a flat on it. There's a picture of the outside of the building at the top of the page, along with internal photos, room specifications, and an inventory of exactly what's included in the rental underneath. 'This one.' She taps the paper.

I pick it up to see if it looks familiar. It doesn't. Inside it's clean and bright but colourless and bland. A blank canvas. I would want to add warmth. Some bright throws over the sofa, patterned cushions, contrasting bedding, Mediterranean colours.

'You wanted a small place. Most of what we have at the moment are for executive rentals, but this one came on our books a couple of days before you walked in. It's a two-bedroom flat on the top floor in quite a nice area. There's communal parking and a security intercom system. I seem to remember you wanted somewhere with intercom that wasn't on the ground floor.'

'And you took me to view it?'

'Yes, the place is empty at the moment, so we went straight there. You really liked it. It was only partially furnished and you wanted fully furnished, but the price is good because the owner wants it rented quick, and it's in a great location. You said you didn't expect to find somewhere so quickly, so you hadn't brought any money with you for the first month's rental. We also require a security deposit and some ID, you see, so you were going to come back with it all later that day, but you never did. I just assumed you'd had second thoughts or found somewhere else.'

'You took her to view the flat in your car? Or did you walk there?' Jordan asks.

'We went in my car. And then I dropped you back here. You said you were going to do some window-shopping for some new things for the flat on your way home. You seemed really excited about it all; that's why I was a little surprised when you didn't come in again.'

'Where did you see her last?' Jordan asks.

'We parked in the council car park behind, and you walked with me back here and then said goodbye outside. I didn't see where you went afterwards.'

My mind whirrs with questions she can't answer. Which shops did I go in? Was I looking for furniture or knick-knacks? Did I talk to anyone? Encounter anyone strange on the way back to Sara's?

'What time was that?' I ask.

'Er . . . probably about five-ish.'

I stand up and give her a smile, but my facial muscles don't seem to be connected to my brain anymore, and it quivers on my face. 'Thanks. You've been very helpful.'

'You're welcome. It's still available if you want it. Just let me know.'

We exit the estate agent, and I stand with my back to the doorway, scanning the shops up and down the street. I could've gone in any of them or none of them. I could've walked back to Sara's with a happy smile on my face and a spring in my step. I could've gone to the moon for all I knew.

'Your purse was still at Sara's, wasn't it?' Jordan asks.

'Yes.'

'And you were intending to go back and get it to pay for the rental. That means it's likely you never made it back there at all.'

'So whatever happened next happened between here and Sara's.'

My bones feel hollow, as if they won't hold me up for much longer. My legs tremble.

'I'm here, Chloe.' Jordan grips my hand more tightly, and I lean against him. 'I won't let anything happen to you.'

Chapter Thirty-One

I've come this far, and it feels like I'm so close now to finding out what happened. I want to know the answer, but at the same time, I'm scared to death. Maybe there's something in what Dr Drew said about the human brain blocking traumatic memories with amnesia. Some things are just too awful to remember. And if I know, if I *really* know what happened, then I'll have to think about it. Relive it. See that horrific underground tomb. Feel the terror again firsthand.

But I have no alternative. I can't spend the rest of my life looking over my shoulder all the time, wondering who might be coming to get me. No, I have to know.

'You look really pale. Shall we find a café and have something to eat first before you keel over?' Jordan says.

'Yes. Maybe that's a good idea.'

Jordan leads me down the street, his hand on my elbow, gently guiding me along through all the people. I wonder what their nightmares are. What's the worst thing that's ever happened to them all? What's the most they can take before they crack and fall apart? I pick out the men in the crowd, scrutinizing their faces for something I recognise. Perhaps it was it one of them. The old man in the anorak. The skinny young guy with long hair and tattoos up his arms. The geeky-looking guy with glasses. The man in a business suit chatting on his mobile phone. The man cycling in and out of cars, with a fluorescent jacket on.

It could be anybody. When you start looking for it, everyone seems sinister or weird. He could be watching me right this second, and I'd never know. How many men were there in the UK? Thirty million? More? How do you find one in thirty million? There could even be more than one of them. Two men working as a team. I vaguely remember reading about two male serial killers once who worked together. I can't remember their names.

I'm barely breathing by the time we arrive at the café, and I grip Jordan's arm tightly.

'Here, you sit, and I'll get you something to eat.' Jordan points to an empty table on the little terrace in front of the building that overlooks the street. Two young women at the table next to me are chatting noisily about the latest celebrity gossip. A lone man on the other side is tucking into a toasted sandwich and typing away on his laptop. None of them looks at me as I sit down.

'What would you like?'

I'm not hungry in the slightest. My tongue feels too big for my mouth. My teeth feel like they don't belong in my jaw. I glance at what the man's eating. 'Something like that, maybe?'

'OK. I'll be back in a minute.' He disappears into the shop and leaves me scanning faces in the crowd.

Ten minutes later, he returns with two golden-brown cheese toasties, a mug of tea, and a frothy cappuccino on a tray. 'I forgot to ask if you wanted tea or coffee, so I got both.'

There it is again, the thoughtfulness that is just Jordan. Despite the worry and fear, a jolt of happiness spears my heart like an electric shock. I smile at him with appreciation.

'Do you know what you would've been window-shopping for?' Jordan sets everything on the table and puts the tray on the empty seat next to him.

'I wouldn't have wanted to take anything with me from home. I don't want to be reminded of everything. Liam can have the lot.' I think about the sparsely decorated flat in the photo. What would I need immediately, and what could wait? What would make me feel more comfortable in my new home? It had the basic kitchen supplies, but I could probably do with things like a decent potato peeler and knives. I wouldn't have worried about pots and pans because a couple of each was listed on the details, and it would only be me now. 'Maybe some kitchen utensils. A bit of furniture, too, probably. Just a bedside table and maybe a lamp. Nothing expensive or fussy.' I glance up and down the street at the shops. 'I like wooden stuff. You know, like your kitchen table. I love Sara's furniture, too. I always wanted a lot of wood in the house, but Liam went for the modern, polished stuff—glass, chrome. Everything with no character.'

'The only shop that sells wooden stuff is Nightingale's.' He tilts his head to the other side of the street. 'And Kitchen Dreams would do the kitchen stuff.' He glances at his watch. 'We could try them first before they close and then do the rest of the shops if we have time. What do you think?'

'I love the stuff in Nightingale's. I haven't been in there much in the last few years because Liam doesn't like it, but, yes, that's probably where I would've gone.'

So that's what we do. We finish our lunch and walk across the street to Nightingale's. It's set on two floors, with lots of Indonesian furniture, oak, mahogany, and reclaimed wood that's been made into all sorts of things. The door is propped open with a tree trunk that's now a plant holder.

It's wood heaven. Things crammed everywhere so you have to wind yourself round the furniture. It's also very expensive. Much more than I would be able to afford on my own.

The middle-aged salesman is dressed in black trousers and a white shirt. He wears a red-and-blue-checked bowtie and reminds me of an old country gentleman. He's chatting with a woman about teak oil, his well-spoken accent drifting towards me. We wander up and down the shop, my hands touching objects as I go by—a candleholder made of driftwood, a wooden photo frame, a carved salad bowl.

As I turn to look at a reclaimed wooden mirror, my reflection stares back, and a spark of memory hits me like a surging pain in between my eyes. I stop and put my hand on a nearby table to stop the room spinning around me.

'What is it?' Jordan whispers in my ear, sliding his arm round my waist for support. 'Do you remember something?'

'I . . . I've been here recently.'

Jordan's gaze meets mine in the mirror.

'I remember. I *did* come in here after going to the estate agents. I had a look around and . . .' I glance over at the salesman. 'I spoke to him. I said I was looking for something a bit cheaper, and he told me about a place. Something . . .' I squeeze my eyes shut, trying to remember it all. 'He told me about somewhere nearby that makes cheap pine furniture. I don't remember where, though, and I don't remember what happened after.'

'OK.' He holds me close, but not too tightly. 'That's helpful, then.'

The salesman is still chatting with the customer, talking about distressing wood now. I want to storm over there and scream at the woman to shut up. I want to grab the salesperson by his shirt and demand to know what he told me. Where he sent me. Hysteria is just a breath away. Jordan takes my hand and leads me towards the salesman. We hover, waiting for him to finish. I shift from foot to foot, twisting my earring round and round. I'm so close to unlocking the answer that I can taste the adrenaline in the back of my throat.

The salesman catches my eye, then gives the woman a patient smile. 'Well, if you need any more help, just ask. Feel free to browse some more. Looking doesn't cost anything.' He chuckles, as if he uses this line frequently. The woman wanders up the other end of the shop, leaving me free to question him.

'Hi, do you remember I came in here nine days ago?' I blurt out, fighting to quell the tremor in my voice.

'What were you looking for?' He gives me the same practised, polite smile he used on the woman.

'Furniture. My hair was different then. Long and dark. I said you had some lovely pieces, but I was looking for something a bit cheaper, and you recommended a place locally that made pine furniture.'

He raises a finger in the air. 'Ah, yes, that's right. I do remember. You know, our wood is very high quality, and it's only made from sustainable sources or reclaimed materials, but our prices are still competitive.'

'Yes, it all looks amazing,' I say quickly, 'but you told me about somewhere else. The place that sells pine. Where is it?'

He nods a little, resigned to the fact he's lost a sale. 'He's an excellent carpenter, but he works with the cheaper cuts, not the kind of discerning craftsmanship we have here.'

'Can you tell us where it is?' Jordan asks firmly. I have the feeling we could be here all day with the salesperson trying to talk to us.

'My boss will kill me if he knew I'm telling you this, so please keep it a secret.' He turns around to an antique wooden desk used as a counter and opens one of the drawers. He plucks out a card and hands it to me. 'This is the place. Tom's Wood Shack. It's not really a shop, more of a workshop, really, but he makes things to order, too.'

'Thank you.' I practically pull Jordan out of the shop.

Chapter Thirty-Two

It's a forty-five-minute walk to the address. The town tapers out here into fields and lanes with views of open countryside all around. After the last house on the road, a dirt track runs along the side of it, with a carved wooden sign on a fencepost that says "Tom's Wood Shack." An arrow points us down the track, so that's where we head. About fifty metres along it, I can see a couple of old barns that must be his workshop, and some ramshackle outhouses. In the distance behind the barns, a dog barks. A car whizzes along the main road.

I stop and sniff the air. The aromatic scent of pine hits my nostrils, and that's when I know for sure I came here before. That smell, sweet and perfumed, triggers something in my brain. Flashing lights pop in my head like an explosion of fireworks. A chill of fear freezes my muscles, and I can't move. The sensation of someone watching me is so strong I almost feel a burning gaze boring into my skin.

Jordan turns around when he realises I'm no longer walking beside him down the track. 'What is it?' He strides back to me, puts his hands on my shoulders.

'I . . . this . . . I . . . not . . .' My mouth trembles so hard I can't get the words out.

'You recognise this place?' His eyes are wide and questioning.

'I . . . horrible . . . feeling.' I'm panting now, sharp jerking breaths. Not enough air. I need more air. 'Something . . . some . . . thing bad.' Reaching deep inside, I struggle to grasp the distant memory and pull it to the surface. Vivid images flood inside my head now. The last time I was here.

One minute Tom was showing me some pine tables, and the next, he grabbed me from behind. One arm around my throat, holding me tight. One big hand over my mouth, stifling the scream of terror. For a moment I was so shocked I couldn't move. I froze. Numb. As if the life were already sucked right out of me.

Then the adrenaline kicked in, and I struggled. But he was too big. Too strong. Couldn't move. I could hardly breathe through his hand, sniffing oxygen hard through my nose.

Then . . .

A blank. That's where the memory fractures.

Before I register what's happening, Jordan is gripping my hand and leading me back up the track towards the main road. There's a bench a little farther along, in front of the houses. He sits me on it and crouches down on his haunches at my side, taking my hands in his and rubbing them vigorously.

'OK, just breathe, Chloe. You need to calm down. Nothing's going to happen. I'm here.' He keeps his gaze on me.

I nod and shudder at the same time. Breathe. In. Out. Yes. Breathe. I take in deep gulps of air. My face is on fire, but my hands and feet are like blocks of ice.

'Just keep breathing. You're doing great.'

I don't know how long we stay like that. It feels like an eternity until my breath slows and the shivers stop. My cheeks are wet, and I didn't even realise I was crying.

'Do you want to tell me what happened?' He sits beside me. 'Did you remember something specific? Did it happen there?'

'At first I didn't, but the smell and the sound of the dog barking sparked something off. I got a really, *really* bad feeling. Like I was going to die. Like someone was suffocating me. And then I remembered him grabbing hold of me, his hand gagging my mouth so I couldn't scream. But that's where the memory stops. After that there's just this big black void again.'

'I don't want you anywhere near here.' He glances around, getting to his feet. 'It's best if I get you home safely, then you can call Summers and let him investigate things. Are you up to walking, or shall I call a cab?' He pulls his mobile out of his pocket.

'I don't want to wait for a cab.' I stand up on fragile legs. 'Let's go.'

He takes my hand and we walk away, but I can't stop looking over my shoulder.

———

When we get back to Jordan's house, I sit on the step outside the kitchen door and light a cigarette. I take deep drags as John winds his way round and round my legs, nudging at me with his head.

'Here.' Jordan hands me a mug of strong coffee and sits next to me. 'Are you OK?'

It's the last thing I want him to ask. I'm not OK. Far from it. 'I just keep seeing that place in my head. Being underground. Wanting to live and not knowing if I would. Running for my life through those woods. Part of me wishing I was already dead because the fear was too much.' Inside I'm a quivering wreck, but my voice sounds surprisingly calm, as if I'm detached from it all. As if it happened to someone else.

'It must've been terrifying.'

'I don't want to think about it, though. I just want to forget it happened, but I can't. I don't want to be scared all the time, but I am. It's like I've exchanged one fear for another.'

'Liam, you mean?'

I take a sip of coffee, and the bitterness hits the roof of my mouth. 'Yes.'

'But you left him, and you escaped being held captive. You can get through the rest.'

'I should call Summers.' I get to my feet and go into the kitchen. I pick up my mobile then dial his number and wait for him to answer.

'Chloe? How are you?' Summers asks.

In the background, I hear phones ringing and loud voices talking urgently. 'I've found out something you need to know.'

'Yes?' he says quickly; and then, 'No, I'll be there in ten minutes.'

'Pardon?'

'Sorry, I was talking to someone else. We've got a major incident going on here. It's all hands on deck. What did you find out?'

'I went to an estate agent in town. The woman there took me to see a flat that I wanted to rent. I said I was going to go back and get some money for a deposit, since I'd left my purse at Sara's. Then she said she dropped me back at the estate agent, and I went window-shopping.'

'No, get the other armed response unit out, too,' Summers says to someone. Then to me, 'Sorry, Chloe, carry on.'

'I went to Nightingale's in the high street, and they told me about a place called Tom's Wood Shack.' I look at Jordan, who's watching me closely. 'When Jordan and I went there, I had this horrible feeling something bad had happened before, and then I had a flash of memory. Tom attacked me. He grabbed me round the throat so I couldn't move and clamped a hand over my mouth. I was trying to struggle, but I couldn't. He was too strong. That's where the memory stops, though, and I don't know what happened after that. But I know I never made it back to Sara's, because my bag and purse were still there.' I expect him to trivialise what I've said, make some excuse about plausible scenarios and rational explanations, but to my surprise, he doesn't.

'Right, Chloe, I'm going to have to go now and deal with what's going on here. But I'll get Flynn to pick up this Tom and bring him in for a formal interview. As soon as we have him at the station, I'll let you know, OK?'

'OK.'

'I'll call you later.' He hangs up.

I smoke more cigarettes, stubbing out one and then lighting another immediately. I'm unable to concentrate when Jordan speaks. My whole body is a jumble of nerves. All I can think about is the police getting Tom off the street so he can't get me again. What will he say when they question him? Will he deny it? Will he be smug and pleased with himself that he's managed to get away with it for so long? Does he have another poor woman tied up in that underground hole to take my place?

'. . . will be OK . . . Summers . . .' I'm so lost in frantic thought that I don't hear Jordan speaking at first.

I shake my head and turn to look at him. 'Sorry, what were you saying?'

'I said it's going to be OK. They'll get him, and this will be all over.' He squeezes my hand. I squeeze it back and give him a tight smile, but I'm not so sure. Will it ever be over? When something like this happens, does the horror ever go away?

My mobile phone ringing later makes me drop my cigarette, burning my finger. My heart kicks out an erratic beat as I answer.

'I just wanted you to know that we've got Tom,' Summers says. 'Flynn's dealing with it until I can get back to the station. I'll keep you updated with any developments.'

'Thank you.' I release the breath I've been holding onto and slump forward with relief. My kidnapper is off the streets and can't hurt me now. I'm finally safe.

Chapter Thirty-Three

Jordan's mobile rings in his pocket. He pulls it out and says, 'Hey, Sis, how are things?' A pause. 'What?' He stands up, shoulders tensing. 'When?' He runs a hand over his hair. 'Is she OK?' A longer pause. 'I'll be there in about twenty minutes.' He hangs up and casts a worried look in my direction. 'That was my sister. Mum's had a fall and broken her hip. She's been taken to A&E. I have to get up there.'

'Of course—you go. I'll be fine.' I make ushering actions with my hands. 'There's no danger now, is there?'

'You're sure?' He looks torn. 'Do you want to come with me? I know it won't be much fun, but . . .'

'No. Really, you go. I'll just go back to my house and collect some more things while you're gone.'

'What about Liam?'

'It's OK; he'll be at work. And, anyway, there's nothing he can say to me now that's going to hurt me or make me change my mind.'

'I'll meet you back here later, then.' He grabs his keys and heads out the door, wearing a worried frown.

I walk to my house and stand outside, a million memories tumbling in . . .

The night I first met Liam. Sara and I were in a club, dancing. I was drunk. I wanted to dance all night, and laugh and flirt. Pretend I was all the things I wanted desperately to be. I was good at pretending by then.

He stood at the edge of the dance floor, watching me. It wasn't the fact he was watching me that made me look twice. It was the *way* he was watching me, as if I was the most beautiful woman he'd ever seen. As if I mesmerised him. Later he told me that the first minute he saw me, he knew I was the only woman for him. He said whatever it took, he was going to make me his.

The day Liam asked me to live with him, after only a month together, I was so happy, hopeful, and in love that of course I said yes. He brought me to life when I didn't even realise I was dead. I was awake for the first time in forever. When he picked me up from the flat I shared with a couple of nurses, we were both so excited about it. He wouldn't let go of my hand as he drove back here, and every few minutes he'd give me these little ecstatic looks, grinning from ear to ear. He carried me over the threshold, even though we weren't married yet, and I laughed so much my stomach hurt. It was going to be my first proper home. My first house. I thought we'd stay here forever.

I remembered the thrill of anticipation as I rushed home from work every day to put my own key into my own front door. I even relished the thought of housework, just because I was doing something useful to keep our place tidy and clean, how Liam liked it.

And I remembered making love on a blanket in the garden one summer's night. The scent of jasmine I'd planted wafting through the air. It was gentle and slow. Afterwards, we lay on our backs, staring at the stars as Liam taught me about the different constellations, with our warm limbs wrapped round each other and sweat cooling on our skin.

A few weeks before we were married, Liam had surprised me for my birthday by paying off the debt from my student loan, still hanging like an albatross around my neck. It was tough trying to survive at Uni alone, with no family support. Even though I worked in a shoe shop at weekends and a pub in the evenings, I was barely surviving. The cost of my rent alone was eating through the loan, never mind all the stuff I needed for my studies.

In the beginning, he took care of me and loved me. I'd been alone for most of my life, and suddenly there he was. He became my family, and I was so grateful for the safety and security he gave me. And I wonder if it's really his fault things went wrong, or mine? If I were stronger, I wouldn't have let it happen. Maybe I'm as stupid as Liam says, for thinking I could change someone who doesn't believe there's anything wrong with him.

Perhaps my childhood made it possible for someone like Liam to come along and manipulate me, take control of me. There was something programmed deep inside, waiting to surface, so I was destined to become a victim. Some inner need to seek love and praise at any cost.

Well, not anymore.

A twinge of regret and sadness hits me as I open the front door. I wander through the lounge and dining room, then into the kitchen. Everything looks the same as when I left it. Everything except me.

I take the stairs two at a time, retrieve a small holdall from the top shelf of my wardrobe, and begin packing. I grab a couple of pairs of shoes from boxes and put them in first. I slide clothes off hangers, fold them neatly, and layer them inside. Underwear from my drawers goes next. I don't want to take anything. I don't want clothes that remind me of this past life, but I can't afford to buy a whole new wardrobe, so I must.

I pack some toiletries: perfume, body lotion, shampoo, and hairspray. Then I go to my dressing table and open my jewellery box. I don't want the jewellery he bought me, but I put it all inside a wash bag. Maybe I'll sell it.

I lift up the top tray of the jewellery box and pick out the personal papers—marriage certificate, birth certificate, passport. I'm stuffing them all inside the wash bag when it hits me with a stark clarity, like a knife piercing through my skull. Icy coldness freezes underneath my skin, leaving me lightheaded and shivery. My knees buckle. I drop down to the stool behind me, warning bells clanging through my brain.

Passport. Birth Certificate. Identification.

I'd told the woman in the estate agent that I was coming back with some money and ID. The money and bank cards were in my purse at Sara's house, but I'd left my ID here.

What if I'd gone to Tom's Wood Shack and nothing had happened? What if I'd just looked at furniture and left? What if the vision I'd had when Jordan and I were there was just some kind of false memory like Dr Drew explained? Maybe I wanted it to be Tom so badly that I distorted the truth in my head.

And if I did leave there, I would've come back here next. Come to get my ID, so I could rent that flat and start to live again. But then I disappeared. I never made it back to Sara's. I just vanished off the face of the earth.

That's when I know it was Liam. Somehow—and I don't know how he did it—Liam did manage to get back from Scotland without anyone noticing.

Chapter Thirty-Four

Three things happen.

I hear a sound downstairs. My heart stops. I freeze.

'I know you're here, Chloe!' Liam's voice, calm but chillingly cold.

I can't move. Can't breathe. I'm just waiting to die. His footsteps echo on the laminate floor downstairs, heavy and rushed. He's searching for me. Then he's going to find a way to kill me. Make it look like suicide or an accident or another bad drug reaction. And hey, if that doesn't work, he'll take me somewhere and leave me to die. Ingenious.

My adrenaline kicks in and I stand up, my gaze frantically searching the room. My pulse pounds in my ears like white noise.

Where can I hide? Under the bed? He'll find me in a second.

In the wardrobe? Ditto.

The bathroom, then. Climb out of the window onto the kitchen extension below. But it's too small.

I rush to the bedroom window. There's about a three-metre drop. I risk breaking a bone, or death.

His footsteps on the stairs. 'You're so fucking stupid, Chloe. So gullible.'

My hand grips the handle as I look down. I'm scared. Terrified. I hate heights. Don't want to die. I try to open the window, but the handle doesn't budge. Every muscle in my body quivers as I yank it has hard as I can.

Nothing. It's locked.

The terror is like a rope coiled round me, squeezing tighter and tighter until it's hard to breathe.

'You stupid bitch.' Liam pulls me back by my shoulder and I slam into him, the back of my head hitting his chest.

I scream. I'm screaming and screaming.

He spins me round as if I weigh nothing. His fist flies towards my face, punching me hard on the cheek.

My head jerks to the left, a cracking sound reverberating in my ears. I taste something metallic in my mouth. Then I'm flying through the air. Banging into the dressing table. Falling to the floor. Landing hard on my shoulder. The breath knocked out of me. An explosion of colours in front of my eyes.

He stands over me, a manic, twisted smile on his face. 'You just won't bloody die, will you?'

I touch my cheek, pulsing from his fist. Tears spill down my face. I scrabble on my heels and hands to get away from him, but when my back hits the wall, I know it's futile. He'll outrun me. He's stronger than I am. He's blocking the door, and there's nowhere to go.

And in the end, Liam always gets what he wants.

Something else replaces the terror. A resigned calmness, like the blood has already stopped flowing through my veins. I know I'm going to die, and I give up. It's easier, just like it's always been easier to give up and give in. The waiting is finally over. No one can save me now. Summers doesn't know where I am. Jordan is at the hospital. I don't have the strength to fight him anymore.

I want him to get it over with. Quickly. I don't want to suffer. Let Liam win. That's what he's wanted all along. And I don't care now. Too tired to care.

He kneels down next to me and strokes my already swelling cheek gently with the back of his hand. I flinch at his touch. 'Look what you made me do.' He tilts his head, like a dog trying to understand a human command.

'Why?' I cry. 'Why couldn't you just divorce me if you didn't love me? Why all this? Why try to kill me?'

'You don't get it, do you?' He shakes his head and makes a tutting sound. 'You're mine, darling. You're my wife. You can't just fucking leave me. *I* get to decide what happens. Not you!' He shouts, and a spray of spit flies from his mouth and lands on my face.

I fight the nausea welling up. 'So you knew? You knew I was going to leave before you went to Scotland?'

'Of course I knew! I'm not stupid. I'm not like you. Not needy and weak and pathetic.'

'What happened, then?' I suddenly want to know. If I'm going to die, and I know I am, then I want to know exactly what happened. I want to finally piece together the hole missing from my head.

'Shut up, you lying bitch.' He slams my head into the wall. Bells ring in my ears, and my whole world turns black.

Chapter Thirty-Five

When I wake up, the bedroom is dark. I don't know whether it's nighttime or the blackout curtains are closed.

I'm lying on my side, facing the door. Someone's making soft whimpering sounds. It's me. My hands are tied behind me, wrists bound together. My ankles are tied, too. I can't open my right eye properly; it's swollen and painful, like my cheek. A gag is tight around my mouth. I run my tongue over my teeth, and one feels loose. I taste blood.

And I can remember something.

I try to move my hands and feet, but plastic cable ties dig into my skin, and my limbs feel heavy and bruised. Pain in my back, my side. A pressure in my chest. It's hard to breathe through it.

Liam laughs. I turn my head slowly towards the sound. He's sitting on the edge of the bed to the side of me, watching. Grinning at his wife, who's trussed up like a turkey. He looks surprisingly normal and relaxed.

I try to speak, but it comes out a gargled sound through the gag. I can't hold my head up any longer, so I let it drop to the floor.

'What? Does Chloe want to say something?' He takes a swig of beer from the bottle in his hand. His Adam's apple bobs up and down as he swallows.

I know what happened now. Not all of it. Most of it. Maybe when my head hit the wall, it did something inside. Or maybe being here with him like this has kick-started my memory spontaneously. Can another trauma recover the memories the first trauma made you forget?

He walks towards me. I don't move. Don't even try to struggle. I just lie there and look up at him.

'What? You don't want to put up a fight? Not like last time?' He kneels beside me. 'Yeah, you were struggling like a wild thing until I injected you with the liquid Silepine. Then you were out like a light.' He laughs. 'Katya fought, too, you know.'

I breathe fast, shallow sniffs through my nose. *Katya? His ex-girlfriend?*

'That's what I liked about you both in the beginning. It's why I picked you. You were feisty and independent, but if you scratched just under the surface, you were vulnerable and fragile. It's so easy to mould someone into what you want. Watch them turn into your perfect woman and know that it's all just for you. Their energy dies, and they become compliant and eager to please. It's all just a matter of control and time. She said she was leaving, too. Said she was going back to Moldova and I'd never see her again.' He smiles, a faraway look in his eyes, as if he's lost in some distant memory. 'Didn't get very far, though. Maybe you met her down there, hmm? Probably not much left now, though. Bet the rats had a field day. Dust to dust and all that.'

I close my eyes, hot tears sliding down my face and soaking into the carpet. I know for certain now I'll never escape. He did it before and got away with it. He killed his girlfriend and never even had a bad night's sleep over it.

My husband is a psycho.

'Why did you cut it?' He strokes my hair and takes another swig of beer, swirls it round in his mouth before swallowing. 'Silent treatment, eh?' He yanks my gag down with such force it feels like he's ripped away some of my skin with it. He leans in close so his face is centimetres away from mine. I smell beer and sweat. The tension radiates out of him like something feral and sour I can almost taste.

My mouth waters with bitterness. I swallow and lick my lips. More blood on my tongue.

'You can scream if you want; no one's going to hear you. The neighbours are still at work.'

I won't give him the satisfaction of it. Instead, I croak out, 'Go on, then. What are you waiting for?'

He shrugs. 'The early hours of the morning. I'll take you somewhere. Somewhere they won't find you. Somewhere you can't escape from this time. I didn't want to make you suffer before. I just wanted to leave you down there to die. But you've lied and cheated and defied me, and I have to punish you, darling. You see that, don't you?' He shakes his head softly, his crazy eyes glazed with an almost serene expression. 'What shall I do? Stab you? Strangle you? Break every bone in your body?'

I don't say a thing. I refuse to let him see how terrified I am.

'I'm surprised you got out of that bunker, you know.' He wags a finger at me, chuckling. He actually thinks this is funny. 'That surprised the hell out of me.'

'Bunker?' I swallow again to bring some moisture back to my mouth.

'It's an old military bunker that was used for storage. Perfectly hidden and camouflaged. Hardly anyone knows it's there, but Dad took me a few times when I was a kid. He was stationed nearby in World War II and was responsible for the supplies kept there. And the best thing . . . it's not marked on any maps. I thought it was a clever choice. Except you had to mess it all up, didn't you?' He runs a fingertip down my neck and along my shoulder. My skin breaks out in goose bumps. 'The memory loss, though. That was good. That helped me. Couldn't have planned it better if I'd tried.'

'How did you travel between Scotland and here without anyone knowing?'

His lips curve in a smile. 'Cousin Jeremy. Do you remember when he and Alice stayed with us the night of my party?' He leans over and kisses my forehead. I squeeze my eyes shut and force myself to breathe. When I open them again, he's peering at me. 'Remember?'

'Yes,' I whisper.

'He left his driving licence here by accident. You know how much we look alike? Only our height makes us noticeably different, so it was easy, really. You don't need a passport to fly to Scotland. All you need is a photo ID, which I had. Jeremy Shaw flew to Aberdeen and back, not me. I had the perfect alibi.

'Doctoring the antidepressants didn't work, so I had to try a different approach.' He sits back on his heels and puts the empty beer bottle on the floor. 'I knew you'd be at Sara's, so it would be easy to find you. I got a cab from the airport. It dropped me off near her house, and I walked the rest of the way. It was getting dark by then. There were no lights on, and you weren't around. I'd already copied the spare key for Sara's door that you used to keep at our house, so it was easy to get in. Then it was just a matter of waiting for you to come back.'

'Out of Sara's bedroom window, I saw you walking down the street, and then you suddenly seemed to change your mind and walked in the opposite direction, so I followed you. All the way back here. How convenient.' He gives me a victorious smile. 'I wasn't going to let you leave me. No way. It's not right, is it? I told you that, didn't I? I told you that you were mine. We promised each other. We took wedding vows, something you obviously didn't take seriously. Till death do us part, forever and ever, Chloe, remember?'

His teeth clench so hard I can see the muscles in his jaw pulsing. I stare at him in frozen silence. He leans in close to me, his breath on my ear. 'Remember?' he yells.

I jump. 'Yes.'

'This is all *your* fault. You made me do it. You gave me no choice. I couldn't let you go. Never. You belong to me.' He raises his hand as if he's going to hit me again. There's an ominous stillness in the air as I squeeze my eyes shut, waiting for the blow to come.

But it doesn't.

Instead, he says, 'I'm hungry. Think I'll make myself something to eat. It's going to be a long night.' I open my eyes, and he's leaning over me. He puts my gag roughly back in place, smiling all the time, his eyes sparkling with what looks like excitement. 'You can't go anywhere, so don't even think about trying.' He walks out of the room.

The key turns in the door with a loud click, sentencing me to death.

Chapter Thirty-Six

They say your life flashes before your eyes when you're about to die.

Mine doesn't. Not my whole life, anyway. Just the last few months.

The baby. My baby. It all started there. I remember now. I can see the images clearly in my head.

When Jeremy and Alice left the morning after the party, I could hardly contain my excitement anymore. For the first time in my life, I had something that was mine. Truly mine. Something Liam or anyone else couldn't take away from me. A life inside me that he couldn't touch. Even though it was an accident, I was ecstatic.

Except Liam didn't feel the same.

I sat him down at the kitchen table, a blissful smile on my face. I had hope. Everything would be different now. It would make things better between us. He'd see how selfish and inconsiderate he'd been. Surely, with a baby on the way, it would make him change. When he held that little bundle in his arms for the first time, I was certain it would make the old Liam come back.

I gave him the positive pregnancy test all wrapped up and tied with a bow. His eyes lit up, thinking it was another birthday present. But when he realised what it was, his features grew hard, his face red and blotchy, blue eyes distant. My smile faltered as I waited for him to say something. Then he stood up, stared me straight in the eyes, and said, 'You never think of anyone except yourself, do you?' A muscle throbbed in his jaw, a sign I recognised that he was about to blow up. 'You're so fucking selfish. After everything I've done for you!' His lips contorted with anger as he pointed an accusing finger at me.

I stared at him open-mouthed, the injustice of his words leaving me speechless.

He thrust his face towards mine. 'You had nothing when I met you. In debt with a student loan! No house! No assets! You fucking owe me. I gave you everything. You should be grateful someone wanted you, and you repay me by going behind my back and getting pregnant! What kind of idiot do you think I am?' He grabbed me by the shoulders, shaking me roughly, his fingers digging in so deeply I thought he would actually pierce the skin. I was too terrified even to cry out. 'I'm not sharing you with anyone. Get rid of it,' he snarled and stormed off to work as tears flowed silently down my cheeks.

Of course, I couldn't 'get rid of it.' I wouldn't. It wasn't just about me anymore. I was responsible for another being now. Even if I couldn't give my baby the gift of life in the end, he or she gave me something precious: the courage to stand up for myself.

He knew. Knew I'd never kill my baby. When he got back from work that night, he had a huge bouquet of flowers in his hand and some champagne. He apologised profusely. He said it had all been a huge shock, and he didn't know how to deal with it. But he'd had the day to think it over, and he was as happy as I was.

He ran me a bath and massaged my shoulders. He brought up a glass of champagne for himself and a glass of the tiniest amount for me, mixed with orange juice. He toasted the baby and us, and as he watched me drink it, the hope returned. I wanted to believe everything really would be OK now, and when you want something so much, it's easy to lie to yourself.

Later that night, the miscarriage started. I woke with stomach cramps, the feeling of sticky wetness between my legs. I rushed to the bathroom and wiped myself. The blood was everywhere. I didn't know then. I couldn't have guessed what I know now. He must've put something in the champagne to make me miscarry. That's what I believe. And suddenly no life was inside me anymore. Just me and Liam again, the way he wanted it.

But I couldn't do it anymore. Existing but not living. I remembered the hope and happiness I'd felt when I was pregnant. The idea of possibilities. I'd wanted that back.

My baby was the last straw.

When the depression hit, I'd thought about leaving him. Thought about it morning, noon, and night. When I got over the grief and felt better, that was it. I was going to get away. But somehow, he knew or suspected I'd end our relationship, and he couldn't let that happen. The antidepressants from the doctor gave him the perfect means to hurt me. He tampered with them, I'm sure. Maybe he wanted me to go mad. That would be my punishment for daring to defy what he wanted. A taste of what would happen if I didn't stay in his control. Or maybe he wanted to kill me then, but something went wrong.

When I came home from the psychiatric unit, I was still unhappy and grieving, but I was something else, too. Suspicious.

No one wants to think their husband can do something like that, but there were just too many coincidences. Losing the baby; losing my mind. I didn't know what he would do to me next. Things were clicking into place, and I no longer believed the doctors when they said I'd just suffered a very rare and unfortunate reaction to the drugs. I knew it was Liam, and it was time to escape. And when I found out about his affair, it justified my decision and expunged any final doubt in my mind. It was the last nail in the coffin.

I just didn't know then that coffin would be mine.

I couldn't tell anyone about my suspicions. Liam is a good actor in company. He's got the perfect husband routine down to a fine art. It was my word against his, and no one would have believed me if I'd told them he'd tampered with my drugs, as I've found out since.

I waited for the right opportunity. When Liam told me he was going to Scotland, I knew it had to be then. He couldn't stop me. I'd take the essentials for a few days. Just get out of the house. Flee to Sara's, then find a place of my own that he didn't know about. I'd have a window of a week while he was away to sort it all out. But again, I'd played into his hands. He'd planned to make sure he left me for dead, and he'd have a clear alibi for the time I was kidnapped.

The perfect murder.

Chapter Thirty-Seven

I hear the door creak open, and squeeze my eyes closed.

'How can you sleep at a time like this?' He kicks my foot.

I open my eyes and stare into the face of a murderer. I don't point out how ironic his words are, coming from a man who can eat at a time like this.

He takes a long, shiny kitchen knife from his back pocket and straddles me, his knees on the outside of my hips, his weight on my stomach, pinning me in place so it's hard to breathe. As he presses the knife to my neck, a smile lights up his eyes. I turn my head to the side, but I can't get away from the blade against me.

He pulls down my gag and traces the knife slowly along my skin. It stings like burning fire. Blood dribbles out, tracking a line over my collarbone and down the back of my shoulder.

'Please, don't do this! Don't hurt me,' I whimper.

'I could make this really slow and painful. You'd deserve it.' He lifts the knife from his handiwork, leans down, and sweeps his tongue along the cut, licking my blood away to taste the very essence of me. 'It would take hours to die. Cut by agonizing cut.'

His weight on top of me crushes my lungs. My pulse whooshes behind my eardrums. Beads of clammy, cold sweat break out on my forehead.

With any luck, I'll suffocate before he can slice me up piece by piece. And If I'm going to die, then I only have one question for him. 'How did you know I was leaving?' I manage to rasp.

'You think you're so clever, but you're just stupid. I like to check up on you when you think I'm at work.' He shakes his head at me, lips pursed together, as if I'm a naughty child. 'Sometimes I follow you, and you don't even notice. Sometimes I come home unexpectedly to make sure you're here when you say you are. I'm a concerned husband who likes to know what his wife gets up to when I'm not with her. Someone has to look out for you, right?'

I grunt out a laugh then. A brittle, pathetic sound.

'I like to know who you're talking to and what you're saying, so I bugged your mobile phone. It's been bugged for years, and you didn't even suspect a thing.' He narrows his eyes. 'Imagine my surprise when I heard you talking on the phone to Sara, telling her you'd had enough of being my wife and were going to leave me. And you and that fucking pussy, Jordan, plotting how you should get away from me. When all the time I was listening to every single move you made.'

'Bugged?' I shake my head with disbelief. 'How could you bug it?'

'It's easy. I installed a simple software programme that uses the phone's own microphone to record conversations. It leaves no visible trace on the phone that anyone's virtually listening in.'

I think about the conversation with Sara. The one I can now remember. How I spilled out my plans to her. How she told me I could use her place indefinitely, but no, no, I'd said, it would only be for a few days, just until I could find somewhere safe that Liam didn't know about. I can clearly hear her voice in my head when she told me I should've done it sooner. That I should go to the police in case anything happened to me. But what would I tell them? I asked her, when he appeared to the world to be just a concerned and doting husband? They would think I was mad, that the drugs had done some kind of long-lasting damage to my brain, and I couldn't go back to the psychiatric ward. I just couldn't. I'd never get out the next time; Liam would make sure of it.

Liam tumbles off me and lies down at my side on the floor. He slips his arm around my shoulder, crushing me towards him so my head presses on his chest. His heartbeat vibrates against my cheek.

I can't stop the tears falling now. I thought I'd given up. Thought I wanted it to all be over, but I don't. I want to live. To survive. But it's impossible.

He'll never let me go, and I can't escape.

'Don't cry, Chloe.' His voice quivers.

I think he's crying, too. But I don't want to look in his eyes. I don't want his face to be the last thing I see.

Instead, I picture Sara and Jordan. Two people who mean a lot to me. Two people who believed me. I wonder what they'll do when I'm gone. Of course, everyone will believe I was kidnapped then. Dr Traynor, Dr Drew, even Summers and Flynn. But they'll all think it was the nameless, faceless man who can't be identified because I couldn't remember anything. They won't suspect a thing. And Liam will get away with it.

Again.

He gently pushes my hair back from my sweaty, tear-stained face. His hand runs down my swollen cheek, my neck, touching me tenderly.

'How could you kill your child?' My voice has almost gone now, my throat closed with the fear of waiting to die.

'I couldn't let it change things between us. It was supposed to be just you and me. I knew you wouldn't get rid of it, so I did it

273

for you. It was a blessing—you must see that now.' He wipes away my tears with his thumb. 'I love you more than anything, darling. I wouldn't do all this if I didn't.' His voice is insanely calm.

And then it happens.

Someone bangs hard on the front door. Liam jerks up into a sitting position, wide-eyed and alert.

'Chloe! Are you in there?' Jordan's voice from outside. More banging.

Liam rushes out of the room. From where I'm lying on the bedroom floor, I see him through the doorway, standing at the top of the stairs, his left hand gripping the knife, right hand balling into a fist.

'Help me!' I yell. 'Jordan!'

'Chloe!' Jordan bangs again on the door.

Liam's shoulders rise and fall with anger and adrenaline.

There's a loud bang and crash from downstairs as Jordan kicks the door in.

Liam's back tenses, and he holds the knife in front of him. 'Come to see your bitch before I kill her, have you, Jordan?' he snarls.

I hear heavy footsteps on the stairs, and then Jordan's head and shoulders come into view. Liam waves the knife at Jordan, slashing it through the air. Jordan swerves back, narrowly missing the blade. Liam lashes out with his right foot, trying to kick Jordan in the face. Jordan ducks sideways. In one swift move, he grabs underneath Liam's ankle with one hand and twists the top of his foot round with the other. Unbalanced, Liam topples sideways and falls to the floor against the hallway wall, landing on his left arm. Jordan throws himself on top of Liam, wrestling to try to get the knife away from him. Liam throws punches at Jordan's face and head with his free hand.

Breathing hard, I shuffle towards them on my backside, arms tied behind me, ankles still restrained.

Jordan grips Liam's left wrist with both hands, trying to gain control of the knife. The blade slices through Jordan's forearm, and he cries out in pain. Heavy blows rain onto Jordan's face as Liam pummels him with his right fist.

I shuffle closer.

All of Jordan's weight presses on top of Liam now, struggling to get the knife away from him. Blood pours from Jordan's wound.

Fighting for his grip on the knife, Liam clutches the handle with both hands now, jerking it towards Jordan's throat. With shaking arms and gargled grunts, Jordan manages to turn the direction of the knife so it's now pointing at Liam's chest.

As I reach them, I lie on my back, ignoring the screaming pain in my arms squashed underneath me. I bring my knees to my chest and kick out at Liam's head as hard as I can with both feet.

Everything happens in a split second.

Liam's head cracks into the landing wall and bounces back. His eyes roll up into his head. His body slumps lifelessly back and to the side.

With no resistance from Liam now, all the momentum of Jordan's weight on top of him forces the knife straight through Liam's heart.

Chapter Thirty-Eight

I sit in the interview room at the police station, with a blanket wrapped round me. The room is hot, but I can't stop shivering. I clench my jaw tight to stop my teeth from chattering.

It didn't really hit me straight away. Too much was going on.

Summers and an armed response team running up the stairs. Jordan being dragged off Liam. Somewhere in the midst of it, me screaming. Cold hands on my shoulder. Voices. Summers untying my wrists and ankles. Jordan—pale, breathless, and bleeding. Paramedics and an ambulance. A ride to Accident and Emergency. Jordan's arm being cleaned and stitched. Doctors questioning me. An examination. My superficial knife wounds cleaned and covered with plasters. Ice on my swollen cheek. Painkillers for the pounding headache. Bruised heels where I kicked Liam's head so hard.

A small price to pay under the circumstances. But I feel guilty that Jordan has suffered injuries just for trying save me.

Summers sits opposite me, Jordan by my side. Just having Jordan here gives me strength and courage.

'Are you sure you're up to making a statement now?' Summers asks me gravely.

Jordan's already made his, not that it was very long. He didn't have much to say, except for how he'd come back from the hospital after seeing his mum and realised I wasn't back yet. How he'd thought I must have been packing a lot of my things, because I'd been away for so long, so he drove the camper to my house to see if he could help me transport everything. How when he arrived, he saw Liam's car parked in the drive. He'd been about to knock on the door to make sure I was OK, when he heard me crying out to Liam not to hurt me. How he'd phoned Summers and then kicked in the door before the police arrived, and—well, you know the rest, don't you?

'I want to get this over with.' I pick up the Styrofoam cup of strong coffee from the table in front of me. My hands are clumsy and sweating, making me spill some down the blanket as I bring it to my lips and swallow.

Then I tell him everything. About how things were in the beginning. The slow passage of time during which love had changed into a dark, controlling obsession. How long it took me to see that our relationship wasn't right, wasn't normal. Liam becoming like Jekyll and Hyde. About my breaking point—the baby who'd made me realise I couldn't live like that anymore. How that fragile little life had finally given me the determination to get away from him. How I'd nearly made it the first time, but of course I'd seriously underestimated Liam.

I tell Summers how he must've given me drugs to start a miscarriage. The depression that followed and the realization I had to leave for my own sanity. How I'd discovered Liam's affair with Julianne, and it confirmed I was making the right decision. I tell him that Liam somehow tampered with the antidepressants. He'd known it was only a matter of time before I would leave him, and he couldn't allow that. He wouldn't. Then I tell him what I remember now of the evening Liam took me. 'After I'd gone to the estate agents, I'd window-shopped for some furniture. I was in Nightingale's when the salesperson told me about Tom's Wood Shack. I'd gone there and found a lovely bedside table. I'd told Tom to reserve it for me, that I'd be back to buy it in the next day or so. Of course, I never returned.'

'So it wasn't Tom who attacked you, like you told me on the phone?' Summers's brows knit together.

'No. That was some kind of false memory I thought was true. Maybe I wanted it to be him, so it would all be over. Or maybe because that was the last place I'd been to before I was actually attacked, my brain distorted things.' I shrug. 'I don't know.'

'So what happened when you left Tom's?'

'I was walking back to Sara's house and suddenly remembered I'd left my passport at my house, and I'd need it for the rental. So I went back home, knowing Liam was still safely away in Scotland. Except he wasn't there at all. Liam used Jeremy's driving licence as ID to fly back here. They look so similar, you see. He was waiting for me at Sara's and followed me back to our house.'

'I was in the bedroom, getting my ID. I didn't even hear him come in. The first I was aware of him was when he put his hand over my mouth and grabbed me round the throat. He banged my head against the wall, and I fell to the floor, dazed. Then I felt a sharp prick in my arm when he injected me with some liquid Silepine to make me sleep. I don't know where he got it. He's got friends at Ashe Pharma who used to work with him, so maybe he visited them and stole it. Maybe he made it himself. He's a chemist, after all. But he was clever enough to use the same drug I'd already been prescribed as a sleeping tablet. The next thing I knew, I was waking up in the bunker, and I'd lost my memory.'

Jordan takes a deep breath beside me and clenches his jaw.

'I don't know how long he planned it for, but he thought of every little detail to make people question my sanity and think I was the crazy one.' I put the now empty cup back on the desk in front of me.

'He's a psychopath.' Summers pauses from writing out my statement and looks up at me with a guilty expression.

'There's something else, though,' I say.

'What else?'

'I think there's another woman in that bunker. He told me about an ex-girlfriend called Katya. How she wanted to leave him and he wouldn't let her.'

Summers looks up at the ceiling for a second. 'Shit.'

I shiver again and rub my arms. 'I told you there was a bone there. The one I used to scrape out the render around the door. What if it was her?' I want to vomit then. I want to cry, too. 'The death of one poor woman was the thing that had managed to save my life and let me escape.'

Jordan reaches for my hand. It's cold and trembling in his warm one.

'Liam said it's an old military bunker. It's not on any maps, so I don't know where it is exactly. It's well hidden, which is why you couldn't find it before.'

'There are a lot of places like that dotted around the UK,' Summers says. 'They've been either abandoned or decommissioned, and forgotten about over the years. I've got a contact in the army who might be able to help with that. They can check through their archives to locate it. When we find the place, we'll need you to come and see if you recognise it.'

'OK.' I pause for a moment, trying to take in every emotion flooding through me. The sadness, relief, pain, grief, hurt, anger, loss. 'Will we be charged with Liam's death?'

Summers shakes his head. 'No. It was a clear case of self-defence. It's not in the interest of the Crown Prosecution Service to try to take this to a trial. Especially not after discovering everything Liam's done.' He carries on writing out my statement, and I stare at the clock on the wall, the second hand ticking round. Tick. Tick. Tick.

Time. That's something I'll have a lot of now. Time to think. To go over things again and again in my mind. Time to question whether I could've done something differently. Time for the nightmares to creep in in the dead of night.

But I'll also have time to heal. Eventually time to fall in love again. Time to have another child. Time to be happy.

I'm alive, and that's a start.

I sign the statement in triplicate with a shaky scrawl that looks nothing like my signature.

'Will you be all right?' Summers asks as he shakes my hand in the doorway.

I glance at Jordan, who smiles warmly back at me, despite the exhaustion etched on his face and the black eyes, cut lip, and swollen cheek. Even after everything that's happened, the ground beneath my feet feels solid for the first time in a long time. The air in my lungs is light. A swell of hope rises deep inside.

I've been given another chance.

'I will be now.' I take Jordan's hand and walk away.

And this time I'm looking straight in front of me.

About the Author

Sibel Hodge has always loved to write. Several years ago she decided to focus fully on her passion.

Hodge is at home in a variety of genres and styles and has written an eclectic mix of books for both adults and children.

She was awarded Best Children's Book by eFestival of Words 2013, was runner-up in the Best Indie Books of 2012 competition by Indie Book Bargains and was nominated for Best Novel with Romantic Elements in 2010 by The Romance Reviews, to name just a few of her many accolades.

Her novella *Trafficked: The Diary of a Sex Slave* has been listed as one of the top forty books about human rights by accredited online colleges.

Her website is sibelhodge.com.